Second DIVE

ALSO BY JASMIN MILLER

Brooksville Series
Baking With A Rockstar - A Single Parent Romance
Tempted By My Roommate - A Friends to Lovers Romance

The Best Kind Series
The Best Kind Of Mistake - A Workplace Romantic Comedy
The Best Kind Of Surprise - A Surprise Pregnancy Romantic Comedy

---

The Husband Checklist - A Brother's Best Friend Romance

Kings Of The Water Series
Secret Plunge - A Surprise Pregnancy Sports Romance
Fresh Meet - A Single Dad Sports Romance
Second Dive - A Second Chance Sports Romance

Second Dive

KINGS OF THE WATER SERIES

JASMIN MILLER

SECOND DIVE
Copyright © 2020 by Jasmin Miller

All rights reserved. No part of this book may be reproduced, distributed, or transmitted in any form without the prior written consent of the author, except in the case of brief quotation embodied in critical articles or reviews.

This book is a piece of fiction. Names, characters, places, and incidents are the product of the author's imagination or are used fictitiously. Any resemblance to actual persons, living or dead, things, locales or events is entirely coincidental.

Published: Jasmin Miller 2020
jasmin@jasminmiller.com
www.jasminmiller.com
Editing: Marion Archer, Making Manuscripts
Proofreading: Judy Zweifel, Judy's Proofreading
Cover Art: Najla Qamber, Qamber Designs & Media

To second chances.
For giving them, for getting them, for taking them.

ONE

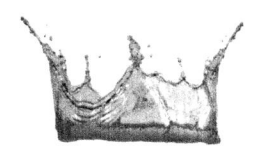

CHLOE

"Are you really sure this isn't some twisted Fifty Shades party? First the masks, now this?" I hold up the small wooden paddle and wiggle my eyebrows, slapping it lightly on my palm for emphasis.

Eadie shakes her head and laughs, her black hair flowing around her cheeks in soft waves. "Man, I'm so glad you're back. I missed having you around."

I grin at her. "Same. It's great to be back. And weird, and nerve-wracking... but mostly great."

Eadie leans closer and bumps my shoulder, while my gaze slips to the stunning skyline in the distance. The yellow-, orange-, and red-peppered sky illuminates San Francisco's Golden Gate Bridge in a way that almost makes it look surreal.

She holds up her paddle and spins it around, using it as an extension for her wild gestures. "My curiosity is going to eat me alive soon. I can't believe they aren't telling us what kind of auction they're holding tonight." She pauses for a moment and studies the object. "Maybe you're right and there'll be some kinky stuff going down. I mean, what better place than a masquerade ball where you can barely tell who's who?"

We both chuckle at the possibility of anything crazy happening.

I turn around and lean on the balcony, gazing through the large bay windows inside the ballroom, mesmerized by the sparkling chandeliers. Everything is stunning with expensive-looking red velvet curtains and a shiny wooden floor, exactly as you'd expect from one of Berkeley's finest luxury hotels. And of course, we can't forget about the attendees, who are mainly decked out in suits and exquisite dresses.

This isn't quite my *normal* circle but it's all for a good cause, the children's hospital. Tell me when and where, and I'll be there.

Eadie turns and mimics my stance, leaning closer so we won't be overheard. "Do you think he'll be here tonight?"

My whole body stiffens at her question, and I turn my wide eyes on her. "Do *you* think he'll be here tonight? I didn't even think about that possibility. I mean . . . he is like a local celebrity. Crap."

I blow out a breath, my stomach queasy at the prospect of seeing the ghost from my past. The person that was partially the reason I moved back to Northern California. Am I ready to see him yet though?

"Sorry for bringing it up. I have no idea if any big names are supposed to be here tonight."

I shrug, opting for the nonchalant route. "It's okay, I should have thought about it too. You threw this gorgeous lace mask at me and told me what tonight was for, and I was game."

"I think we should be safe with our disguises." She moves her head left and right, bringing her hand under her chin like she's modeling her feather mask.

"Not sure I'm in disguise but you sure are. Yours is huge, practically covering half of your head."

A snicker sounds from somewhere inside, drifting through the open door.

Eadie glances in the direction for a moment before she shrugs. "Anyway, let's forget about it. Nothing can overshadow the fact that you're here with me tonight."

"You're right. I'm so glad you invited me."

A waiter steps out, balancing a tray of drinks on one hand. Impressive. I'd probably tip over the whole thing in two seconds. Graceful has never been my strong suit.

Eadie grabs a glass of champagne while I opt for the orange juice. She lifts her glass and clinks it with mine. "There's no better plus-one than you, Chloe. Not in middle school, high school, or beyond. Well . . ." She purses her lips. "Except maybe Jordan Brewer in sophomore year. He was wicked good with his tongue."

I laugh and give her butt a soft tap with my paddle. "You're so bad."

She tilts her head. "Well, it's not like you weren't busy with you-know-who."

The groan escapes my lips louder than intended, and I look around to make sure no one heard me. Even though I probably won't ever see most of these people again, embarrassing myself during my first week back in town is still not on my to-do list.

"I know you're nervous to see him, but you shouldn't be. Whether that's tonight, or another time." She's lowered her voice and I'm grateful. "It's been ten years since high school, he can't possibly still hold a grudge, right? I'm sure things will be fine once you guys get to talk."

My mouth opens but a commotion at the door steals my attention. A group of guys stumbles onto the balcony, laughing.

They pass us and head to the other side. All but one of them.

He's dressed in a navy-blue suit and a silver mask. From the way he's wavering on his feet, he's looked a little too deep into his glass tonight. His gaze roams over Eadie first and then me, not even attempting to hide the hungry look in his eyes.

Gross.

It's almost impossible to make out any of his features in the dim lighting. His eyes could be purple, and I wouldn't know. All I see is short, dark hair and a normal-looking jawline.

The smile he gives us is probably supposed to be charming and seductive, but it only looks smarmy, especially when a wave of alcohol hits my nostrils. "Well, hello there, ladies."

Eadie and I share a look before she nods at him. "Hi and bye."

Without another word, we make our way past him and back inside.

Eadie pulls me to the side. "Total douche alert."

"Agreed. No one needs a drunken idiot."

She goes up on her toes, her eyes settling on something behind me, and I follow her gaze to the stage. "It doesn't look like anything will happen soon, so I'm going for a quick bathroom break."

"Sounds good. I'll wait right here."

I take out my phone to check my emails while she's gone. Might as well see if there's any news from my agent. Less than a minute later, someone clears his throat, and my head snaps up. Ugh. Douchey guy is back. Right in front of me. Damn it. I should have paid better attention.

Manners kick in—as well as a hint of annoyance—and I look him straight in the eye. "Can I help you?"

Apparently, he takes that as an invitation and steps closer, and I immediately take a step back. "Oh baby, I'm sure you can help me. Especially with those pretty lips of yours."

I narrow my eyes at him and refrain from crossing my arms over my chest. The neckline of my dress covers me up to my neck, but there's no need to invite his gaze to stray to my breasts in any way. "Wow."

"What do you think about you and me getting out of here?"

That guy. "No."

"Or we could sneak into a dark corner somewhere."

"No."

"Oh, come on. Don't be like that." He lifts his hand toward me, and I tense.

If he's going to grab me, I will punch him in the face. Or kick him in the balls. I have no patience for anyone who thinks no means yes, even less so when they're about to manhandle me.

But his hand never makes it anywhere near my body. Instead, someone grabs his wrist and pulls him away from me. Another man. The two have a quiet conversation where douchey dude nods vehemently before ducking his head and turning around to briskly walk across the room toward the exit.

My defender turns my way, and I get my first good look at him. His black suit must be tailored because it hugs his tall frame like a glove, accentuating his body shape of broad shoulders and narrow waist in a way that's almost . . . sensual.

"I wasn't too late, was I?" He leans closer while still keeping an appropriate distance.

His face is covered by a smooth black mask from his nose to his hairline, not allowing me to catch a real glance of his face. Besides his lips, which are definitely noteworthy. And his voice . . . it's deep and smooth, setting off a little alarm in the back of my head. It's familiar, yet not.

Stop staring and say something.

"No, nothing happened. Thank you." While I could have handled myself just fine, I still appreciate that Handsome Suit stepped in instead of looking the other way.

He nods, putting his hands in his pockets before taking one out again and extending it my way. "It was nothing. By the way, I'm—"

"Attention, everyone." The host's voice booms from the stage, making most conversations stop immediately. "Would the participants of tonight's auction please join me by the stage?"

A woman in a stunning red gown and a silver mask appears out of nowhere, grabbing his arm and pulling. "I'm sorry to interrupt, but we need to talk. Right now. It's urgent."

He turns toward her. "What's going on? Everything okay?"

"Yes. I'll explain."

He huffs out a frustrated breath and nods at her.

Then his gaze collides with mine, and my breath catches in my lungs at the intensity. "I'm so sorry. Maybe we . . ." He shakes his head. "Never mind. Enjoy the rest of your evening."

His gaze holds mine for another heated moment, and this time, my body reacts. It's buzzing, like someone just coated my whole skin with a light sheen of electricity.

How the hell is that possible from one glance? Who is he?

The woman gives me one more look, her eyes wide, before she grimaces and mouths "Sorry." Then they spin around and leave, pulling and tugging at each other's arms as they disappear into the crowd.

Oookay.

Welcome home, Chloe.

From douchebag, to saved by a stranger, to lover's quarrel?

All in less than ten minutes.

"What did I miss?" Eadie stops beside me, a fresh glass of champagne in her hand and a gorgeous smile on her face.

My mouth opens and closes as I try to find the right words.

I'm not sure what she sees on my face—the little she can see—but her expression falters in response. "Hey, is everything okay?"

I nod as I try to make sense of my body's reaction to this stranger. There was a definite sense of familiarity. Which is bizarre. The only person I've ever felt this with is . . . *No, that's impossible.*

Wouldn't I have recognized his voice?

Not if it's been ten years since you last heard it.

My mind is spinning when the host steps onto the small stage on the side of the room.

He used to be a popular TV host and is still handsome with silver hair and a charming smile. "Who's ready for our auction?"

Eadie leans in. "Ooooh finally."

The host walks to the other side of the stage. "Ladies and gentlemen, welcome to our bachelor auction."

I snort. Thankfully, the applause covers that up.

"You brought me to a bachelor auction? Eadie . . ." I moan. My best friend shrugs.

"You know I had no clue either." She smiles. "But what better way to welcome you home than with some eye candy to enjoy?"

I chuckle. She has a point. Why not be here? "And free drinks. Let's not forget about those."

"There you go. Here's to a fun night of hot bachelors." She holds her glass up for a toast.

With a shrug, I tap mine against hers. "And watching women trying to outbid each other."

Especially knowing I won't be one of them.

TWO

NOAH

I have no one but myself to blame for this shitshow. I should have known better and listened to my gut when I thought my sister, Daisy, was up to something.

Instead, I kept quiet and now I have to look into her pleading doe eyes.

"Please don't be mad. It'll be good for you ... and fun."

I close my eyes and count to three. She's just gone through a divorce. She's bound to be emotionally unstable. She's a single mom of two boys.

I ... cannot ... kill ... her.

Damn it, I still have the urge to, because I don't want to participate in this fucking bachelor auction she signed me up for without telling me. But if I back out now, I'll look like a total ass. So, to go back to our mom's favorite childhood mantra: *It is what it is, and we'll make the best of it.*

Or *suck it up and eat that fucking lemon with a smile on your* face as Daisy and I liked to call it as we got older. Only behind our mom's back, of course.

Fucking hell.

The proceeds go to the children's hospital. The proceeds go to the children's hospital.

I close my eyes and repeat it a few more times.

Shooting the reason for my current misery a narrowed look, I straighten my suit jacket. "We'll talk about this later."

"Sure thing." She stands taller, tilting her chin at me defiantly, and I bite the inside of my cheek to keep from smiling like I want to.

Despite everything going on in her life, and all the necessary adjustments, she's still got a backbone made of steel. Sometimes I have to remind myself that she's four years older than my twenty-nine and that she can take care of herself. I doubt the need to help her, in whatever way I can, will ever fade. Younger brother or not. We've always been a great team.

Someone walks up behind me and claps me on the shoulder. When I turn my head, I'm faced with a cocky grin I'd recognize anywhere.

Hunter Kinney, my Olympic swim teammate and one of my best friends—along with Ryan and Jace—winks at me. "Hey, dude. I didn't know you're going to participate too."

"That makes two of us." I half growl the words and shoot a glare at Daisy, still not looking forward to this ordeal.

Of course, Hunter chuckles like the almost-constant fucking sunshine he is and ignores me and my foul mood. "Come on, it'll be fun."

"That's what I said," Daisy says, unhelpful as ever.

"Hmm."

Hunter turns to my sister and gives her a quick hug. "Hey, gorgeous. Are you here to bid on me?"

She puts a finger to her mouth pretending to think really hard before she laughs. "Not really, but I mean . . . it's for a good cause, right?"

Is she checking him out? I think I'm going to puke.

Hunter puffs out his chest. "It most certainly is."

I only manage to contain some of my groan.

Why did I come here tonight? This isn't my scene.

Oh, that's right. Because my sister begged me to be her plus-one so she didn't have to show up by herself. I'm such a sucker.

She'd planned this whole thing in secret because apparently, I'm being auctioned off tonight to one willing bidder. What a nightmare. I'd much rather be home watching a movie, or hanging out with my nephews.

The line in front of me has steadily moved forward, one guy after the other being shown off on stage like a piece of meat. Now that I'm actually paying attention, I'm not sure what's worse. Hunter openly flirting with my sister while I'm standing right next to them, or Cade Hartley—quarterback for the San Francisco Bears—strutting down the stage like he owns it.

Wait a second, did Cade just . . .?

Yup, he just shook his ass like he's a damn Chippendale. And of course, the crowd's eating it up, those paddles hitting the air like bras at a fucking boy-band concert.

And it's almost my turn. Well, they'll be in for a big disappointment, especially after that little show. My minute on stage won't be anything like his.

I zone out this madness while still dutifully keeping up with the line.

Deep breath in. Deep breath out.

This is for a good cause. This is for a good cause.

Yet again, the words turn into a chant in my head until someone slaps my ass.

I don't need to turn to know it's Hunter, who's already leaning closer to whisper in my ear.

"Your turn, Noah. Show 'em how it's done, tiger." He and my sister chuckle and I ignore them.

After another deep inhale that does absolutely nothing to calm my irritation, I make my way up to the stage and to the host.

"Ladies and gentlemen, please welcome Noah Winters. Our very own star swimmer and Olympic gold medalist. Insider sources tell us he's also a master in the kitchen, knows how to rev up your engine, and enjoys getting a good sweat in." He wiggles his eyebrows and the crowd eats it up, cheering and catcalling.

Master in the kitchen? Since when?

I send a silent promise of revenge to my sister that will most likely be happening in the form of obnoxiously loud and super messy toys for her boys at the next chance I get. The sooner, the better. Maybe I'll go online the second I get done here to place a big order.

The crowd calms down and the host proceeds to the actual bidding part. I lose track of the bids as I scan the crowd with my hands deep in my pockets and a scowl on my face. I'm not really looking for anything or anyone specific, but I stop when my eyes find the gorgeous mystery woman I saved from that asshole earlier.

That dude clearly couldn't take a hint if it hit him straight in the face. And there was no way I could stand by and watch him bother her, especially when it looked like he'd put his hands on her. No way in hell.

And well, well, well . . . look at that. Her arm is in the air, that paddle as high as it can go. She's bidding on me. Maybe this night won't be as boring as I thought. Keep that arm up, Mystery Girl.

The host yells, "Going, going, gone," before he sends me off the stage to wait for further instructions. Hopefully, someone will enlighten me soon as I need to find my sister. My mystery woman made it a little better but still . . . The auction is for a good cause, sure, but a little warning would have been nice.

Naturally, she's disappeared.

Instead, I'm forced to watch Hunter make a fool of himself on stage, striking poses and flexing for the crowd. His bidding goes on for what feels like hours, but I'm unable to tell who won with so many people—mostly women—having pushed closer for a good look.

Just like I haven't been able to see where my mystery woman has gone.

I was hoping to talk to her some more after Daisy barged in on our conversation. I don't even know her name, but it seems like I will get my chance now after all. Unless seeing her win my bid was a mirage of wishful thinking on my part.

There was something about her, something that drew me in. It doesn't surprise me that I found her in the crowd, yet I'm surprised how eager I suddenly am to go on our "date."

I haven't felt like that for years.

A woman—Debbie, according to her name tag—comes up to me and explains the reservations at different restaurants for the winners and that mine will take place next Saturday at Skates On The Bay, down by the marina. The highest bidder was already informed and will meet me there at six o'clock.

Debbie gives me a look that I think means I'm excused, but I'm not ready to leave just yet. "What's the winner's name?"

"Oh, I'm sorry, Mr. Winters. I can't disclose that. I think she's trying to maintain the secrecy, which sounds like you're in for a fun night."

Although Debbie's words are polite, I sense that she's not really wanting to spend time educating a swimmer on the etiquette of bachelor auctions.

It's times like these that I need Hunter. He knows how to put the flirty on. "It will be a little strange turning up at the restaurant not knowing who will be there to meet me, don't you think, Debbie?"

She chuckles. "I hear you, and I'm sorry, but she asked if we could keep her name confidential at this moment. Actually, she was quite specific about it."

What the hell? Debbie smiles a sheepish smile and apologizes again. I can't be mad at her. *It's for charity, Winters.*

After I say goodbye, I spot my sister across the room and hurry through the crowd to get to her, grabbing her arm gently before she can disappear again. "Look who we've got here."

Her eyes go wide. "Oh hey. You looked great up there, and your auction went super well. Congratulations."

What a bunch of horse shit.

The mask is hiding most of her face, but I'm ninety-nine percent sure her right eyebrow is doing that traitorous twitchy thing it always does when she's nervous or when she lies.

I point my thumb to the side of the expansive room that offers more privacy. Her shoulders slump and she sighs dramatically.

When we're away from prying eyes and ears, I face her. "Want to tell me what the hell you were thinking signing me up for this bachelor auction? I'd have happily written an extra check instead of standing up there."

She blows a long breath through her lips. "I'm sorry, okay? I didn't want to make you uncomfortable. But you've been so lonely lately, and I wanted to help."

I scowl at her. "Why on earth would you think I'm lonely?"

"Noah, you're hanging out with the boys and me more than usual." Daisy takes a step closer and touches my arm, her voice lower than before. Soothing.

My mouth opens but she holds up a finger.

"Let me finish. We all love you. Mason and Alex say you're their best friend—the best uncle—in the whole wide world, and I appreciate your support so much since Daniel and I divorced. But if you spend all of your time with us, how are *you* ever going to find someone special?"

I cross my arms over my chest. "I don't need anyone special."

"I think you do though, and I think you know it too." Her voice is so gentle, I hate it.

Because I'm not looking for anyone.

I don't want anyone.
I don't need anyone.
I haven't needed anyone.
Not since that night ten years ago.

THREE

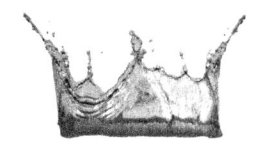

CHLOE

"He won't know what hit him." My mom's mouth curves into what can only be called an indulgent mother's smile as she stares back at me in the mirror—unapologetically blind and sweetly optimistic.

But she's right about the fact that Noah won't know what hit him. It just won't be the way she thinks it's going to go down.

I see it in her eyes, in the spark that's inescapable when I lock gazes with her. She's a believer in happily ever afters and second chances.

This time for *me*.

I'm a believer too, just *not* for me.

As of right now, my main goal is to keep Noah at the restaurant long enough tonight to say what I want to say. To not have him leave the second he sees me. Even though I dare say my chances aren't very good.

Not that I blame him.

I've tried putting myself in his shoes about five thousand

times over the years. How would I have reacted if the roles were reversed? How would I react now?

Would I be happy to see him? Shocked? Disgusted?

Would I even give him the chance to talk to me?

So many different options that make my head spin and my heart rate pick up in sync with my nerves.

"Hey." My mom grabs my chair by the back and spins it around before she crouches down so we're eye level. "I think you're incredibly brave for doing this. I know you've been carrying around a lot of guilt over how things ended with Noah, and I'm sure it doesn't feel good. Guilt never does, and there's probably a good reason for it. Your dad would be so proud of you."

My dad.

Of course, she has to bring him up.

He's one of the reasons I moved back here with my mom, to follow through with the things I'd promised him. To take good care of my mom, of course. But also, to not have any regrets, to right past wrongs . . . to do the right thing.

Why does it have to be so hard though?

"Now, let's suck it up and get you ready. Just because you're about to beg the love of your life for forgiveness doesn't mean you can't look like the goddess you are."

"Ugh, Mom." I sound every bit the petulant child I feel right now. "No one said anything about begging or love-of-my-life stuff."

"I know." She presses a kiss to my temple before pushing back up and spinning my chair once more.

We share a silent moment when our gazes meet in the vanity mirror. She knows how hard all of this is for me, especially my dad's passing and making the decision to seek out Noah. It's been over a year now since we lost Dad, but oftentimes, it still feels like it was just yesterday. And I know that bringing him up pierces her heart a little every time too.

Things have slowly gotten better for us over the last few months. We've actually shared several moments where we laughed together about a memory of Dad instead of being sad. Those moments still don't happen often, but they've definitely become more frequent.

The bathroom door flies open and Francesco blasts in. He's been my mother's best friend for as long as I can remember, making him like an honorary uncle before he became my real one by marrying my mom's brother.

I feel like there's an uncle joke somewhere in there.

Either way, I love him, both of my uncles, and I missed them like crazy after we moved. Thank goodness for video chatting, and their love for road-tripping down the California coastline.

"Ciao, bella. Look at you, Chloe. I knew the lavender hair would look gorgeous on you. I officially approve." The corners of his eyes crinkle in that familiar way, even though I haven't seen him as often as I'd like in the last decade since my parents moved us from Northern to Southern California practically overnight.

"Thank you. I'm glad Eadie talked me into it this week."

"Me too." He shares a look with my mom before glancing back at me. "If that boy isn't nice to you, I'm sure I know a few guys who'd love a shot with you."

My mom shakes her head at me while I grin. Francesco tried to set me up with one of his nephews once when I was a teenager. That was before he and Uncle Cody became a thing and then . . . well, then, Noah happened.

Which brings me back to what he just said. "You know I'm not looking for anything. I just want him to know the truth."

Francesco purses his lips and nods. "Uh-huh, sure. Have you seen that man lately? I'm not sure you'll be able to help yourself. Especially with all of those feelings still involved too."

My ribs tighten, and I shake my head. "It's been ten years since we were together, so there definitely aren't any feelings anymore. For all I know, he still hates my guts and will leave the second he realizes it's me."

My mom tilts her head. "Orrrrrr he might not. Give him a chance too, okay? Sometimes it takes a little longer to make amends."

It's easy to hear my dad's influence in my mom's words. They did a lot of soul-searching together after my dad was diagnosed with stage four prostate cancer several years ago. It made it easier and at the same time harder for us to know there was no cure for him, and that he wouldn't be with us for much longer.

The limited time amplified all of our relationships, and I'm eternally grateful for that bond we shared and will always have. Nothing will take that away. His diagnosis—and ultimately his death—changed both my mom and me. But in the end, it was also the major reason we moved back to Berkeley. I guess both of our hearts were still in Northern California.

Now we're here . . . to start anew.

To be with our friends and family.

To try and mend old wounds.

Because how can you expect your life to change for the

better, for your soul to be nurtured, when you don't show someone else—someone you once loved—that you're sorry?

Even when it's not easy.

Even when I'm ready to pee my pants just thinking about facing Noah tonight.

Bidding on him during the bachelor auction wasn't planned. At that point, I was still wondering how I'd actually get in contact with him.

But when the host announced Noah's name, and the mysterious man—the one who rescued me from the drunken douchebag—walked onto that stage, I couldn't believe it. I mean, what were the odds?

He stood up there, and the mask didn't take away a thing from his looks. With his short brown hair, and a body built to beat competitors in the water, all wrapped up in a suit that fit perfectly in all the right places, I couldn't help myself.

Without a doubt, he has turned into an even hotter version of his teenage self. I looked him up for the first few years after we left Berkeley, but when it entered an unhealthy stage, I had to stop. Seeing him in any form kept me from moving on, from trying to live a normal life. My unhealthy obsession—a deep and dark sadness—over my old boyfriend didn't do me any favors.

Francesco snaps me out of my thoughts when he squeezes my shoulder. He hums deep in his chest. "No old feelings, huh?"

"What?"

He points toward the mirror and therefore, me.

At my wide eyes *and* flushed cheeks. Thank goodness they can't see past the high neckline of my gray dress because my skin feels like it's on fire everywhere.

Meeting up with Noah has been long overdue. Knowing we're in the same city again drives my mind crazy, and I hope my thoughts will calm down after I see him.

And of course, I wonder if the glimpse I caught of the man at the party mixed with the memory of the boy I knew so long ago matches my wildest dreams.

Because even though the chances of him forgiving me are very slim, I can't lie to myself.

I've been imagining this meeting, this conversation, for the past decade.

When I step out of the Uber at the Berkeley Marina, I feel slightly lightheaded. My brain's been getting even crazier on the drive over, and I'm questioning everything. Because is this really a good idea? Waking up and confronting these old ghosts?

I've gotten pretty good at ignoring the guilt and regrets over the years—or at least, I've tried—so maybe it would be better to just leave things be. What if I only make things worse by confronting him, by opening up that Pandora's box I've tried to keep as tight a lid on as possible?

Promise to live your best life. Don't let the past weigh you down. If there are things you can fix, bridges you can mend, patch them up. There's nothing worse than being at the end of the road and looking back at a pile of remorse. Especially when there's a chance you could have made things better.

I bite back the sting of emotions that threaten to surface at my dad's words.

I close my eyes and breathe in for four counts before

breathing out for four. I do this several times until the familiar calmness settles over me like a comforting veil. It's not as effective as it normally is, but a ton better than before.

Taking out my phone gives me a welcome distraction. A look at the time confirms that I'm fashionably late, on purpose. The last thing I wanted to happen was to be there first and for him to see me and walk right back out the door again.

This way—if Noah's still as punctual as ever—he should already be in his seat, which will hopefully give me the advantage I need.

My screen lights up with a reminder of a waiting text message from Francesco.

> **Francesco: You're fire on heels, baby girl. Don't forget that. Go grab that gorgeous man by the nuts. Not literally, of course . . . unless you want to. More in the grab life by the balls. Text me when you're done, or if you need backup. I'm expecting a full report. Love you.**

I laugh when I see the parrot emoji at the end of the message. The one emoji that portrays him without any words as he likes to proclaim he's as gay as a parrot. We're all used to it, and it's been a running joke in the family for years. But as so often, Francesco went above and beyond and actually turned it into the branding for his bar *Parrot Lounge*.

> **Cody: Checco's getting out the parrot costume, but I'll try to contain him. Sorry I wasn't able to see you**

earlier, but he showed me the million pictures he took. You look beautiful.

Goodness, I love my uncles. Since Dad's diagnosis, they stepped up so amazingly to become two solid rocks in my life. I doubt I could have gotten through the last twelve months without them.

After another deep inhale, I put my phone back in my purse, and pull back my shoulders as I walk toward the entrance of the restaurant.

Ready or not, here I come.

FOUR

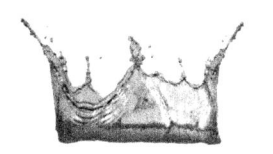

NOAH

Legs.

Tanned, toned legs.

They almost make up for my mysterious date being late. Almost.

I need a moment before I deal with the rest of the woman. So I quell my curiosity and focus on the hostess instead.

The same hostess who's aiming a bright smile at me like she just won an award for a stellar performance. "Your date has arrived." Her cheeks redden when our gazes collide. "The server will be right with you."

I tip my head down. "Thank you."

With her smile still in place, she turns and heads back to her hostess station. My gaze stays on her for an extra moment, a weird sense of dread pooling in my stomach over facing my date. I'm not even sure why. Because I felt an odd connection to this mysterious woman?

At the same time, this is also the person who spent money on me so we could have this tonight. It's still a strange feeling to go on a date that has been bought. Can it even be considered a real date under these circumstances?

Or I'm overthinking all this shit, my sister is right, and I'm just extra grumpy lately.

My date clears her voice. "I'm so sorry I'm late."

Her voice.

It's so eerily familiar that it throws me back in time for a moment, hitting me like a punch to the chest.

But it does the trick and snaps me out of my stupor, allowing my manners to kick in. I swiftly get up to pull out the chair for her, disappointed when I finally look at her and see a curtain of hair because she's turned the other way to place her purse on the table.

"It's no problem." I push in the chair under her, looking at the back of her dark hair. It has a hint of purple to it. Interesting. Was it already purple last week when I saw her at the ball? I definitely remember it was dark but don't recall any vibrant color like this.

My gaze wanders away from her hair to where I'm greeted with a stunning view of a toned back and a whole lot of exposed, smooth-looking skin.

Spending most of my time at the pool means I see a lot of skin, and barely ever notice it anymore, least of all get excited over it.

There's definitely excitement going on at the moment though, but that could be because I haven't seen any bedroom action in a while. And by a while, I mean in over a year.

After a silent threat to my libido to not embarrass me in a restaurant full of people, I sit back in my chair and catch my first real view of the woman across from me.

At this point, I'm feeling high on the anticipation of

seeing her, like all this has been some weird form of foreplay between us.

Time screeches to a complete halt. Like "after a major pileup accident" complete halt.

Because what the fuck?

My chest feels so tight, I have the urge to rub it so the intense pressure on my ribs eases.

How is this . . . What is happening? No . . . This is . . . this is impossible.

The woman smooths her long waves back, breaking the blazing eye contact between us and therefore, allowing me to fully take her in. And I take in every single fragment of her like a starving man.

Her bronze skin, which is peppered with a slight array of freckles. Her full lips. Her beauty mark under her almond-shaped eyes that are still as unique as before, the inner green rings competing with the beautiful gray-blue irises. Her heterochromia that I always found fascinating. And her nose with its . . . nose ring?

The jewelry throws me off so much that I look straight into her eyes again.

Big mistake.

She tilts her head to the side, her lips pulling up a fraction at the corners. "Hi, Noah."

The connection is intense. Too intense.

There's so much I want to say, so many things I've wanted to say for so long, but it's like something's squeezing my throat in a way that no word could ever make it past that constriction.

This time, I break eye contact with her and lean back in my chair, rubbing my hands over my face like I'm trying to get rid of a layer of skin. Or maybe the memory of her. Fuck. Maybe I'm imagining this whole thing? I take a deep breath, and our waitress chooses that moment to stop by to take our drink order and leave us with the menus.

The words all blur on the page, and I know neither one of us is paying attention to the listed food. I'm not the only one who keeps stealing glances at the other.

By the time the waitress comes back with our drinks and we give her our order—I have no idea what either one of us ordered, I just pointed my finger somewhere—my body has almost fully rebooted.

Shock and disbelief shift into something else that I'm not sure either one of us is ready for. Not to mention, it's probably not the place for whatever strong emotions are torpedoing their way through my system anyway.

"What are you doing here, Chloe?" My voice sounds strange to my own ears. Maybe that's due to the fact that my throat is finally less constricted but instead feels like I just forced a serving of nails down.

And saying her name out loud after so long makes my stomach clench.

She swallows a couple times before she picks up her water and drains half of it. It's impossible to miss her shaky hand that she puts back under the table the second the glass is safely on the tablecloth. "I wanted to talk."

Something inside me snaps, and heat rushes through my body like it's trying to burn me up from the inside. I'd like to say I'm the bigger person here but I'm not. I shake my head and snort. "*Now* you want to talk?"

She nods and bites her lip. Why does she have to bite her damn lip and draw my attention to it?

"After *ten* fucking years?" I lean across the table as far as I can without pushing things over with my chest. The distance between us shrinks, and my next inhale is filled with her scent. It's fresh and sweet, and so *her*. Which makes me even angrier. "Is this all a joke? Did you come to the masquerade ball so you could set all of this up?"

"No, of course not. I had no idea you'd be there. I didn't even know about the auction. I swear."

Now she's the one leaning in, and I don't know if she expects me to lean back at her approach or what, but I'm immobilized. I'm not sure I could move even if I wanted to.

What kind of spell is she putting on me?

This can't be happening, not again.

Never again.

I need to move. I *have* to move for my own sake and put this whole charade to a stop.

The look she gives me couldn't be more opposite of me. It's gentle and soft, maybe even pleading, contrary to me sporting the scowl of the year and grinding my teeth. My jaw is so tight, I'm afraid I might crack a tooth.

She swallows. "This isn't easy for me either, but can you please give me a chance?"

I scoff at her comment, the spell finally broken by her words.

Not easy for *her*. As if she wasn't the one who ripped out my heart all those years ago, leaving behind a vastness that no one and nothing has ever been able to fill.

I should get up and leave. Right now. Just push back the chair and walk out without looking back. Easy-peasy, lemon squeezy, as my nephews would say.

But of course, things aren't ever simple.

They used to be easy between Chloe and me, but that's long over. Just like us.

I wish I could also say we're a distant memory, but alas, I can't.

There's this sick, clearly very delusional part of me, that *wants* to hear what she has to say.

Since I'm apparently a masochist when it comes to her, I indulge that part, happily—and very irrationally—opening my arms wide to the pain. "Talk."

Her eyes widen, like she's actually surprised by my willingness.

Good. Maybe that'll throw her off, and we can just cut this ridiculous meeting short.

She nods and wrings her hands. "Okay, thank you." Then she puffs her cheeks and blows out a breath.

Damn it. Another familiar thing. She always did that when she was nervous.

We're interrupted by the waiter bringing our food and filling up our water, which doesn't really matter. Most of this evening could be a mute movie, and no one would miss a thing.

She picks up her fork, then puts it back down. "Back then . . . you know when I was moving away. Um . . . Do you remember I wasn't feeling very well?"

I raise my eyebrows because of course, I know. I was the idiot who called her about five million times, because I couldn't reach her when I wanted to make sure she was okay.

Her lips flatten and she tips her head once, probably knowing I'm not a willing participant in this conversation. "Well, I got worse when we went to visit my grandparents."

Fuck, I don't want to know about this. This was my nightmare back then. Literally.

Her tongue slips through her lips to wet them. "They have some good doctors down there, and you might remember that my grandma had just broken her hip too, so my parents decided it might be best to move there to help her and take care of everything."

I blink at her before looking away. Her gaze is too much. It holds meaning and history. It holds *us*. Too much us.

Instead, I focus on my water glass, running my finger over the condensation that's already left a wet spot on the pristine tablecloth.

A strange laugh escapes her throat, and I look up again, unable to escape this pulsing link between us.

"Well, anyway, I got worse after we left. But both my grandma and I are good now. And I'm . . . well, I'm here I guess." The corner of her lip disappears in her mouth as she chews on it and stares at her hands.

All the while, my brain has no clue what to do. Talk about too much input with just a few words. Yet not enough. I'm still trying to wrap my head around the fact that she's actually here. Sitting right in front of me. More gorgeous than ever, pushing my fight-or-flight urge into total overload.

"Anyway, I wanted to apologize for the way things went down. I should have talked to you and explained what was going on. I hate that I left you hanging like that with just a message, but I thought I was doing the right thing. I'm really terribly sorry." She lifts her head a fraction, and her eyes zero in on me once again. They're shiny, and I look away, focusing on the setting sun in the distance instead.

Studying the orange and purple hues in the sky seems a lot safer than looking at Chloe.

I'm . . . well, I'm here I guess. Her words repeat in my head.

And that is part of the problem. Chloe is here now. I should be asking what was wrong with her. What was so wrong with her that she left without saying why? I should be communicating how angry and hurt I was that she left. But I've got nothing.

There are no words.

Because she left and never said goodbye.

And took my heart with her.

FIVE

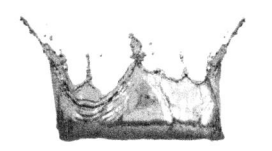

CHLOE

"And then he just left?" Francesco pats my hair as I'm hunched over, with my head on my forearms on the bar of the Parrot Lounge. After wiping it down with some disinfectant wipe, of course. The last thing I need is getting someone else's nasties during my meltdown.

Even Francesco's stink-eye couldn't keep me from doing it, or his reassurance that of course, his tiki bar was spotless.

My motto: better safe than sorry.

Always.

"Yup, not that I can blame him." My answer is muffled, just like my ego is bruised, and my brain is a bit wishy-washy at the moment, still not a hundred percent sure what's going on. "I basically cornered him, making him feel like a freaked-out animal."

"More wild animal. Rawr."

His roar sounds more like a cute kitten than a wild animal, and I smile against my warm skin before I peek up at him just as he smiles at someone behind me.

"Oh hey, babe."

I turn around at the approaching footsteps, my mood instantly lighter when I see my uncle's face.

"Hey." He leans over the bar to give Francesco a kiss.

They are so dang cute together.

Francesco immediately fusses over him, his gaze roaming over his face, his hand fluttering along his cheek. "Stressful day at work?"

"Yeah."

"Want me to make you your special drink?"

"Yes, please."

Francesco smiles widely at him. "You got it."

"Thanks."

"Always for you." Then he nods into my direction. "You take care of this one while I make your drinks."

Cody plops down on the wicker barstool next to me and gives me a solemn look. "Your date didn't go well, huh?"

"You know it wasn't a date." I let out a long breath, trying to get rid of all these mixed emotions that have been pestering me ever since Noah left me at the restaurant. Who am I kidding? This roller-coaster ride of feelings has been an ever-present shadow since my mom's announcement about moving back to Berkeley. "And no, it didn't go well."

I really didn't have any expectations when it came to the dinner. My mission was clear and simple: apologize to Noah. And that's exactly what I did.

So why do I feel like it didn't go well? Why don't I feel relieved like I thought I would? Wasn't that the whole point of meeting up with him? To not carry around this crazy amount of guilt and regret that has been with me for so long, it's become a part of me? A living, breathing fragment of myself that feeds off me, happily dancing along with a smile on its face while I succumb to its darkness a little more each day.

I groan and plop my head back on my arms.

Talk about being melodramatic.

That's what Noah Winters does to my heart. My poor, poor heart that didn't know what to do when it saw that vision of a man. With his short, slightly wavy light brown hair, his five-o'clock shadow, and those eyes . . . the stunning blue gray I remember so much, the ones I dreamed of so often. There was an instant reconnection with a part inside of me that no one and nothing else has ever reached.

I'm officially screwed. So, so screwed.

My uncles' voices are muffled as Francesco fills in Cody on what happened while I try to drown out the noise. And my thoughts. Not sure what's louder right now, but it's exhausting.

Where's that off-switch button when you need it?

"Give him some time, Scribbles," Cody says.

It's impossible to keep the corners of my mouth from tilting up at the use of his nickname for me. He gave it to me when I was little because I was always drawing, scribbling on whatever surface or material was available.

Today, I choose my surfaces wisely, but I still don't shy away from a napkin or other unusual material if nothing else is available and inspiration hits.

I look at him, at his adoring smile and my mood lifts. Slightly. Maybe by one-ninetieth.

Let's yank that up a notch because Francesco has perfect timing, finishing up our colorful drinks while swinging his hips to the exotic music coming from the hidden speakers.

"A zombie for you, babe." He places one of the orange-red drinks in front of Cody, and the other one in front of me. "And a hurricane for you. Virgin, of course."

"Thanks," Cody and I say in unison before taking a sip.

The sugary taste hits my taste buds immediately, and I sigh in pure fruity appreciation when the passion fruit flavor hits my tongue. There's nothing quite like it, and it will be worth having to drink about five green juices to counteract all these calories and sugar. Even though Francesco already makes me a healthier version.

Cody bumps my knee with his. "I bet it's a lot for him to process. You're like a ghost from his past."

I stop mid-sip, trying hard not to choke on the juice concoction that's halfway down my throat.

"Yeah. You probably gave that poor guy the shock of the century." Francesco leans against his side of the bar. "I mean, you had time to mentally prepare yourself for seeing him again, while he went in there like a blind man. Maybe he was expecting an old, lonely woman who was going to try and hump him. This date was *bought* after all."

I blink and turn to Cody.

He shrugs and scratches his neck. "As much as it disturbs me to say this, he does have a point."

"Ugh." This time, I take several sips. Maybe I can fall into a sugar coma for a little while and escape this madness.

"Hey." Cody's voice is gentle, and he gives my shoulder a squeeze. "You knew this wouldn't be easy, but it's done now. You did what you wanted to do. Maybe things will be better when you see him next time."

"Next time?" My eyes widen when I look at him.

"Berkeley isn't a small town, but it's not a metropolis

either. You both live and work here, so it's possible you'll run into him again, right?"

"Oooooh, this will be so juicy. I can already taste it." Francesco's voice is the opposite of Cody's. He sounds like he's already looked too deep into the cookie jar, ready to bounce off the walls from excitement like a five-year-old on a sugar high.

"Checco, not helping." Cody gives him a look that makes Francesco raise his hands in defeat.

"Fine, fine. I'll go make sure the stage is ready for tonight's karaoke session. You two talk about whatever boring, non-juicy stuff without me." He sighs and leaves.

His theatrics make me chuckle. "Gosh, I missed this. It's never as good in text or any other form of electronic communication."

"He's one of a kind." Cody smiles his special smile that's reserved for when he talks about his partner in crime. Then he looks at me. "Speaking of work though. How are things going?"

I welcome the change in topic and try to push Noah out of my mind.

At least, for now.

Plus, I love talking about my work. I love thinking about my work. The doodles I did as a chubby toddler have matured and developed to the point where I became a children's book illustrator—with the occasional dabble into other areas like middle school or young adult if the job sounds interesting, and the pay is fair.

It brings me a joy I don't think any other job could ever match. There's just something about the sweetness and innocence, not to mention the pure joy that practically jumps off the pages, and I enjoy being a part of it.

I shrug. "It's going okay. Good. Between the publisher and my indie authors, my schedule is full."

"So the freelancing is working out, then?"

"It is. I wasn't sure if anyone would hire a random illustrator for their books online, but they do." The pride is easy to hear in my voice, and I wear it like a crown because I'm proud of myself. I worked incredibly hard for what felt like a gazillion years, and it paid off.

After taking another lazy sip from his drink, he tips his head to the side. "And what about the competition?"

I draw a breath before speaking. Now that's a totally different topic. "I really want to win it because I just *know* it would make such a big change in my career, but . . ."

"But?"

I bare my teeth in a grimace. "According to Gina from the office, it will come down to me and this other guy. Joe. He's a good illustrator but also a major asshole. We've gotten into a few arguments online because he thinks he's better than me, and that they'll pick him anyway because the execs are guys and well . . . he's one too."

Cody's brows shoot up before he exhales sharply. "That's bullshit."

"Yup. Pretty much."

"Do you think she's right?"

I swallow, not sure if I want to be honest not only to him but also to myself. "I don't know. It's possible. Wouldn't be the first time they pick a man over a woman just because they have an extra piece of meat hanging between their legs."

Cody chokes on his drink, and I slap my hand over my mouth.

My breath makes a hissing noise. "Sorry."

He wipes his mouth on a napkin before dragging it down his smooth-shaven chin. "Just didn't see it coming, that's all. You know I've seen my fair share of inequality just because I'm gay."

"Why are people like that? I will never understand it. It's just stupid." It might sound like a juvenile answer but that's really what it comes down to. "I hate it."

"I know you do. You've always had a gentle heart and wanted everyone to get along." He places his hand on my arm and squeezes gently.

I did and still do. The thought alone of people hurting because of others' idiocy makes me incredibly sad *and* angry.

We're both quiet, and I'm glad I have a moment to get my emotions under control.

Cody nudges me with his elbow. "And you're volunteering at the hospital too?"

My spine straightens at his question, a lightness spreading through my body that wasn't there a minute before. "Yes, I'm super excited. It's been a while since I've done a bigger project like this. It will be a nice break from my normal work a few hours a week."

"It's about time they catch up with the outpatient building after enhancing the main hospital last year. The kids will love having murals on the walls." The gentle smile on his face proves once more why he makes such a good doctor for the little ones.

"I think so too."

Even though I don't know everything about nephrology—

his field of expertise—his general medical knowledge has come in handy on more than one occasion.

"Anything to make the little ones smile, right?" He downs the rest of his drink before he turns around to the sound of the microphone being tapped. The light on the small stage across the room dims just as the music starts.

In less than five seconds, Cody is engrossed in the power ballad Francesco is belting out for him, both of them wearing matching dorky smiles. Neither Francesco's exotic shirt nor the palm thatch and bamboo decoration around him takes away from how romantic this moment is.

The fact that the bar is still closed, and we're the only ones out in the actual lounge part, makes me feel like I shouldn't be here. Like I'm intruding on a private moment. On their love.

Even though it thrills me that they're still this happy after so long.

I've often wondered what that would feel like.

To have someone to come home to.

To share a bed with someone every night.

A whole life.

A *long* life.

My throat feels scratchy, like always when thoughts like these take over my mind.

But I push them away as much as I can, knowing I should get home so I can lose myself in my drawings. It's the escape I so often seek—my favorite kind of escape and self-induced therapy—filling my bucket with much-needed happiness and a sense of accomplishment.

After seeing Noah again, there's a chance my fingers will try and draw him like they so often do. Even though this time it's a new Noah. The older version of him, different than his younger self yet in some ways the same. Without a doubt more mature, more muscular, and manlier. And most definitely sexier. Shit, it won't be easy, but I have to resist that urge.

He used to be my most favorite thing to draw, but times have changed.

He's not that one person for me anymore—my person—the one I'll spend the rest of my life with.

I should be glad that chapter is now officially closed after my apology.

So why do I feel like I just lost him all over again?

SIX

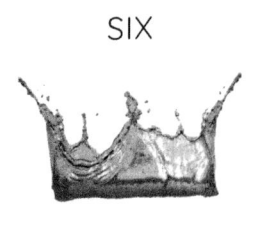

NOAH

Two hands tap the side of the pool to get my attention when I'm almost done with the lap. I slow down, swimming to where my coach is now crouching next to the starting block.

Coach Diaz has trained me since I was a little kid, and his now weathered face is as familiar to me as my parents', if not more. His salt-and-pepper eyebrows draw together as he stares at me, the breath he releases heavy and filled with so much meaning.

After working together for two decades, it's almost natural to know the other person's body language like it's your own. Particularly important with swimming where we often have to communicate without words.

I hold on to the edge of the pool as we exchange a loaded look.

Since I'm busy slowing down my breath anyway, I wait until he starts to talk. I know something is up from the way he looks at me, and because he usually doesn't interrupt me unless it's important.

After giving me a small nod, he leans down to clap my shoulder. "Let's wrap up your main set and cool down, okay?"

"Okay."

With a low hiss, he straightens to his full height, which is several inches below my six foot three, and hugs his clipboard to his chest. "Drop by the office on your way out?"

My stomach rolls at his question and what's about to happen, but I nod anyway. "Sure."

Because I know. I just *know* why he wants to see me. What he wants to talk about. The immature child in me wants to cross his arms over his chest and huff out a "But I don't want to." Alas, I'm almost thirty years old and that shit doesn't fly anymore.

He breaks eye contact and tips his head once. "Good, good. Now get your ass moving and cool down."

With a turn on his heel, he takes off, and so do I. Weaving in and out of the water, diving below the surface, just to launch myself out of the water again and into the air. Repeat and repeat. Dolphin dives are one of my favorites, even when I do them slower to relax. There's something liberating about this particular move that has always spoken to me.

The movement clears my head. It's only me and the water, which is the way it's been for such a big part of my existence. I can tune out my life and everything that bothers me, completely focus on my body, and the work I'm putting into my performance. It's been the one constant thing in my life.

At least, it used to be.

My cooldown—or rather, warmdown that allows waste products to be effectively removed from my muscles—is distracting enough that my head stays mostly clear and undisturbed until I finish up and shower.

When I knock on Coach's open door, he waves me inside, and my brain's back in overdrive. We train here at the university most of the time because Coach is their swim team's trainer, and wherever he goes, I go. The competition with the youngsters also helps keep me on my toes.

There aren't a lot of people here, so it's quiet after my training session, and I leave the door open. That way it feels less restricting.

"Hey, Coach."

"One moment." He lifts a finger off the computer. "Sit."

I don't need to be told twice, so I walk over to the chair and plop into it. This was only my morning session, and it's not even noon yet, so why do I feel so exhausted already? My terrible sleep in the last few days is probably one of the reasons, and I blame *her* for it.

Seeing Chloe over the weekend has thrown my equilibrium more than I'd like to admit. How can someone you haven't seen in a decade have so much impact on your life?

Coach puts his glasses on his desk and rubs his eyes. "Okay. Let's get straight to the point. What's going on with you?"

"Nothing." My standard answer.

"I see." His groan is barely audible. "Well, if you think it's nothing, let me tell you my two cents."

My next swallow is harder to push down as the wave of uneasiness creeps back through my body.

"I've had a lot of students, most of them come and go, but you and I have been training together for a very long time. I know something's off with you. I can see your mind hasn't been in this lately, and you know that too. I can't even remember the last time your times were this shitty."

I lean on the back of the chair and stare at the ceiling. "I know my times have been crap this week."

Thanks, Chloe.

"No doubt about that. But I'm not just talking about this week. They were already getting worse before then too. They haven't been your best for a while, but you were able to scrape it together for the Olympics and barely anyone noticed."

Ah, yes. The Olympics. Winning those medals. Adding them to the others I won at previous Games I've attended in my career. It was an amazing feeling. Something that would never get old, or so I thought.

But . . . here we are.

At a loss of words, I shrug.

That elicits another frustrated groan from Coach. "All right, here's the deal. I think you have another great four years and an Olympics in you, but my opinion doesn't mean shit if you don't put the work and effort into it."

"I know."

"Well, isn't that just peachy that you know that?"

I raise my head at his retort and look at him.

He leans forward as far as the desk allows. "I want you to take some time off and think about what you want. Your volunteer work starts this week, right?"

I nod.

"Good. Maybe doing something else will get you out of this funk, or at least, give you some clarity. Sometimes it's good to push, necessary even. But there are also times when you're at a crossroads without realizing it. At that point, pushing only forces you down a path that will lead to misery and disappointment. That's not our goal, you hear me?"

"Yeah."

His eyes turn toward the ceiling, and I give him a moment. Especially when he starts massaging his temples. I know when to shut up with this man. The same way he knows me, I know him too. And I have no desire at all to push his buttons today.

"Is there anything I should know about? Are you in any kind of trouble?"

A long sigh leaves his body when I shake my head.

What does he expect me to tell him? Because I honestly don't have a clue myself. It sounds stupid, but one day I just woke up and felt incredibly tired. Bone-deep exhaustion. I didn't feel "it" anymore, that inexplicable, invisible force that drives you to push yourself harder than you ever thought you could be pushed. To achieve the unimaginable and continue doing so.

He studies me, probably knowing I'm full of it. "That's something I guess."

Weirdly enough, my brain's blank right now. I know he's right about my times, and that something's going on, but I'm not exactly sure what it is either. Or why.

Sure, I can blame Chloe for the extra distraction in the last few days, but not before then. What or who can I blame for that though? No one but myself probably.

He rubs his chin. "Go talk to someone if that helps."

That gets my attention. "Like a therapist?"

"That's why we have sports psychologists. They know what they're doing."

"Hmm."

He wags his finger at me like he's done so many times before. "Noah, you might be a grown-ass man, but you don't need to give me attitude. Figure this shit out. Take some time off. Do the volunteer work at the hospital. Hang out with your friends. Do nothing. But do something that helps. This isn't just about your swimming, this is about your life. Something has to change."

My fingers tap on the armrest in a fast rhythm before I cross my arms in front of my chest to keep still. "Will do."

"Good." He brushes a hand over his face, the golden band on his finger reflecting the light. "You know where to find me if you need me. Now get out of here, or you'll be late."

With my bag in hand, I stand in the doorway less than a minute later. "Thanks, Coach."

He only grunts and waves me away.

"Noah."

I turn around and look for my sister. And there she is. In all of her nurse glory. Brown hair atop her head, dark scrub pants paired with a Dory scrub top, and a paper tray with two large cups from the coffee shop by the entrance.

When she reaches me, she's a little out of breath. "What are you doing here?" I'm just about to reply when she groans, "Oh right, the painting starts today, doesn't it?"

"Just a preliminary meeting of sorts to make sure we know what we're doing, who we'll be working with . . . that sort of thing. Some prep work. And then we'll start over the weekend."

After transferring the tray to one hand, she reaches out to grab my arm as we walk to the bank of elevators together. "I'm glad you're doing this. It sounds like a lot of fun."

"Hmm." Grunting seems to be my specialty today.

"Is everything okay? You seem grumpier than usual."

Yes, it seems I'm grumpy most of the time, but what can I say? I'm under constant pressure to perform virtually three hundred sixty-five days a year. Well, at least it feels that way sometimes.

But am I grumpier than usual? Hell knows.

I close my eyes for a moment, trying to decide how much to share with her. Do I tell her about the tongue-lashing I received from Coach?

Besides the guys, she's the closest person I have in my life. I'm close with our parents too, but they've been on a mission to save the world—currently in Africa. That's great for them and everyone they can help, but they also left Daisy in a bind when she had to figure out life after her divorce.

But, as usual, they told her they believed in her, and that she was capable of managing it all, half a foot already on the next airplane. Metaphorically, of course, but it might as well have happened. Being supportive and overly loving while at the same time being absent. That's our parents in a nutshell. Loving from afar. Not as available to us as we'd often like.

The elevator ride is quick, and I feel her eyes on me the whole time.

When we step out together on the third floor, her gaze is gentle. "You know you can talk to me, right?"

"You're the second person today to say that to me."

Her eyebrows go up. "Really? Who else said it?"

"Coach."

"Mmm. Interesting."

"Is it?"

"Yes." She brushes a stray hair from her forehead. "Lorenzo usually doesn't say anything until he really has to."

"Maybe."

"So what's going on?" She's not going to let this go. Once she knows something is going on, she's like a ferret. Their latch-on bite is brutal, and you have to cover their nostrils in hopes they'll let you go.

Talk about random tidbits in my brain.

Naturally, my gaze flickers to my sister's nostrils. It might distract her from digging deeper, but yeah, no, thank you.

Instead, I exhale dramatically because I feel like it today. "He said I need to figure out what's going on and what I want to do because my times have been shit."

"Ouch." Daisy grimaces. "I'm sorry."

I shrug, because I still don't know what to say or think about it.

A flicker to her watch has her eyes widen. "Dang it, I have to hurry. But let's talk about it some more later, okay? I want to help if I can."

"Sure." The only acceptable answer right now, not that I want to talk about it again.

With another quick squeeze to my arm and a wave, she turns around and speed-walks away.

After releasing a pent-up breath, I turn the opposite way and head in the direction I was told to go for the meeting.

When I get to station five, I stop dead in my tracks at the scene in front of me.

A man and a woman laughing together. The guy bends down to kiss the woman's cheek before he disappears behind a door that leads to the exam rooms.

The woman's smile still lingers on her face, lighting it up like a Christmas tree. She looks absolutely stunning. Radiant even.

Most importantly, it's the last person I was planning on—or was ready for—ever seeing again.

Chloe.

Once the love of my life.

Now, at the top of my shit list. Could my day get any worse?

SEVEN

CHLOE

The smile on my face drops when my gaze collides with Noah's.

Noah?

What the hell is he doing here?

If his squished-together eyebrows are anything to go by, he's as confused as I am.

A small woman walks toward me before I can say anything to him—or rather decide *if* I'm going to say anything to him—her hand stretched out toward me. "Hi. You're Chloe Williams, right? I'm Tammi Brown, the healthcare interior designer. We talked on the phone."

Until she contacted me and introduced herself, I had no idea there was even a job like that.

Forcing my face muscles to work, I put that smile back on my face as I shake her hand. "Hey, Tammi, it's so nice to meet you in person. Thanks again for this opportunity."

She shakes her head and chuckles, her hand going to her chest. "Believe me, thank *you*. I cannot wait to see your painting on the wall. I adore the sketch and know the kids will absolutely love it."

Several artists are working on this project, spread out across the hospital and outpatient center. I was assigned to the outpatient clinic, level three, and stations three to five to the right of the elevator. That was the info I got along with measurements and pictures of the space so I could draw the design on paper before I transferred it to the computer.

I was thrilled when they let me choose the theme, because I didn't even have to think about it. Ocean life. Plain and simple. There's always been something about the underwater world that fascinates me.

Which, coincidentally, has always been a link between Noah and me. Whereas he liked to be the fish in the water, I was never more than an average swimmer but loved anything water-related. It calmed me. The smooth movements of a person or animal—small or big—in the water is intoxicating to me.

"Chloe? Is that okay?"

I jolt when Tammi says my name, and heat flushes my face when I see her worried face. Did I just zone out in the middle of this conversation with her? Dang it.

Get a grip, Chloe.

A chuckle escapes my lips and I shake my head. "I'm so sorry. What did you say?"

Her smile stays in place as she blinks at me.

Hopefully, I didn't screw things up and they'll get someone else for this job. Even though it doesn't pay since it's a community project made up of volunteers, I've always wanted to do something on a larger scale. So this is the perfect opportunity.

"No worries, it's Friday afternoon, so I totally understand. Even though you'll be stuck here over the weekend, while I'll try my best to not even think about this place."

We both grin, as I will my body to relax and to stay present. "It's been a long week, but I'm excited to get started. I'll listen now, I promise."

"Okay, let's see." One of her fingers goes to her chin and taps there. "Every artist has one or two assigned volunteers to make things easier. Yours should be here soon too."

No, no, no.

She can't mean . . . It can't be . . .

I almost choke on my saliva at the sheer possibility of—

"Oh, Mr. Winters. I didn't see you there. My apologies." She walks to where Noah stands, his expression unreadable. She shakes his hand and waves in my direction. "Thanks so much for volunteering. This is Chloe Williams, the wonderful artist you'll be working with."

My breath catches in my throat and unapologetic heat rushes from my chest up my neck and all the way to the top of my ears.

Holy Batman. This can't be happening.

Noah's gaze stays fixed on Tammi. "We know each other."

Tammi claps her hands together. "Oh, that's fantastic. This should be so much fun for you, then."

Fantastic is the last word I'd use to describe this situation, and Noah's answering grunt seems to be in line with my thoughts.

Thankfully, Tammi seems to be unaware of the negative emotions buzzing between us, and I try at all costs to keep my eyes on her. If I catch one of Noah's murderous gazes, I might go up in flames, and that really isn't on today's agenda.

Tammi gestures to a short hallway close to us. "Let me show you the storage closet we were able to utilize for you. It should have everything we talked about. The weekend security guard in the lobby will have the projector for you tomorrow when you arrive."

I nod. "Perfect, thank you."

"Of course." She opens the door to the closet and steps aside so I can get a good look at everything.

Cans of paint, brushes, a ginormous bag of rags, rolls of painter's tape, a couple of drop cloths, some paint rollers, cups, a stepladder, a ladder, and a few palettes.

My heart sighs in anticipation, and I smile at Tammi. "Looks like everything we need. Great."

"Awesome. I'm glad." We take a step back and she closes the door again. "Please let me know if anything's missing, or if you run out of any material. The hardware store is ready for us if we need more."

"Okay, thanks."

"Great. Your other helper should be—"

"I'm here. Sorry for being late. I got held up." A tall man jogs toward us. After winking at Noah—wait a second, he *winked* at Noah?—he slows down to a stop in front of Tammi and me.

He must be as tall as Noah, or at least close to it, with a similar build. And that smile he's giving Tammi and me. Phew. I bet that can melt some panties into nothingness. It's crooked, which makes it cocky *and* endearing.

After shaking Tammi's hand, who's suddenly very quiet, he takes mine in his. "And you must be Chloe. I looked you up, and your artwork is amazing. I'm Hunter Kinney." His eyes roam over me, the corner of his mouth going up another notch. "And I'm at your service. Use me however you need me."

Noah groans behind him, and my eyes flitter to him, despite my earlier pledge to *not* look at him. His eyes are closed, his head tilted back slightly as he scrubs a hand over his face.

Hunter chuckles before looking over his shoulder. "I'll give you some attention in a moment too, Noah, no worries. But ladies first."

Oh my gosh, they *know* each other. Could this situation get any worse?

Just then, Tammi's phone rings and she gets it out of her pocket. After checking the screen, she gives me an apologetic look. "I'm so sorry, but I have to take this. Let me know if you need anything, okay? I'll check in with you next week to see how things are going. Have a great weekend, everyone."

And just like that, she's gone. Leaving me alone with these two men.

One who looks like he'd rather be anywhere than here, with me.

And the other one seems to be a flirt and possibly friend to the man I once thought of as my soulmate for life.

Since I'm not sure where to look, I decide to stare at the wall. The blank wall that was thankfully primed and is ready to go.

"Well." I clear my throat and try to be as un-awkward as possible. My face still feels hot, and since I pulled my hair back into a ponytail, I can't even hide my flaming cheeks behind it. "Have you painted walls before, Hunter?"

"Yes, ma'am." He beams at me, his eyes crinkling at the corners.

I've had guys hit on me before and have dated a little over the last few years, even though nothing ever lasted very long. But I don't think anyone's ever been as flirty and charming—without seeming like a douchebag—as Hunter.

Of course, things were different with a certain someone, but I'm still doing my best to ignore him. Plus, we were teenagers. Kids, really. That doesn't count that much, right?

"Noah's experienced too." He hooks his thumb over his shoulder but keeps his gaze on me.

I wave him off. "Oh yeah, I know. We've done—" *Shit.*

What am I doing telling Hunter about Noah's and my past? About the times he helped me paint my bedroom walls, because I loved it so much and he wanted me to be happy and spend as much time with me as possible?

My mind is off on a crazy ride again, images of Noah and me filling my head. The laughter, the joy, the pure bliss of not knowing what ugly things might lie ahead of us. The roadblocks so high they'd seemed impossible to pass. And the pain that would be waiting at the end of the road . . . so much pain that life would sometimes feel like too much to bear. No, we definitely didn't know about any of that when we were together.

I blink and look down, trying to swallow past the thick lump in my throat but the feat seems almost impossible.

Pulling at the high collar of my shirt, I hope no one notices my shaky fingers. How embarrassing. First I zone out with Tammi, and now I'm having a small emotional breakdown in front of Hunter. Being around Noah is screwing with my brain a lot more than I thought it would.

"Hey, are you okay?" Hunter's voice is quieter than before, the cheerfulness now missing. When I look at him, the smile is gone too.

I nod, clearing my throat several times before I manage to push out some words. "Yes, sorry about that. I swear, I'm not usually like this."

"No worries."

Another set of footsteps comes closer, but I can't look *his* way. I barely just got my emotions back in check, and I can only take that much.

Work. I need to work. Lose myself in the familiar throngs of what's always been my escape. Just like I did last week at home when I poured all of my energy into the kids' book I'm currently illustrating.

Sadly, I still haven't gotten much further with my draft for the competition with the publisher, but I'll get there.

Another deep inhale, and my spine straightens infinitesimally.

I've got this.

I knew there was a chance of running into him, just like Cody had predicted. But I didn't think it would happen like this. Not here, not in my space. Now, I have to figure out how to deal with him because this project will take a few weeks to complete. At least.

So, new motto for this task: finish it as soon as possible to get away from this strange connection with Noah. The faster, the better. Then we can go our separate ways again.

Turning my back to them, I walk to the storage closet and pull three rolls of painter's tape from one of the shelves, pushing them over my hand and onto my wrist. The ladder comes next before I close the door again.

With everything in hand, I walk the few steps back to where Noah and Hunter stand together, heads close as they whisper to each other. Noah's jaw is tight, the muscles working overtime. Those poor teeth.

The ladder scrapes across the floor by accident, and both look up at the noise.

I hold up the tape. "Are you guys ready to tape?"

Hunter smiles and grabs one of the rolls from me. "Let's do it. Do you want me to start on the other side and work my way back over here?"

"Sure, thank you."

With another smile and a nod, he turns around and leaves.

Did his smiles look less flirty this time or did I imagine that? Oh my gosh, did Noah say something to him about me? Maybe he warned him about me. The thought alone ticks me off.

My head whips around just for my gaze to clash with Noah's.

It's spellbinding just like the first time our eyes met. He sees through my shell, through any barriers or defense mechanisms, and straight into my soul.

Exactly like so many years ago. It was my first day of high school and Eadie and I stood in the hallway when Noah walked by and our gazes locked. A normal moment, nothing extraordinary, yet my whole world shifted in that instant, and I was never the same again. I felt like I had found a missing puzzle piece of myself without actually looking for it or knowing it was missing.

The current coldness in Noah's eyes brings me back to the moment. It's clear I'm the only one still stuck in the past.

When he takes the tape from me and his fingers brush mine, I pretend to be a statue.

There are still no words from Noah. Just complete silence. I know he's hurt . . . was hurt . . . but this utter silence is deafening.

We used to talk about anything and everything.

We used to be each other's everything.

And now we're nothing.

EIGHT

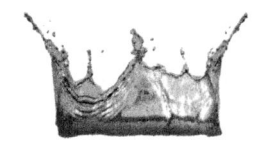

NOAH

Splashing cold water on my face barely makes a difference to my mood, so I just stare at myself in the mirror. The water drips down my chin, and my eyebrows are drawn together in such a tight frown, I'm not sure I can ever get them back to their normal positions.

Fuck.

After another load of cold water to my face, I wave my hands in front of the hand towel dispenser, and dry my face and hands before making my way out of the restroom.

This whole afternoon was a shitshow. Sure, on the outside everything looked normal. At least, as normal as possible to someone who doesn't know me. But on the inside, I've been battling a vicious hurricane ever since I saw Chloe again, and it has just picked up speed.

Somehow, I have to figure out how to handle that she's back. That she's here. Not just in this town but also in my life. Surely, I can handle a few weeks of volunteer work with her, right? I mean, I should be able to. Maybe next time I can bring my headphones and drown everything else out. Focus on the work in front of me. The same way I've always done with swimming.

Hunter and Chloe left several minutes ago, so it's just me at the elevator bank.

So what if I hid in the bathroom for a while?

I didn't just have to escape Chloe, but Hunter too. Since his inquisition when Chloe was distracted by Tammi, he's aware that I know Chloe.

And Hunter is like a bloodhound—once he gets a sniff of something good, he won't let it go until he gets whatever info he wants. Kind of like my sister, actually. Huh. I never realized that before. Speaking of Daisy, did she know about Chloe working on this project I'm volunteering for?

The elevator ride to the lobby level is quick, the hospital quieter now that it's evening.

Outside, it's the opposite. Sometime in the last hour, a rainstorm has decided to show up. It's only September, so rain is rare, but apparently, it's happening anyway. At least, it's usually short-lived.

I take it as an omen of my mood.

Of my life.

Trying to let out some of my frustration with a big exhale, I mentally prepare myself to get wet, as it's coming down hard.

The automatic doors open, and all I manage to see is a flurry of purple before a wet body smacks straight into my chest. And I know exactly what—or rather who—just hit me.

"Oh crap, I'm so sorry. My car won't start, and I was just trying to get back into the—" Chloe's gaze meets mine as she tilts her head back enough to see who she ran into.

Damn. She's so beautiful.

The other day at the restaurant, I was staring at her, but I was surrounded by a cloud of shock and anger that subdued my senses.

All afternoon, I was trying to ignore her as best as I could, never looking at her for longer than I had to; and when I had to, it was never this close.

Those damn freckles on her nose and cheeks are still as adorable as they used to be. My gaze stays on her nose ring for a moment, intrigued by it. Somehow, it fits her, accentuating the small curve at the tip of her nose.

Her mouth is slightly parted, her body still pressed against mine. And those lips . . . fuck. I spent so many hours devouring them. Sucking on them. Licking them. Biting them. Would they still taste as good as I remember?

That thought snaps me out of this weird spell she's got over me, and my gaze goes to hers as I take a hasty step back. She almost stumbles forward at the sudden movement but catches herself at the last moment.

When a shiver ripples through her whole body, I look her over. Her black leggings and her blue T-shirt that is now drenched and clinging to her upper body.

"You know better than to be out without a jacket at night."

Wow. Way to be a jerk, Noah.

Rubbing her arms with her hands, she scrunches up her nose. Her version of an eye roll. I used to tackle her whenever she did it and kiss her nose until she giggled in my arms.

"Sorry, *Dad*. I forgot, okay? My weather brain's still in Los Angeles. And I'd be okay if I could sit in my car with the heat on. But since it won't start, that's not going to happen."

The passionate fire in her eyes makes me want to put her

over my knee, but no fucking way are we going down that road. "Could it be the battery?"

She shakes her head. "It shouldn't be. I just had it changed last month."

"Hmmm." After an almost non-existent debate with myself—because my masochist side seems to run strong where this woman is concerned—I get out my phone, pull up the number I'm looking for, and press the call button.

"What are you doing?" Chloe stops rubbing her arms, even though she's still shaking like a leaf.

"Calling my uncle."

"Why?"

"You don't want him to take a look at your car and fix it?"

"Oh." Her lips form an o-shape, and I know being so close to her isn't good for my sanity. "Of course. Thanks so much."

"It's nothing." I push the words through grinding teeth. No clue if they're even audible or not, but thankfully, my uncle picks up at that moment.

"Hey, Noah. What's up?"

"Hey, Chris. I have a favor to ask. I'm at the hospital for a charity project, and the car of one of my . . ." I glance at Chloe, her eyebrows lifting at my pause. "Uh, one of my *friends'* cars won't start, and I was wondering if you might have time to look at it."

Why did I just call her my friend? We are *not* friends. There's nothing friendly about us.

My uncle clears his throat. "You bet. We just had an appointment fall through, actually, so I can head out with Larry in a bit."

"Thanks, man. I appreciate it."

"Sure thing. Just text me the license plate number and location, and leave the keys under the floor mat if your friend is okay with that."

"Sounds good. Thanks again."

"No problem."

I hang up after saying goodbye and rehash the conversation to Chloe who keeps nodding.

I press the message button on my uncle's contact and lift my gaze to meet Chloe's. "What's your license plate number?"

"8CAN386." She looks away from me.

My hands halt mid-type. *CAN* for Chloe and Noah. "You still have your old license plate?"

And why shouldn't she? She didn't move out of state, after all. But to keep her old license plate, *our* license plate.

She nods and chews on her bottom lip. I'm positive she's out to kill me. That's the only reason that makes sense.

After sending the text message to my uncle, I try to find my inner Zen. The same one I've worked on for over a decade and usually isn't a problem for me to slip into. When I can't get into it right away, I briefly wonder if Chloe broke it. If she broke *me*.

The desire to retreat and go somewhere quiet to rethink my offer to drive her—and possibly taking it back—is at the forefront of my brain. Not even a second later, my manners kick in though and I sigh, "Let's get you home."

"Uh what?" I walk around her to the sliding doors, looking over my shoulder to make sure she's following.

Of course, she's not.

Placing my hands on my hips, I let out a loud breath,

speaking slowly. "Obviously, I'm going to drive you home. Unless you'd rather try to get an Uber on a Friday night?"

"But why?"

She's staring at me like I've grown a third eye.

I let my hands drop to my thighs. Loudly. "Because I'm not an asshole?"

It comes out more as a question, even though it shouldn't have. It's clear that I'm trying to be a stellar citizen—and just a straight-up stellar person—by doing the right thing.

Naturally, she has to make even that more difficult.

"But you don't even like me." This time, her voice has less bite, and I feel like massaging my temples. Now I know what my coach felt like earlier.

I take a step in her direction and bend my head to be on eye level with her, ignoring all the memories that want to haunt me when I get a good glimpse of her eyes. "I don't have to like you to be a decent person. Are you coming now, or what? I'm not going to beg you."

With that, I turn and make my way through the sliding doors and out into the cold rain. Thankfully, it has calmed down and there is only light drizzle now.

This time, she follows, and I gesture for her to lead the way to her car. We walk quietly until I spot our destination and stop dead in my tracks. "You're kidding me, right?"

Chloe lets out a little snort and goes straight for the silver Honda that's parked a few feet in front of us. "Nope. She's still alive."

I shake my head as I watch her grab a few things out of the trunk, wiggling her ass in the process. I contain the groan that wants to escape, and of course, I'm totally not staring at it. Nope.

And that car. The same one we drove around for years. The car we did *things* in. Dirty things. Orgasmic things.

When she's done, she shuts the trunk, and looks at me over her shoulder. Her purple ponytail whips to the side as I keep staring at her. "You said to put the key under the floor mat, right?"

"Yeah."

"Okay."

After putting it in place, Chloe closes the door, and we walk to my car two rows down. It's a black sedan and only a few years old. The most important thing: it doesn't hold any memories of us.

I unlock the car and get a few towels from the trunk. Fortunately, I always have some extra in case my nephews and I need them for swimming or a mess they made. I hand her one and put another few on her seat before we both get in. Chloe throws her things in the back and almost whacks me in the head.

After securing my seat belt, I glance toward the back. "A puzzle?"

"Yes. I'm going over to my mom's tonight and she loves them. But I need to get home first and get changed. Then I'll catch an Uber or cab to her place."

My fingers go to the spot between my eyes and I rub it. Pinch it. "I'll drive you to your mom's after you get changed at home."

I'd better get brownie points for this. Lots of brownie points.

"You don't have to, Noah. You already did so much by taking care of the car and getting me home."

My hand goes to the shifter to put it in reverse, my fingers turning white from pressing so hard. "Chloe, what's your address?"

"814 Westminster Avenue."

My head snaps her way so fast, a sharp pain shoots through the back of my scalp. Son of a . . . "Are you serious right now?"

"Yes. Is something wrong with that address? Do you want me to pull it up for you on my phone?"

"Nope. I got it."

My breathing grows heavier as I try to hang on to my emotions by a thread.

Chloe Williams is back in my life.

I'm stuck with her for this volunteer project.

Chloe Williams is also my fucking neighbor.

NINE

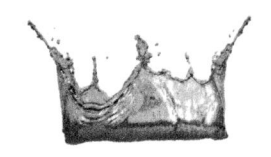

CHLOE

This is the strangest car ride of my life, and Noah has been acting extra weird. I don't really blame him for avoiding me at the hospital. It was clear as day that he was as surprised as I was about being there. Because what are the odds? Fate is clearly laughing at us—or at me, at least—rubbing her hands together in poor glee over screwing all of this up so badly.

When I signed up for the project, I had no idea where my volunteers would come from. Painting the mural was supposed to be my safe haven, my fun project to distract me from too much free time that usually leads to thoughts of my dad, or of Noah—and especially the fact that I'm in the same city as him.

Things were supposed to be done with him. Cleared up. Forgiven or not, done with. Without anything left.

Instead, I'm stuck with him in his car. It's not a small car by any means, but I might as well be rolled up with him in a blanket for all it's worth. His presence is astronomical. And his scent . . . Goodness, the scent of him is so overwhelming to my senses I feel a little intoxicated. Or high. Maybe both.

Car rides with him used to be my happy place. Our main teenage hangout spot where we could be alone without watchful eyes on us. The place where we crossed lines and whispered naughty things to each other. The place where we explored and learned.

Sure, there had been tears too—they seem to come naturally to a teenager, especially when you're in love—but I mainly remember the fun times. The joy and bliss that only a teenager without a care in the world can feel.

The car stops, pulling me out of my thoughts.

I look over at Noah whose gaze is locked on the house behind me. My house. For now, at least. It was one of the only affordable rentals in this area. Close to my mom, the hospital, Eadie, my uncles, and everything else I love and need.

At some point, I might look into buying a house, but that wasn't anything I wanted to do online without seeing it in person. Maybe next year.

It's close to the neighborhood I used to live in, and I was thrilled to find this place available.

"I'll be right back." I open the door to get out but turn to him when he doesn't say anything. "And you're really sure you're okay to drive me to my mom's? It's no problem to call an Uber or cab."

"Go. I'll wait." His voice is gruff as he turns his head in the other direction, successfully dismissing me.

Grouchy butt.

Not for the first time, I wonder if he's like this with everyone, or if he saves his moodiness specifically for me.

It's so contrary to what he used to be like. He was never the life of the party, the classroom clown, but there was more lightness to him. Now, there hasn't been one smile or form of levity whenever I've interacted with him.

I make my way to the front door while rummaging through my bag to find the keys. Somehow, they always disappear in there, no matter how hard I try to keep them in the same spot.

Once I'm inside, I make quick work of my clothes, changing my T-shirt and leggings for another set, but this time also putting on a sweater. I take the extra minute to hang up my wet clothes in the laundry room, so I don't have to deal with them later.

After locking the house, I make my way back to Noah's waiting car—the light drizzle has mostly stopped—ready for the second leg of our odd car ride.

This time, he doesn't react all weird when I tell him the address. I take a moment to send my mom a quick message to tell her what happened and to let her know I'm on my way.

"Thanks so much again for driving me. I really appreciate it. And also for the help with the car. I'm sure I wouldn't have been able to get it done so quickly otherwise."

"No problem."

That's it. He doesn't give me an inch, and I can't even blame him. Shit. I'm not sure I've forgiven myself for what happened back then. I know I wasn't planning on getting sick, but the way I ended things between us was brutal. For both of us, even though he doesn't know that.

To him, I was the evil one.

To him, I was the one who ripped out his heart while mine stayed intact.

And that's what I let him believe—what I wanted him to believe—even though it couldn't have been further from the truth.

Because even when my heart was ripped out and there was nothing left of it, I could still feel his imprint deep inside of me like it had never left.

He was a part of me, engrained so profoundly within my essence that I would never be able to let go of him entirely for as long as I lived.

And yet I did.

That doesn't change the fact that there's no future for us though. I have to live with this new life, and there's no room for him in it. It wouldn't be fair to him or to us.

As so often, my body isn't in line with my thoughts. Inhaling his scent deeply, I feel like he's around me. Taking in this still-the-same yet slightly-unfamiliar, older version of him whenever I can, committing every single detail to memory, even though I know it will only make things harder for me.

But as before, when it comes to Noah Winters, I'm unable to deny my senses what they crave. Most of them, at least.

Thank goodness the drive to my mom is quick. When we get there, I jump out of the car before it fully stops, slamming the door shut after mumbling a quick "Thank you" in Noah's direction.

I'm almost at the front door when two things happen: my mom opens the door and smiles at me, and Noah calls my name.

Sending a few stern words to fate, or whoever's doing all of this for shits and giggles, I give my mom a forced smile and give myself a second to think about what Noah might want. Has he gotten over his aversion to me? My body, my memory, and everything in between are obviously drawn to him.

Maybe we could be friends? Friends sounds good, right? Everyone needs friends.

A spark of something I don't want to name ignites in my chest, spreading warmth through my body. I take a deep breath and shoot another glance at my mom before looking at Noah, who's walking up the drive. How bad is this going to be?

Then I see it. The bag in his hand, just as he stretches it out toward me.

Damn it. Of course. I was so focused on getting out of his overpowering presence, I totally forgot that I still had my bag in the backseat.

Taking it out of his hand without touching him—okay, maybe just a small, torturing brush of my fingers against his—I'm glad the sky has gotten darker because my skin's on fire. "Thanks."

My mom gasps behind me. "Oh, I can't believe it. Is that really you, Noah Winters?"

I hold my breath, and then I die because Noah smiles. A disarming smile that is breathtaking.

Wow.

Unfortunately, it's not aimed at me, but my stupid heart doesn't seem to care. It latches on to this rarity like it's never seen it before. Which I guess it hasn't. Teenage Noah's smile had me enchanted from the very beginning, but adult Noah's smile is something else entirely. It's meant to steal my sanity, along with other things. Which is not an option. No. Nope.

Not going to happen. And now I won't ever be able to unsee it.

"Hey, Mrs. Williams."

"Oh my. I didn't know you two were getting together today. What a surprise." She shoots me a meaningful glance that silently portrays "You owe me an explanation," before her focus is back on Noah. "And look at you. You're all grown up."

"I guess I am." Noah chuckles once and shrugs. "You look as lovely as ever."

It doesn't escape my notice that he didn't comment on the "getting together" part. Also, I never thought I'd say this, but I think I'm jealous of my mother. Who needs that?

My mom touches her cheek, probably because she's another woman who's fallen victim to the Noah-made-me-blush syndrome. "Would you like to come inside? I just set up some tea for Chloe and me."

I feel like I'm watching a tennis match, my gaze flickering back and forth between my mom and Noah. I'm actually not sure which team I'm on though. And who do I want to win?

His gaze meets mine for a nanosecond before he scratches his neck with one of his oversized hands. That guy has always had big hands, or rather paws as I'd called them. Strong and very, *very* capable. "I have some things to do, but thank you for the invitation."

She waves him off. "No worries. Maybe next weekend? You could come over for Sunday lunch if you want to."

He's about to open his mouth to decline, I just know it.

And I don't even blame him. What on earth is my mom doing?

Apparently, she's prepared for him to decline this invitation as well. "I insist . . . for old time's sake."

Guilt card, here we go. I think I might need to have a stern talk about this with her later.

Noah's Adam's apple bobs with a thick swallow as he closes his eyes. "Okay."

"Great. That's great." My mom seems to be the only one who thinks this is anything but a disaster, and also the only one who's oblivious to the tension radiating off Noah. Or she's a better actress than I thought.

He clears his throat. "Well, I better get going. Have a good night."

With that, he turns around, leaving me to enjoy the view. And by view, I mean that tight, round ass in his low-hung sweatpants.

"Well, well . . ." My mom's hand lands on my shoulder as she spins me around and we walk into the house. "Looks like there's a lot you have to tell me."

"There's nothing to tell, Mom."

"That didn't look like nothing to me."

We make our way through the hallway—where I stop to look at our family photos, sending my dad a smile, as always—and into the kitchen. The two mugs on the kitchen bar are steaming, the herbal tea tags hanging over the edges.

After slinging my purse and the bag on the bar, I plop onto the barstool, and drop my head on my folded arms. Seems to be my new thing, especially after seeing Noah in any capacity, or when recounting anything involving Noah.

What a mess. This wasn't supposed to be like this. None of it.

This was supposed to be a new start. Bringing me

comfort to be united with my friends and family. Instead, it has unleashed chaos.

I listen to my mom's movements around the kitchen, the clinking of the mugs on the counter, the opening and closing of the trash can drawer.

She's always been the patient one out of my parents, which sometimes drove my dad and me insane. Do I want to talk to her about Noah? We're close, even closer since my dad passed away, but talking about boys . . . about men has never been our *thing*.

And what's there even to tell? Nothing on the outside since we aren't anything. But there's so much going on inside my head. Things I don't want to say out loud, let alone think about. Not that my mind or heart care about any of it.

"Noah was assigned to me for the volunteer work at the hospital." I accept the mug she holds out to me, knowing she's already added the honey. "Thank you."

"Oh wow. That's unexpected." She grabs her mug and we move to the dining room table.

I'm not sure why she even needs one since she's living by herself, but in my eyes, she's got free rein on whatever the heck she wants to do. Between me and my dad, she's had a lot to deal with in the last decade, and I just want her to find a slice of happiness. If a giant dining room table makes her happy, so be it.

I catch her up on the hospital work and my broken-down car. There really isn't much else to tell.

After spreading out her puzzle mat, we spend the next hour hunched together over her latest obsession, a three-thousand-piece edition of Flowering Paris.

It will look gorgeous and has me completely engrossed.

My thoughts don't sneak off to Noah at all.
Not one bit.

TEN

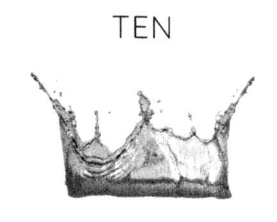

NOAH

Is twenty-nine too old for a round of ding-dong ditch?

Or maybe a mental assessment would be more appropriate because, at this point, I'm seriously doubting my mental capabilities.

I clearly seem to be incapable of making wise decisions when it comes to anything Chloe-involved, and shouldn't be around her at all.

The last few days alone are proof enough.

First, the hospital project. Maybe I could have gotten out of that one. I probably should have tried the second I saw her, but I was too dumbfounded.

Then, not only driving her home, but also to her mom's? Definitely reckless. Maybe even stupid. Clearly, I was asking fate to smack me upside the head.

Which brings me to my third point. A lunch invitation from Chloe's mom. How on earth could I have said no to her? She's always been incredibly kind and supportive toward me.

I shake my head at my own . . . I'm not even sure what to

call it. Idiocy? Weakness? Either way, I turn around. I have to leave. Right now. Before—

"Noah?"

That voice.

That damn voice that torments me, even in my dreams.

I wait for a heartbeat before I turn around—just to immediately wish I hadn't. Because Chloe's in only a workout T-shirt and shorts.

Both are tight. So very tight.

Just like my balls all of a sudden.

I hate them. *Loathe* them.

Of course, my body has to betray me when it comes to the one woman that's on our shit list.

"Sorry, I'm a mess. I just got done working out." She brushes her hands over her hair, trying to calm the flyaways. Unsuccessfully so.

"You work out? Voluntarily?"

Her mouth twitches before a chuckle escapes. "Yeah. Every day, actually. Who would've thought, right?"

Something feels off about her voice, her smile never fully reaching her eyes, but what do I know? She's clearly not the same person she was ten years ago, and why should she be? Neither am I.

"Right." I try not to flinch when I hear the bite in my voice.

She hasn't done anything—at least not since she came back—but I can't seem to let go of my past anger. How can I still feel so . . . *much* after all this time?

It's suffocating.

My muscles clench, trying to erase some of the tension in

my body. My hands form into fists by my side, almost crushing the book in my hand. Wait a second. *The book.*

With almost stiff movements, I lift my hand and wave the book in front of me like I've lost my mind. Which might be a pretty solid representation of my current state of confusion.

Chloe slaps a hand over her mouth, her already red face turning a shade darker. But this time, it's not from working out. Nope. If I had to guess, my money would be on the half-naked guy on the book cover. And the ripped bodice. Let's not forget about that little detail.

"Whoops. That must have fallen out of my bag in your car." The words are muffled since she still hasn't taken her hand off her mouth.

"Uh-huh. Must have." My eyes track her every move as her gaze flitters between the book in my hand, my face, and the ground.

Why can't I look away? Why do I still feel the same pull that was like second nature to me all those years ago? I always thought it had something to do with being in love. Something extra mushy you tell yourself only happens because you're a teenager and your hormones are out of fucking control.

I can't say I've dated a ton over the years—at least no lasting relationships—but I've not once come close to feeling any sort of pull to any of the other women. Not the way I did with Chloe.

And here we are. The devil from my past gets thrown back into my life in more than just one way and zap, that intense feeling is back.

But this time, it feels almost cruel. Bitter. With an underlying thrill to it, which marks another notch on my way to officially becoming a masochist.

And who needs that?

Being around her clearly screws with my brain.

Her hand stretches out toward me, palm up, and I stare at it like the idiot I am.

"I'm so sorry about leaving that behind."

Oh, she wants the book. Of course.

She takes it from me and almost drops it when I pull my hand away too quickly. Anything to try and avoid touching her.

Her gaze lands on the cover and she snorts. "Historical romances are my mom's other new obsession, besides puzzles. I totally forgot I got this for her too."

"Oh."

"Thanks for dropping it off. You didn't have to come by just for that."

Right. She still doesn't know I live across the street.

"No problem." Nope, still not telling her.

"And thanks again for last night too. I really appreciate your help with everything. Your uncle called earlier. He doesn't have the part he needs at the shop, but he's already ordered it for me. That means the car won't be ready until Monday, but at least he said it's an easy fix, so I can't complain."

"That's good." I push my hands into my athletic shorts. Why am I still here? "You can ride with me to the hospital later."

Fuck. Why did I just say that?

Her eyes widen. "Oh." She brushes her hand down her neck. "No worries, I already have a ride, but thank you."

I nod. Thank God she does. Right?

Hopefully, it's someone trustworthy.

"Well..."

"Hey, I know this sounds lame, but I was just about to push the button on the blender, and you've always loved smoothies. Would you like to come inside and have a shake? I always double the recipe. I promise it's delicious and super healthy." The words rush out of her mouth, and she bites on her lower lip when she's done.

My mind is blank.

A total shutdown.

"As a thank-you for all your help. It's the least I can do." Her eyebrows move up in question.

My brain finally reboots, powering up with a big, fat "Fuck no, absolutely not," as I lift my shoulders and say, "Sure."

I mentally shake my head at whatever part of me that's acting like a total loser. I've lost sight of who's in charge of me right now, but it certainly isn't the rational part of my brain. To make a point, and show my utter displeasure, I scowl like my life depends on it.

Since it doesn't seem to deter Chloe, I follow her into the house, keeping my eyes up, on the back of her head. That's a safe spot. I will absolutely not look at her ass. No fucking way.

The kitchen is just around the corner. It's small and clean. Simple. Wooden cabinets, light countertop. A few random items strewn around. The backyard is just beyond the window and patio door, flooding the kitchen in bright morning light.

"Let me just get this started quick." Chloe picks up the blender from the other side of the counter where she must have put the ingredients together.

The blender base is right next to where I'm standing by the stove, and I barely move out of the way before she touches me when she clicks the jar into the base.

Her finger pushes the smoothie button as she turns toward me, and that's all I remember for the next few seconds as total chaos descends on us.

"Oh my gosh!" Chloe squeals, her hands flailing around amidst the smoothie attack. She bumps into me as we both try to shield our faces from the liquid the blender continues to throw at us and pretty much everywhere else in the kitchen.

I beat her to the button by a second, and the monster machine turns off.

Our gazes collide, both of us wide-eyed and looking like . . . I'm not even sure like what. We look hideous, that's for sure. Covered in muddy-green goop that's dripping down our hair, skin, and clothes.

Chloe looks back at the offending machine. "I swear I pushed the lid on tight. At least, I thought I did."

When her gaze meets mine again, I press my lips together.

I mean, what is this? After all the strange meetups in the past week with this woman. Now this. And it was supposed to be her thank-you to me, and look at the mess.

Is this the universe's way of telling me to listen to my inner voice that's telling me to turn the other way whenever Chloe is involved? Because that voice sounds incredibly legit, now more than ever. It actually couldn't be any louder. Yet, here I am. Ignoring it over and over.

Neither one of us moves, too shell-shocked.

And then Chloe laughs. Full-on laughter accompanied by her signature snort. She laughs so hard, that after only a few seconds, she's gasping for air. Right before she slaps her hands on her thighs several times. Something she's always done when she has a laughing fit like this. She also manages to fling some more smoothie my way, hitting me almost in the eye with it.

Me, on the other hand . . . all I can do is stare at her. It sounds so much like the Chloe I knew. It's subtle, and I'm almost ready to admit that I miss it—miss *her*—but I'm not there yet. However, under the surface, something shifts inside of me.

Things have always been effortless with her, and I suddenly crave it like nothing else. This easiness. The familiarity. Something that isn't loaded with a ton of pressure and a million responsibilities or expectations like everything else in my life seems to come with these days.

Swimming used to be easy for me. It used to be my happy place where I could let go of everything and just be. But something has changed there too in the last year. It's started to feel lonely. Too lonely.

Damn it, my sister was right. My whole life's started to feel lonely. Even with all the people in my life. Not only do I help my sister with her two sons a lot, but there's also the guys, my swim buddies Ryan, Jace, and Hunter.

But since Ryan and Jace have found their other halves and welcomed kids into the world, and Hunter's been more busy than usual too, I haven't seen as much of them as I used to.

And there really isn't anyone or anything else.

Sure, there are my parents, but since Daisy and I have left the nest, so to speak, they've been traveling the world a lot. Working with charities, making rural areas in Third

World countries a better place. Their work is admirable, and important, but it's definitely not the same without them here.

Which means my life has mostly revolved around watching my family and friends move forward with their lives. Taking steps I once thought I'd someday take too. Witnessing it firsthand has only amplified how stagnant my life has become.

Chloe hiccups. "I'm so incredibly sorry, Noah. I don't know what to say."

I hear her words, but my mind is still busy with my latest realization.

Do I have any "old" friends I could add back to my life?

Chloe is an old friend.

Could I ever be friends again with her?

This is messing with my head.

As if to prove a point, she touches my chest, and a current of electricity zaps through my body.

"I can't believe I made such a mess."

My thoughts exactly. Although, I'm not sure she's talking about now or what she did to me ten years ago.

ELEVEN

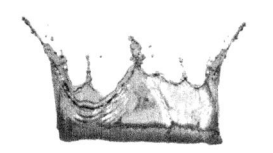

CHLOE

I didn't mean to touch him.

I mean, I kind of did, but not in an I-want-to-rub-myself-all-over-him way. But that's exactly what my body is yelling at me to do right now.

Rubbing, rubbing, and some more rubbing. With lots of touching in between.

Knowing that's the last thing Noah wants is a huge help though. He's scowled at me over fifty percent of the time, which is an excellent indicator that we haven't gotten anywhere.

Not to mention, he openly admitted yesterday that he doesn't like me.

Can't get more transparent than that.

But that's my doing, and I have to live with it.

Obviously, my brilliant idea to give thanks in a small way by offering him some of my smoothie—as strange as that sounds—couldn't have gone more wrong.

Now we both look like mud monsters, and I'm sure we'll smell like some sooner or later too.

Somewhere in this whole debacle, I snatched a towel to dabble at his chest. Which I'm still doing. My hands are on autopilot, and I'm not sure there's an end in sight. Because it's not awkward enough yet.

But I also haven't been this close to a guy in way too long, and despite the smoothie-smell—that's slowly taking over my sense buds—I'm weirdly enough enjoying this moment.

Maybe, I should find a therapist here after all. Can't hurt to check. My last therapist can attest that I'm a stellar client.

"Chloe." Noah's raised voice pulls me out of my thoughts, a second before his hands grab my wrists.

He's touching me, actually touching me—not just pulling me off him or pushing me away—and I shiver, especially when I glance away from the spot where he's holding me and up to his face. Our gazes lock, and I go weak in the knees.

This man has always done it for me. From the first moment until the end, and actually well beyond that. And seeing him again has only confirmed my suspicions from the last few years . . . No other man will ever consume me the way he does.

Too bad I'm not looking for anything long-term. It's just not in the cards for me.

If it was, Noah would definitely be in my number-one spot. That is, if he stopped disliking me and actually wanted me.

Yet, knowing all of that, it's still impossible to ignore the electricity that almost vibrates under my skin from his touch. His thumb sits right on my pulse point as the current zips its way up my arm and through the rest of my body like it's supposed to light me up from the inside. Maybe I'll start glowing from the sheer power of it soon.

"Stop rubbing my shirt, it's fine." He still isn't smiling at me, but at least his scowl is gone. Mostly.

The smoothie has started to dry in places, and it looks like we're having an awkward—and very unplanned—spa day.

Definitely no thanks-so-much-for-everything feelings going on here.

My gaze flickers to his filthy shirt for a second. "You can't get in your car like this. You'll get everything dirty."

He could always take off his shirt, of course, but somehow, I don't think he'd appreciate that suggestion.

He huffs. "Don't worry about my car."

"What? Why?" I swear there was more I wanted to say but he's started rubbing his thumbs across my wrists, and it's distracting as hell.

The motion is barely noticeable, but my body is on high alert.

What is happening? I feel like I've entered the Twilight Zone.

My eyes aren't sure where to look, flicking back and forth between his face and the spots where his big hands encircle my much smaller wrists.

Then his movement stops. When I notice that his gaze is fixated on my left wrist, I realize my mistake. *Major* mistake.

I try to pull my hands out of his, but he only tightens his grip.

Shit. Shit. *Shit.*

"Chloe, what is this?" His voice has dropped an octave, a dangerous edge to it.

I ignore it. I ignore him. Continuing to pull.

"Stop trying to get away and answer my question."

Sweat starts to form at the back of my neck, but I stop

moving. I push away the sensation of not being able to get enough oxygen into my lungs and inhale deeply. Only then do I meet his gaze and immediately wish I hadn't. The intensity of it heats up my body even more as adrenaline floods my system like it has an expiration date and needs to be used up right this second.

Despite everything, I lift my chin and ignore his flaring nostrils and dull eyes that don't blink. With one more hard yank, I finally get out of his grasp and get some distance between us, almost slipping on the messy floor.

Wrapping my arms around myself, I refuse to look away first. "It's nothing."

The words didn't come out as strong as I wanted them to.

"What . . . the . . . fuck . . . is that on your wrist?" Noah's words are quiet, but so piercing, they reverberate through every particle of my soul.

He takes a step toward me, and I take one back, which puts me flush against the kitchen counter. If he comes even closer, there's nowhere for me to go. Unless I try to get around him to make a run for it. And let's face it, the chances of making it past him are slim to none, especially on the slippery floor.

Thankfully, he stops.

Looking up at the ceiling, he clasps his hands behind the back of his neck and takes several deep breaths. "Was it you? Did *you* do it?"

The backs of my eyes burn.

Why did I invite him inside my house? Stupid. I shouldn't be so close to him. Even less so when we're alone.

I wanted to apologize to him, and I did that last week at

the restaurant. That should have been the end for us. For good this time.

The fact that we work together on the volunteer project was unexpected, but we're adults, so what the heck. We can manage to co-exist and work together for a few weeks, right?

But *this* . . . it's a lot.

It's too much when all I want to do is curl into a ball and have him hold me.

To have him soothe my many wounds, especially the ones invisible to the naked eye. I have plenty of those too, but they don't hurt nearly as much as the ones I hide on the inside.

His hands fall back to his sides, his posture sagging like he's about to fall in on himself.

Why does that make me want to comfort him?

This is all so screwed up.

And so confusing.

His Adam's apple bobs several times before he clears his throat. "Why?"

"It doesn't matter."

He bares his teeth at me, and his clenched fists are almost vibrating next to his body. "The fuck it does."

"Noah, please."

He closes his eyes, his jaw clenching like he's trying to crush his teeth.

When he opens his eyes again, they are softer. Only marginally, but it's better than nothing. "You can't expect me to just walk out of here and ignore the fact that you have a scar on your wrist from cutting yourself. It doesn't matter if you cover it up with a tattoo, it's still right fucking there."

"I know."

My thoughts are all over the place, and it's hard to focus

on any one of them. The past mixes with the present. The present mixes with the past. It's too much.

A moment later, my ears start ringing, and I'm a little lightheaded. I lean more of my weight against the kitchen counter and put my hands on it for extra support. "I'm . . . I'm sorry about your clothes. Let me know if you need me to pay for anything or want me to clean them or whatever."

He sends me a murderous look.

We're both a total mess, and Noah and I stare at each other for a prolonged moment. It's awkward. It's strange, yet familiar. Overwhelming. Comforting. How is that even possible?

Have I thought about what it would be like to see him again after so long? To talk to him as my friend? To confide in him? To fill in the many gaps of our time apart? Of course, I have. Plenty of times.

But the whole time, I was so focused on figuring out the words that I needed to apologize. That was my top priority and made me anxious enough. I didn't think much beyond that point.

"You know you don't have to pay for anything or wash things for me. Don't insult me."

"I wasn't trying to."

With his hand squeezing his neck, he looks around the kitchen, probably inspecting the mess. "Shit. Let me help clean up."

Since I feel steady enough, I take a step forward and lift my hand, almost reaching out to him again before I think better of it. "No."

We both stiffen when I pretty much yell at him.

I cringe. "Sorry. I meant no, thank you. I'll take care of it."

"Are you sure? It's pretty bad."

Crap, he isn't wrong. It's more than just bad.

The green goo is everywhere. On every available surface, every appliance, plus the floor and ceiling. Nothing has been spared by my green smoothie that I thought could be my helper today in smoothing things over with Noah. Pun totally not intended.

And look where that has gotten me.

I release a pent-up breath and press my lips together. "Yeah, I've got it."

"I see." He nods before bending down to untie his sneakers.

Of course, they're filthy too.

"Why are you taking off your shoes?"

He doesn't look at me. "So I don't carry the mess to the front door?"

Of course, he has to be thoughtful now.

What a jerk.

"Well, I better get going, then, I suppose." His words are stiff, and how can I blame him?

This morning has turned into a total clusterfuck.

With his shoes in his hands, he stares at me, and I take that as my sign. After quickly wiping off my feet, I lead the way to the front door and open it. Right before stepping back as far as I can to make as much room as possible. If I could, I'd dissolve into the wall.

He walks off without another word, and I shut the door behind him the second he's out.

Is that rude? Maybe.

But right now, there can't be enough space between us.

Nothing is safe where Noah is concerned.

"You can't expect me to just walk out of here and ignore the fact that you have a scar on your wrist from cutting yourself."

He's wrong.

That's exactly what I need him to do. To walk out of here forgetting what he just saw.

TWELVE

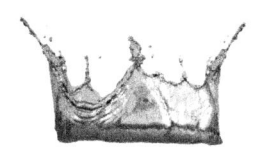

NOAH

"Dude, where the hell have you been? I was ready to kick in your door soon." Hunter rushes past me and stops several feet away.

My breathing is so labored, I can barely hear anything over the sound of blood rushing through my ears. Maybe I overdid it just a little bit with my gym session today.

But it's been my only outlet all week. Working out until I'm so exhausted I can barely stand straight anymore. Until I'm so exhausted my brain can't do anything but shut down. To drown out all the unwelcome thoughts while I do my best to ignore everyone and everything in my life.

Especially thoughts about a certain someone and her scar.

"Chloe said the hospital lady informed her that you'd called in sick this last week." Hunter lifts his hands in question. "You don't look sick to me."

I raise my eyebrows because I have no energy left for more than that. Or rather, I need every last ounce of it to flip this monstrous tire one more time to finish my set.

Gearing up, I take several deep breaths as I retake my wide stance, tighten my core, and grab the underside of the thick rubber to lift it. My body fights the weight of the tire with the small amount of strength it has left while also being reluctant to not let the crushing weight win. My hands slip once, but I steady my grip and make that tire my bitch.

This is where I'm in control.

Just me and my body. My physical work takes over my mental state.

It's all physics. Cause and effect. Logic.

There aren't any surprises waiting around the corner that smack me in the chest like a freight train.

The opposite of anything that involves Chloe.

In just two weeks, she's given me more sucker-punching surprises than I've had in the previous few years combined.

An image of seeing her for the first time again at the restaurant pops into my mind, followed by one of her wrist, and then the look on her face when I asked her about it. When I realized what the scar is from. And the little birds she had tattooed over it.

Little bird. My nickname for her etched into her skin forever. Total mindfuck.

So I push my thoughts away. All of them. Just like I've been doing since I left her house after smoothie-geddon.

My life had already started to slowly unravel at the seams before she waltzed back into it, but at least, there was still plenty of time and several ways to fix things.

Enter Chloe, and it feels like she took that seam and tore it open as far as it would go, before tossing everything around. Now, I don't even know where to start fixing things. If they're even fixable.

And I hate it. I fucking hate that life seems to be slipping through my fingers at the moment, and I don't know how to control a fucking thing.

With one last enormous effort, I let out something that sounds eerily similar to a war cry, flip over the tire, and let it crash onto the floor with a loud *thud* as I try to catch my breath.

The heaviness in my body, the tightness in my chest, it both goes beyond this workout session. They've been my constant companions while my brain tries to make sense of everything.

Which is why I needed to be alone to at least attempt to process what happened. I still go swimming—at the aquatic club rather than the university though where my coach is—and do my gym sessions, but I do everything by myself.

For as lonely as I am—thanks for planting that seed, Daisy!—I don't want company right now either.

The only people I saw this week were my sister and nephews, but they immediately noticed something was wrong and kept their distance. At least once they realized I wouldn't talk more than the bare minimum.

"Hey, you okay?" Hunter rushes over to where I'm now bent over because my body is done. Utterly depleted. There isn't enough air going into my lungs, and I don't have the energy to stand upright anymore either. "Come on, let's go sit down somewhere."

He leads me over to the side where I lean against the wall and slide to the floor. Or rather drop like a sack of potatoes, but who cares anymore at this point? Hunter does the same next to me—except the potato-sack action—and stays silent. Which I know isn't an easy task for him.

After a minute, he shuffles next to me, and I turn my head in his direction.

"What's going on, man?" He holds up a blue water bottle. "That's yours, right?"

I nod and grab it from him, greedily emptying the contents in large gulps. I have to hold it with both hands because my hands are shaking from exhaustion. "Thanks."

"No problem." He lets his head fall back against the wall, and we're quiet again.

I ignore his other question and go back to my previous position. My knees pulled up in front of me with my quivering arms folded on top. The most comfortable place to rest my head right now.

"This can't possibly have anything to do with Chloe, can it?"

I grunt without looking at him.

"Mmm. I thought so." He exhales loudly. "What's going on between you two?"

"Nothing." The word shoots out of my mouth, muffled. My throat is scratchy. Maybe I'm coming down with something.

"Is that the problem?"

"Huuuuuuunt." I lift my head to glare at him before I switch my position and rest it back against the cold wall.

Oh yes, that feels nice.

Not as comfortable but the cold surface feels good against my overheated skin.

He holds up his hands. "Sorry. I'm just trying to help."

"I know." Shit. I can be such an asshole sometimes. "Sorry."

He mimics my position, and we both stare at the gym.

Thankfully, the back area we're in is isolated and mostly deserted at the moment. The last thing I need is extra ears or eyes on our conversation.

"No worries." He stays silent for a moment and I close my eyes. "I know you haven't been training either."

"Coach told me to take a break."

"Yet you're here busting your ass."

"Mmm."

"You know you can talk to me, right?"

"Yeah."

More silence while my heart is finally slowing down.

"Can I ask you something?"

I open one eye and peek at him. "Huh?"

"Is she the one who pissed in your Cheerios? Chloe, I mean."

My eyebrows draw together at his words until my brain puts two and two together. The conversation we had at Ryan's house last year when Jace had screwed up with Millie. Something Hunter said to me about wanting to know who pissed in my Cheerios. Not that I remember what I said.

Shit. I don't know how much to tell him. It's not that I don't trust him. We've been friends for many years. All of us. But do I really want to dig up more crap from the past? Would he even understand? I've never really talked much about what went down with Chloe and me.

After we broke up—or rather she left to go on the vacation she never came back from—I focused on swimming. I turned all of my thoughts and anger into energy and used it to my advantage in the pool. It turned me into a beast in the water, yet no one knew there was a reason for it.

The guys and I first met at camp when Chloe and I were

still together, so of course, they knew she wasn't in the picture anymore at some point. But I didn't talk a lot about her, didn't like to share our private stuff with anyone. The guys didn't know much about her or what was going on with me. We were still teenagers at that point and easily distracted.

With a heavy sigh, I close my eyes again. "I guess she is."

"No fucking way. I knew it."

Hunter's way-too-cheerful response makes me snort, which is progress, I suppose.

He whistles under his breath. "Wow."

"Okay, Hunt. I got it."

"Sorry, dude. But wow. And now she's back . . . and the hospital work. Man, she's fucking hot."

"Ugh." I grit my teeth, a headache slowly forming behind my temples.

"Shit. Sorry." He grimaces. "What are you going to do? Are you going to skip the volunteering?"

A question I've been asking myself all week long.

"Now I feel extra bad. My agent landed this new campaign for me last minute, and it will collide with the times at the hospital, so I won't be able to help out as much as I had hoped, if at all. If you're dropping out too, she's gotta do the whole thing by herself." He stops talking, and I look at him. His gaze is focused somewhere far away.

It's rare to see Hunter this focused and serious outside of swimming.

He huffs. "Now I feel like a total dick. Maybe I can move around some stuff. Talk to Coach and my agent to see if we can shift around some of my schedule."

Even if I've been half the problem, the thought of Chloe

being there all by herself without any help doesn't sit right with me either.

Yes, she still screws with my mind.

Yes, I hate the things I've discovered about her since she returned. *Loathe* them.

That she wasn't feeling well. That she . . . that she tried to harm herself at some point.

But I'm an adult, and I signed up for this project.

I can push aside my differences and be civil, friendly even, right?

Just for a few weeks, and then I'll make sure to never see her again.

With a groan, I turn to Hunter. "I'll help her. I'll go back to the hospital."

His head whips my way. "You will?"

"Yeah." Not sure who's more surprised about it. Hunter or me.

But it's the right thing to do.

This isn't just about Chloe and me. This is about the hospital and doing something nice for the kids. I've never been one to back out of projects I signed up for, and I won't start now.

I shouldn't have flaked on her this week, but it's not too late to make it right.

It's time to face the music, or rather paint in this case.

Hunter stretches his arms above his head. "She'll be there this afternoon."

"Awesome." I don't think I could sound more unenthusiastic if I tried.

He jumps up and holds out his hand to help me up. "I gotta get going, and you need a shower."

"Thanks."

"Always." And there is Hunter's signature cocky grin, and I shake my head.

After a long hot shower at home rather than the gym, some lunch, a cat nap, and a quick grocery trip, I enter the third floor of the hospital.

Since it's the weekend, it's mostly quiet, which is both good and bad. When I round the corner, I spot Chloe immediately at the far end.

Taking this moment to study her as I make my way over, I can't help but notice how different she looks when she paints. It's her element, always has been, and her focus is similar to mine when it comes to swimming. The only difference is that I don't stick out my tongue at the corner of my mouth when I concentrate like Chloe does so often. I'd suck in way too much water if I did.

Her purple hair is knotted on top of her head and she's wearing a large men's shirt. It looks old and heavily used, covered in paint splatters that look like they've been washed more than just a time or two. She's on top of the stepstool when I stop behind her.

I didn't mean to stand so close, but I can't help it.

My attention shifts to the octopus she's working on. Wow. It's mind-blowing. Absolutely fascinating. I have no idea how a painting can look so real.

"Amazing." I take a step closer to get a better look when Chloe turns and screeches.

She takes a step into nothingness and looks like she's

about to faceplant. And what do I do? I open my arms to catch her.

Does that make me the knight in shining armor? Nope.

I'm so distracted by her and her painting that I stumble backwards, barely catching myself before I land on my ass. With Chloe half in my lap and half on top of me.

"Hey."

Well, I guess that's a way to tell her I'm back after ghosting her for a week.

THIRTEEN

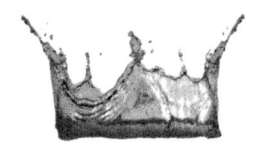

CHLOE

"*Hey?* That's what you're going with?" I close my eyes for one deep breath in an attempt to calm the pounding in my chest. "How about 'Sorry, Chloe, for almost giving you a heart attack'?"

"Yeah." He grimaces. "Sorry about that."

I was so engrossed in my painting, with the music as a nice background sound coming from my headphones, that I didn't notice anyone was here until Noah was standing right freaking there and started talking.

My poor, poor heart.

It's definitely been getting an extra workout this week.

First, the whole smoothie murder scene at my house. Like any murder scene—I assume—it took a ridiculous amount of time to clean up.

Then, the whole wrist and tattoo thing that has caused me several sleepless nights.

And now this. Whatever *this* is.

All I know is that I feel way too comfortable in his arms, with no desire to move. At all. And who could blame me?

Noah is built with a capital B. Muscle after muscle is my cushion, which is a lot softer than it sounds. He definitely didn't have all these muscles when we were teenagers.

Given our strange circumstances, I probably should move, right? I mean, smarter choice and all that shebang.

Why does nothing ever go according to plan?

I didn't expect to want to be around him this much after all is said and done.

Okay, maybe I did. Or maybe not? I don't even know anymore, but I probably should have anticipated it.

Because do I still feel insanely attracted to him after all this time? A big, fat yes.

So where does that leave me when I know I can't possibly get back together with him? Not that I think he'd want that anyway.

One-sided friends? Frenemies?

What would being friends with Noah look like anyway? We were never *just* friends. But since we were so young, and under a lot of adult supervision from both of our parents, the friendship portion might have actually been the biggest part of our relationship.

No matter what we did, I always loved being around him.

He was my person.

My safe place where I could forget about teenage drama, school stress, and all the other things we like to worry about as teenagers.

"Ehm." Noah clears his throat and looks at me with raised eyebrows.

Of course. I'm still draped across him.

A hot tingling sweeps up the back of my neck and across my face. "Dang it, sorry."

I climb off him as gracefully as I can, which isn't very graceful at all.

I knee him in the crotch by accident before dropping my weight on his chest so I can get off his penis. I definitely don't want to crush *that*.

That would be a shame. Teenage me blushes at the memory of exploring that specific part of his body.

No, don't think about his penis.

Nope, nope, nope.

How did I just jump from thinking about possibly being friends or frenemies with Noah to his penis?

Maybe because it's not the first time I wonder how sex would be like with him now? I mean, we were kids back then. Inexperienced. Each other's firsts. There was fumbling. Lots and lots of fumbling. No orgasms. Quick orgasms. Great orgasms. We had it all.

"Uh, Chloe."

I wince. Damn it, I was gone in la-la land again.

All because of Noah.

The same Noah I still haven't gotten off.

Nope, not going there.

This man turns my brain into a squirrel.

"Sorry." I finally crawl off him and straighten my clothes as we both get up. "It's been a long day."

And then, we just stand there. Staring at each other like it's the most normal thing in the world. For once, he doesn't frown at me. Okay, maybe a little, but at least not as much as before.

"Sooooo." Noah rubs his hands on his sweats.

"Sooooo." I rub my lips together and rock on my heels.

"Should we just—"

"Is this too—"

Our words mash together when we talk at the same time, and I point at him. "You first."

This time, he rubs his hands together in front of his body. "First, I want to apologize. I shouldn't have pushed you the way I did at your place. Like you said, it's none of my business. I also shouldn't have flaked on you and your work. I'm sorry."

I shrug and try my hardest to keep my facial muscles relaxed. On the inside, my blood is heating up, my heart is pumping faster, and a light sheen of sweat is forming on the back of my neck.

His apology isn't only unexpected, it also means a lot. I absentmindedly rub my wrist, unable to stop myself even when his gaze goes there. My flight of swallows tattoo that's so important to me. Knowing it's there always helps me. It settles me, calms me.

During our abrupt move to Los Angeles, I thought I'd lost my beloved bracelet that someone very special gave me as a gift. It was a delicate bracelet with two swallows that are supposed to symbolize love, loyalty, commitment, and also freedom.

That special person was Noah, of course, and I was devastated when it disappeared.

By sheer luck—or fate as I'd like to think—I found it in an old jewelry box a few years later when I was going through a really tough time. But at that point, I was yearning for more, for something more permanent that I'd never lose again, and that would add a special meaning to my scar.

Less than twenty-four hours later, I had my first tattoo. Every time I look at it, it gives me hope. It makes me feel strong and free, and grateful to be alive. Because things could have turned out differently in so many ways.

And now Noah's apologizing to *me*, even though I hurt him deeply all those years ago and will never be able to forgive myself for it. But it was the right thing to do. I have to believe that.

So, I lift the corners of my mouth and shrug. "You're here now."

"I am."

"Aaaaaaand are you planning on staying, or did you just drop by to tell me you won't be coming anymore?"

One corner of his mouth lifts the tiniest bit before it drops again. "I'd like to stay and do what I promised I'd do. If that's okay with you?"

You've got this. You can work with him. It's just for a few weeks.

I swallow. "Of course it is."

He rakes a hand through his hair. It's so much shorter now than it used to be. It definitely suits him though. "Great."

"Great."

Just how awkward is this going to be?

He points toward the wall. "What do you want me to do?"

I rub my finger along my chin. "Ehm, you can start painting Nemo if you want. I was going to do him next but now you can get started on him."

"Really?"

I snort. "Yes, really. What did you think you were going to do? Watch me do all the work?"

He thinks about that for a moment. "Not sure, actually. I

obviously missed a lot this week, and Hunter didn't mention what you guys did."

"Ah, Hunter. He's something else." Something in my brain clicks. "Wait a second. That's not the same Hunter you went to swim camp with all those years ago, is it?" His eyes go wide at my question, and I hold up my hand. "Sorry, I won't ask any questions. Let's just focus on the painting."

His hand lifts for a second before he shoves it in his pocket. "Yep, that's him. And, of course, you can ask questions. I mean, we're . . . friends, right?"

The way he bites the inside of his cheek once the question leaves his lips is adorable but also speaks volumes. And can I really blame him? Wasn't I just wondering too if I could be friends with Noah? Not that there are a lot of alternatives. If there are any at all.

I tilt my head. Friends . . . with Noah? "I guess we are."

"Well, *friend*, show me what to do." He gestures toward the supplies, and I nod.

"I did the outlining with the help of a projector most of the week, so now it's basically just coloring in. I can write down what color goes where and turn it into a paint-by-numbers kind of thing if you want."

"Sure. I'll try my best to not screw anything up."

I barely catch myself from bumping my shoulder into his side in an attempt of reassurance. I don't think we're those kinds of friends.

I grab one of the extra aprons from the supply closet along with everything else he needs. A few paintbrushes, a palette, his own cup of water to clean the brushes, and a couple extra rags, just in case. And then we get started. I get back to my octopus while Noah is working on the clownfish.

The minutes tick by, but it's a comfortable silence. I forgo my headphones this time because I don't want to be rude. My gesture backfires when my thoughts take over, and my awareness of him rises with every little movement.

I can't take it anymore and need to look at him. I'm compelled to. Intrigued to figure out how he's still the same, and how he's different. This friends thing might be a bit weird, but I *do* want to get to know this older, more mature version of him.

Because if I'm honest, something about him is off. He looks . . . sad. I thought that was from seeing me, that the anger I saw wasn't his default personality.

Yet, after seeing him a few times, I'm finding it hard to reconcile this serious, contemplative Noah over the driven, mischievous Noah. He had a certain earnestness to him when he was a teenager. It was necessary to achieve his dreams. But that seems to have changed to something darker.

His eyes are focused, tiny slits as he moves the paintbrush across the wall. Slowing down when he gets to the corners, careful to not color over the outlining.

"So, how's swimming going?" It's the first question that bubbles to the surface. But it should be an easy one since it's well . . . swimming. Noah's number-one passion that always brings a smile to his face and a shimmer to his eyes.

But neither one of those things happen. Instead, he sighs heavily and lifts his shoulders before letting them drop like they weigh a ton.

I blink at him, my brain needing a few extra seconds to process this strange realization. I've never seen a reaction like this from him when it's about swimming. "Uh-oh, that bad?"

He lazily dips his brush into the paint, continuing to work. "I wish I knew."

"I'm sorry."

"Don't be. It's not your fault." He turns to me, and I can't explain it, but his gaze . . . it's too much, yet I can't look away.

My throat clogs from the intensity in his eyes. The rawness, and the fact that he's letting me see it. "What happened?"

"Nothing really." His voice is flat and he focuses back on the wall.

After a moment, I do the same, the quiet sound of our brushes on the wall the only noise.

"Do you ever want more from life but don't know what that more looks like? All you know is that you're not happy with the way things are going. That something is missing."

The need to rub my chest at his words is almost impossible to resist.

And why is my chin trembling? Shit.

I know he's probably talking about swimming, but it's like he's talking straight to my soul.

The only difference is that I know what's missing, or rather who. And that I'll never get him back.

FOURTEEN

NOAH

Why the fuck did I just say that to her?

Is it because there's some sort of leftover familiarity with Chloe after all this time? Or because she's almost like a safe zone, a stranger—yet not—that I feel compelled to open up to?

Or do I just have no willpower when it comes to this woman?

I haven't talked to anyone about what's going on, or rather, how unhappy and restless I've been. Sure, my coach seems to have an inkling, but that's it.

Just saying these few thoughts aloud made my chest feel lighter and my breathing a little less confining.

Wait. Why hasn't Chloe said anything yet?

I just answered her question, about a topic that has been filling me with nothing but dread and confusion lately, and she doesn't reply?

After another moment of silence, I peek at her and find her staring at me.

And her eyes.

Shit.

It's like she knows exactly how I feel. Just like the bond we used to have where one look is enough to connect us on a level I've never had with anyone else.

Over the years, I formed a decent link with the guys, and especially Coach Diaz, but never with this intensity.

A long time ago, when Chloe looked at me like this, with a pained look that somehow still managed to feel comforting, I wouldn't have wasted a second. I would have grabbed her and pulled her close. Wrapped her in my arms and kissed the top of her head.

Finding solace in her arms used to be one of my favorite things. Sometimes it ended in more, other times not. But it always left me satisfied because it was her. Everything was better with her.

Now, I have to fight the urge, the instinct, to be her shelter. It's like my brain is battling with itself, the thoughts racing through my head so quickly, I can barely make them out.

Comfort her.

No, stay strong.

She's not your problem anymore.

But look at her. She's clearly hurting.

My head's starting to pound, but one question remains on my mind after I shut up the rest. Who am I trying to protect by not giving in to this need to comfort her? Her or me?

I clear my throat awkwardly. "Are you okay?"

She blinks and sniffles quietly. "What? Oh yeah, sorry."

If she cries, I'll lose my shit. I'm not the best at handling tears anyway, but with her? Not on my list of things I want to test today.

Chloe turns back to the wall and continues the finishing touches on her octopus. It's enormous, its tentacles spreading along the whole length of the wall. "I'm sorry things aren't going as planned for you."

"I always thought I'd have a family by thirty. You know, the stereotypical two and a half kids, a dog, and a white picket fence." And there goes my mouth again. Throwing out those words like it gets paid for it.

Her paintbrush slips out of her grasp, and reflex has both of us trying to catch it. Our hands collide, but we immediately pull back as if burnt. Thanks to this stunt, there's now a zig-zag path of coral paint smeared across the wall.

"Damn it, I'm sorry. How bad is it?" I stare at the splatters across the outlines of the sea turtle, the stingray, the whale, and the hammerhead shark, while she grabs one of the rags to wipe off most of the mess.

She studies the wall and rubs some more. "There. It should be fine."

"You're amazing." Her head snaps around at my words, her eyes wide as she gapes at me, and I gulp. "Your paintings, I mean." Shit. What is wrong with me today? My mouth is just out of control.

"Thanks." She doesn't say anything else and gives me a tight smile.

Crap. I totally just made it worse.

She wrinkles her nose and shakes her head softly, before going back to painting. "You know, about what you said before, there's still time to go after everything you want. It's not like there's a cut-off age when you turn thirty, or something like that."

I wait for her to look at me so I can read her expression, but her gaze stays firmly on her work. Is she avoiding my scrutiny on purpose?

Her words sink into my consciousness, my brain mulling over them. On a rational level, I know there's still time for everything. That I haven't run out of options yet. But something's nagging me about it. Maybe my gut? Something just doesn't feel right, almost like I *have* run out of time. Like I've missed my chance but don't know about it yet.

It's hard to imagine a life without getting what I've always thought my future will look like. No wife, no kids, no dog, and no white picket fence. When I try to imagine it, it's all just blurry.

"Yeah, I guess." My brain wants to go to places I don't want it to go. Fictitious places where Chloe and I had a future. Kids. I shut that train wreck down real quick. I need to keep my brain occupied with something else. "So, is this what you do for a living? Paintings like this?"

She shakes her head. "No, this is just a fun project and something I've been wanting to do for a while. Professionally, I illustrate children's books."

"You do?"

"Yeah." The corners of her eyes crinkle when she smiles. It's new, something my brain stores away.

"Do you like it?"

"I do." She exhales loudly. "There's just something about creating a whimsical world for kids that fascinates me. Their minds are so pure and beautiful, and I love being able to add my pictures to them. In a small way, I help shape the way they see the world. There are so many terrible things going on everywhere around the globe. To be able to create something for them to escape to is special to me."

This. *This* is the Chloe I know, the Chloe I lo—

Nope, not going there.

"That's amazing. I'm so glad you were able to do what you love. And you're so good at it too." And I mean it. Her work is amazing, always has been. I don't think there was a medium she picked up that she didn't turn into something magnificent.

Art is in her blood, like swimming is in mine.

Only I seem to have lost my spirit. Or whatever the hell has happened.

"Thank you. That means a lot. I'm just glad I get to do what I've always wanted to do. I know not everyone's that lucky." After a few more brushstrokes, she takes a step back to inspect her finished design. It's perfect, almost too perfect, like it could glide out of the painting at any second. "How about you? Will you participate in another Olympic Games?"

Well, isn't that just the million-dollar question?

"Not sure yet."

"Really?"

This time I feel her eyes on me, but I keep my gaze forward to finish the next clownfish. "Yeah. We'll see."

I don't feel like talking about it because there isn't much to say.

All I know is that I just don't *feel* it anymore.

Swimming never used to be a *thing* I did, it was a part of me. But now, it has become a thing, and I don't know how to handle it, or if I'm even equipped to handle it. Because what happens if I don't . . . if I can't? Because so far, I haven't done a very good job, it seems.

Chloe clears her throat. "Oh and by the way, before I forget it."

This time I turn her way.

"I was going to talk to you about it sooner, but since I didn't see you all week . . ." She scratches her neck. "Anyway . . . about tomorrow, you don't have to come. At all."

Tomorrow? What's she talking about?

My confusion must show on my face because her cheeks turn red.

"I meant lunch at my mom's."

Oh shit, I totally forgot about that. Or rather, I've blocked it from my thoughts as much as I could. "Oh yeah. What about it?"

"You don't have to come. Really. I'll make up an excuse for you. My mom shouldn't have pushed you into it like that."

"What if I want to come?" *What the heck?*

"Do you?" Her eyebrows lift as she looks at me expectantly. It's still the same *you can't fool me* look she's given me about a million times in my life.

I nod. Of course, I don't. I mean, I do.

Might as well bathe in my misery. "Sure, why not? Your mom's a fantastic cook, and I've always liked your parents, you know that."

She winces, and her whole face crumbles in front of me. The color drains from her skin before she gazes down, hiding as much of her from me as possible. "Mmm, about that. My dad. He . . . he died last year."

What?

Fuck. No.

"I'm so sorry, I didn't know."

"I know you didn't, but thanks." Her voice cracks, barely

able to push out the words as she continues to stare at the floor.

Shit. I feel like a total dick.

I quickly put down my supplies, grab her, and pull her against my chest.

She loved her dad so much. *I can't imagine the pain she's experienced.*

Our hug isn't very close. I don't crush her to me as tightly as I used to, especially since she's still holding on to her things, but it's the best I can do in this screwed-up moment.

Her shoulders sag further into my embrace, like she's allowing herself to let go.

With me.

My chest tingles from the close contact, and I don't move, not even an inch. I don't want to break the moment, especially since she seems to need it. So I just stand there, offering her what little comfort I can give her, hoping it's enough to soothe the hole in her heart. At least, a little.

Chloe has always been closer to her parents than I have been to mine. Her parents were actually present while they were loving and doting on her. The pain this must have caused her. And her mom.

After another minute, she clears her throat and sniffles before pulling back. Her eyes are watery, but I'm not sure if she cried or not.

"Thank you."

I nod. "No problem."

"Um." Her voice cracks and she clears her voice several times. "Sorry about that. But I was planning on telling you anyway so you're prepared, you know?"

"I'm so sorry you lost him."

"It was better for him. He was in a lot of pain at the end after battling cancer for years. It was hard to let him go, but we knew it was coming, so at least we were able to enjoy the time we had left with him and say our goodbyes." She tilts her head back and blinks a few times, inhaling and exhaling deeply through her nose.

She was able to say goodbye to him.

Her words trigger something, and even though I know it's irrational and incomparable to her actually losing her dad, all I can think about is that I never got to say goodbye to her.

I was never able to get the closure I wanted, maybe even needed.

She disappeared out of my life like a ghost, taking everything with her except my memories that drove me insane for a long time.

And now she's here, and we're having a conversation.

Apologizing. Dancing around our pain. Trying to empathize with the other.

But for what? After we've finished the mural, that's it. Chloe will be gone from my life.

Again.

FIFTEEN

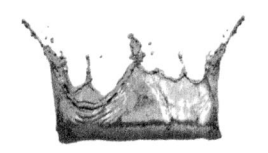

CHLOE

When I come back from my run the next morning, my mind is still a mess.

Noah's confession yesterday, the way he opened up to me like we're still . . . *something*. Like he still trusts me and wants to confide in me.

Then the mention of my dad, and the way he cradled me in his arms. So gingerly, like I'm fragile and he doesn't know how to hold me properly. Definitely not like it used to be. He once knew exactly how to hold me.

But I guess it's a good step in the friendship direction, right? Talking about meaningful topics, confiding in each other, and offering comfort.

When I'm almost home, I exhale all my conflicted emotions and push the Bluetooth speaker in my ear to disconnect from my phone, then stop short.

What?

Two of my elderly neighbors—who've been nothing but welcoming since I moved into the neighborhood last month—are walking on the strip of grass next to the sidewalk.

That's not the unusual part about this, but rather the fact that they're both dragging lawn chairs behind them in one hand, and big mason jars with straws in the other.

What on earth are they up to?

And where are they going? They aren't going . . . wait a moment. To *my* lawn?

Bessie huffs when she stops and leans on the back of her folding chair, gasping for breath. "Oh hey, Chloe. There you are. I knocked a few minutes ago to check if you were home, but no one answered. It's okay if Agnes and I relax on your front lawn for a little while, right? You have the best view, and we'll be gone as soon as the show is over, I promise."

Agnes is just a few feet behind her, taking a sip from her mason jar. The orange-red liquid reminds me of . . . Wait a second, *is that a cocktail?*

When she stops next to Bessie, she grins at me. "Hey, sweetie. Are you going to watch with us? It's our favorite show in the whole neighborhood."

"What show are you guys—"

"Oooooh. I think I saw movement." Agnes whistles, frantically trying to open her chair while Bessie is scrambling to do the same.

I, on the other hand, stand there like a total idiot, no clue what the hell is going on. Both ladies have plopped in their chairs, their straws to their mouths, as they quietly whisper to each other between sips.

Since they're both staring straight across the street, I look too. Something glorious must have caught their attention after all. Whatever mysterious show they were talking about.

The yard gate at the side of the house opens, and someone pushes a lawn mower through the opening.

"Here we go." Bessie does a little shimmy with her shoulders, and they both giggle.

The man pushing the lawn mower has a cap pulled low over his face, making it impossible to get a better look.

When he rounds the corner to align the lawn mower with the edge of the sidewalk, he looks straight at us. His eyes go wide for a moment before he waves. Not sure if he's waving at the two ladies or me.

What. The. Ever-loving. Hell?

"Is that . . . Is that Noah?" His name pops out of my mouth, and I'm too stunned to fully wrap my head around this scene in front of me.

Why is Noah mowing the lawn across the street?

"Look at those calves."

"And those biceps. They look extra muscly today."

Loud slurping noises accompany Agnes and Bessie's chatter, which I'm only listening to halfway.

My feet move on their own accord, compulsion carrying me across the street. There's no other explanation for it.

And goodness, the ladies were right. I don't know where to look first. In his sleeveless shirt and shorts combination, there's so much to explore for my eyes.

The strong muscles under the stretched skin, the veins standing out loud and proud.

I want to lick him all over. From top to bottom, and back up.

Noah clears his throat when I'm only a couple feet away and staring at him like a crazy person.

When did he turn off the lawnmower?

He turns the hat around on his head, and my knees go weak. Is he doing this on purpose? He knows I have a thing for *that*. I mean, wearing a baseball hat backwards raises the hotness levels by like five hundred billion points.

"Hey." He looks over my shoulder and waves. "Good morning, ladies."

A unified "Good morning, Noah," echoes across the street.

"What are you doing here?" My gaze strays to the house behind him. The same house I've seen several times before without paying too much attention to it. The same house I've never seen anyone going in or out of.

He rubs his jaw, and my gaze follows his hand, zeroing in on his five-o'clock shadow. Gosh, it looks so good on him. Back in high school, we didn't have a lot of guys come to school without shaving. Swimming is another reason to shave. There's absolutely no denying that the scruff shoots him up on the sexiness scale like nothing else.

Backwards hat plus scruff. I'm ready to melt into a puddle about now.

The scruff also makes him ridiculously manly, which is something I'm still not entirely used to.

This Noah, with the facial hair, with all the new muscles that are also more substantial than before, and then those dang fine lines in his skin. Veins. The matured face. It's hard not to stare at him, which is exactly what I'm doing right now. Again.

He bites the inside of his cheek. "Well, we're kind of neighbors."

"Kind of . . . neighbors?"

"No, I meant we *are* neighbors. Definitely are. I live here"—he points behind himself before pointing across the street at my house—"and you live there."

"How is that possible?" I gather my ponytail from my neck and scoop it to one side to play with the ends. "I mean, of course I know how it's possible that we live on the same street. But . . . wow. I had no idea."

He stays quiet and looks away from me.

I narrow my eyes at him. "And you didn't think I should know about this? Why didn't you say anything?"

And then, I shove his shoulder.

Hard.

Well, *that* gets his attention.

Mine too, because why on earth did I just do that?

We've actually had several moments in the last few weeks where I caught myself thinking about doing it, but I never acted on it.

Before now, I guess, even though I shouldn't be too surprised.

These weird moments keep happening where this old familiarity seeps into my pores, and I'm thrown back into *us*. Into the previous version of us that is slowly mixing with the here and now. It makes me not think about what I do or say and things just happen. Almost like I'm using muscle memory from past Chloe and Noah to navigate present Chloe and Noah.

The question is, is that a good or a bad thing?

Pulling my hand back, I interlace my fingers in front of my body to keep them from touching him again. "Sorry."

"No problem." He crosses his arms over his chest, accentuating those fine muscles, and I pinch my lips together.

Will this attraction to him be a problem? Because holy hell, he's still doing it for me.

If the sudden excited chatter behind us is anything to go

by, my senior friends approve very much of Noah. Or maybe they'd like their piece. Who knows with these ladies?

"I was going to tell you. That we're neighbors, I mean." His gaze roams over my face, one corner of his mouth twitching. "Eventually."

"Eventually, huh?"

"When I found out, I didn't particularly *like* you."

Copying his stance, I also fold my arms over my chest. I can be like this too. Staring him down like it's no one's business. Well, I'm still staring up at him, but who cares about specifics?

His chin lifts in a small nod. "So, wanna carpool to your mom's later, *neighbor*?"

I narrow my eyes at him. "Fine."

Then, I spin around as quickly as I can before he can see the corners of my mouth lift.

When I walk past gaping Agnes and Bessie, I wink at them. "Enjoy the show, ladies."

They mutter something I can't make out as I disappear into my house. I have to shower and a lunch carpool to get ready for.

"Thanks so much for lunch, Mom. It was delicious, as always." I give my mom a hug before stepping back.

"Yes, Mrs. Williams. Thanks so much for the invitation. It was as good as ever."

My mom waves both of us off as she opens the door. "Thank you, guys, for spending some time with me."

Even though she smiles, her words still tighten my chest.

I know she's "doing okay" as she always likes to tell me, but sometimes I wonder if she lies, or rather, how much she lies.

I know from my own experience how often we tell others we're okay even when we're not. My mom isn't any different.

Losing my dad was tough for both of us, even though like I told Noah at the hospital, we knew it was coming. That allowed us to prepare ourselves mentally, at least somewhat. Yet it also meant that our grieving process started a lot earlier than normal.

Grieving someone while they're still alive is a distinct and bizarre mind process that screwed with my brain more than once.

How are you supposed to let go of someone when they're right in front of you? When it's impossible to erase them from your memory—or at least suppress them until you feel like you can breathe again? When your mind's hard drive wants to pull up all of their memories, constantly, at the most inconvenient times, therefore dissolving you into a living crying machine.

I reach out and squeeze her. "Bye, Mom. I love you."

"I love you, honey. And thanks for coming today, Noah. It was wonderful to see you."

"The pleasure was all mine."

They share a smile, like so many times during our visit.

Lunch was good. Eerily normal.

The conversation flowed easily, mostly, while Mom was getting the CliffsNotes on Noah's last decade. The three Olympic Games he's attended, what medals he won, how his sister and parents are doing. All totally ordinary details, although I was sad to hear about Daisy's divorce.

I ate up every single word. Storing it in the back of my

mind like it was the most important information, and I'm not going to think about the reason behind it.

"Back home for you?" Noah's shoulder lightly brushes mine as we walk down the narrow walkway to his car.

When we get there, I shrug. "Yeah. I don't really have anything planned for the rest of the day."

His hand plays with the car keys as he looks at me. His head cocked, his eyes slightly narrowed as his gaze roams over my face.

Does he like what he sees?

No, don't think about that.

We're barely friends.

I chuckle. "What are you thinking about so hard?"

"If I should go to the movies or not."

"Sunday movies, huh?"

He bites his lip and nods. "Yeah. Just like we—"

Just like we . . . used to do. Crap.

And why the hell does he need to bite his lip? Screw him and being so damn attractive.

My body loves him, heating up in all the right places, and I'm not sure how to feel about that. Of course, he's hot, but it's the history we share that burns the brightest.

And I can't deny that he makes me happy. Being in his presence fills me with a peace I haven't felt in a very long time, and it's addictive.

The more I'm around him, the more I crave his presence.

Does it make me selfish that I long for this blissful feeling? That I actively seek it out even when I know I shouldn't?

But then, who doesn't want to go after things that make them happy?

Is there even a right way for me in this? A smart way that will keep my heart in one piece?

Noah pushes the button on the remote before taking a step closer.

There's only a foot separating us, and the air between us vanishes like it was sucked out by some magical force. His breath hits my face as he leans in even closer, the sweetness of the cheesecake he had for dessert making my mouth water.

The anticipation—the agony—is too much, and I close my eyes.

When the car door opens behind me with a click, and I open my eyes again, Noah stands next to the door, holding it open for me.

His gaze scans my face before settling on my eyes. "Want to come with me?"

I swallow the disappointment of staying un-kissed and force an enthusiastic smile instead. "I thought you'd never ask."

He smiles . . . slowly . . . and good God. Be still, my heart.

"Uh, what are we watching?"

"Does it matter?" he whispers.

Not in any way. Noah Winters asked me to go to the movies with him, and that's the only thing that matters.

"No," I whisper back. I slip, albeit dreamily, into the passenger seat and watch Noah as he closes my door and walks around the hood to the driver's door.

Is this a smart idea? To spend more time with him?

Especially when I'm starving for more?

The thumping heart in my chest seems to think so.

SIXTEEN

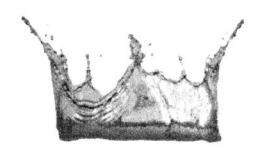

NOAH

THE PARKING LOT OF THE MOVIE THEATER IS ALMOST deserted, as usual.

It's nothing fancy. Just one of those small ones that plays old movies.

I put the car in park and kill the ignition.

Chloe gasps next to me. "I can't believe this place is still standing."

"Yeah. It's definitely seen better days, but they've been doing a good job keeping up with it on the inside."

"Wow."

I get out and Chloe joins me at the front of the car. "Ready?"

She nods, an eager expression on her face. "Yes, I'm excited. It's been so long since we've been here."

I swallow past the lump in my throat. It's not like I forgot. I couldn't come here for a while after she left because I couldn't stomach the memories of this place. I was such a fool. And so fucking in love.

And look where that got me.

We walk inside, and I raise my hand at one of the employees. He's tall and skinny, wearing a burgundy suit.

"No way." Chloe grasps my arm as we get closer, although I'm sure she's unaware of her grip on me. "Is that—"

The man comes out from behind his ticket counter, quietly whistling under his breath as he takes us in. Together. "Miss . . . Chloe? Is that you? What a sight for my old eyes."

That man has a memory like I've never known before. I might have also told him that she's back when I came here a few weeks ago.

"Ernie." Chloe blushes. "Still as charming as ever, I see. Thank you. How are you?"

He shrugs and shoots me a look. "Same old here."

Chloe clasps her hands together and leans a little closer to him. "Well, you look great."

Ernie smiles, the dark skin around his eyes breaking into lines. "That's what I always tell Mr. Noah. I'm so much better looking than his lonely self."

Chloe laughs, and I shake my head. That man is as unique as this theater, and he's been a constant in my life once I started coming back here. I always stop to chat with him for a while before and after a show.

And now, he's telling Chloe I'm lonely? Good to know where his loyalty lies.

Even though he's not wrong. Lately, I've been here more than usual. Wanting to get out of the quiet house.

Sundays used to be our guy day where we often hung out, played poker, or watched a movie. A relaxed day after a gruesome week at the pool and the gym.

Then Jace and Ryan found their other halves and welcomed kids into the world, and Hunter's been busy with new endorsement deals. As a result, I haven't seen as much of them as I used to.

And my sister and my nephews don't always have time to hang out with me either. Since Daisy told me she wants me to find someone, I sometimes wonder if she pushes me away on purpose, thinking that would get me "out there" as she likes to call it.

As if that *someone* would just be waiting around the corner for me.

I don't think going to the movie theater by myself is what she had in mind though.

"What are you kids watching today? We got *Transformers* and *Across The Universe*." Ernie walks back behind his desk to click on the outdated computer.

Chloe and I lock gazes. What are the chances they play two movies today that we binge-watched when we were younger? Maybe *Transformers* a bit more than *Across The Universe*, but they were both great movies.

"Ladies choice." I tilt my chin at Chloe, waiting.

"*Transformers*? I haven't seen that one in forever," she blurts out, not wasting a moment to think about it while grinning at me. "Is that okay?"

I can't help but smile back at her infectious enthusiasm. "Sure."

Grabbing my wallet from my pocket, I turn to Ernie. "You heard the lady. Two tickets for *Transformers*, please."

"Already done."

"Thank you."

I pay and we catch up with Ernie for a moment on how his wife is doing since she broke her hip. When we head to the concession stand, I look back at him, and he gives me an encouraging smile along with a thumbs-up. I shake my head at him and fall back in step with Chloe.

She looks at the board and puts her hand on her stomach. "I'm still pretty full from lunch."

"Want to share a popcorn?"

She studies my face. "You don't mind?"

"Not at all." And I really don't. I mean, things are good. And sharing popcorn doesn't mean anything.

We order our popcorn and drinks, and this time, Chloe flashes her money to the teenager behind the counter before I can even get my wallet out.

Shit. I just paid for our tickets without a second thought. Old habits really die hard sometimes. At least we should be good now that she paid for the food and drinks, right?

After a bathroom break—where we switch spots outside the restroom to hold our food and drinks—we head to theater two.

The red not-so-plush-anymore seats welcome us, along with the familiar smell of stale, recycled air-conditioned air and buttery popcorn.

Chloe lets out a loud sigh.

"Same old, hey?"

She nods, and I watch her take everything in. The theater isn't huge, but it's still a decent size. The red seats, the old movie posters on the sides, the small cutout at the top for the projector to shine through.

Luckily, there are only a few people toward the bottom rows as I follow Chloe up the stairs and toward the middle of one of the top rows.

We settle into our chairs just as the theater turns dark.

The previews start on the screen, and once we're settled in, our gazes are focused on the screen.

A few minutes into the main movie, Chloe leans in, her arm brushing against mine. "Is the popcorn next to you?"

I nod and whisper, "Yeah, let me get it."

I don't know if she didn't hear me, or if it's one of those strange moments when you hear the other person but don't fully process it until a few seconds later, but the result is the same. We bump heads when I lean in again to tell her and she tries to lean closer to get the popcorn.

Out of reflex, my hand shoots to her head, touching the spot she hit, feeling if she's okay. Wanting to soothe it because I hate when she gets hurt.

Reality sinks in, my brain registering what I'm doing—what I'm thinking—and I freeze. That's when I notice that Chloe's been frozen this whole time, while I was touching her . . . exactly like I would have all those years ago.

Like she's *mine*.

But it's not like that anymore. It hasn't been for so long. Shit.

How can a simple touch feel so good?

I pull my hand back, slowly, while brushing her skin one last time like I'm an addict and she's my drug. Like I *have* to feel her skin under my fingertips, hoping it will imprint there forever.

Fuck.

I'm in so much trouble.

"Sorry, you okay?" Thank goodness I have to keep my voice to a whisper, and she can't hear how strained my words sound.

"Yeah, thanks." Her hand goes up to her cheek, brushing away a strand of hair.

"I'll get the popcorn, okay?" I hold up my hand and wait until I see her nod.

Leaning away from her, I grab the popcorn from the seat beside me and hand it to her. The scene on the screen has switched and the earlier brightness is gone. Instead, the room is almost pitch black, and Chloe's fingers brush over mine when she tries to get a hold of the paper container in my hands.

"Thanks." This time, she pauses for a moment before taking the popcorn, and therefore, eliminating the contact.

Does she feel this electric connection between us too?

It's as intense as it used to be but different. The tie between us is definitely still present though. And I can't be the only one feeling it. Is there something like physical memory? That my body remembers her, searching out that contact it used to enjoy so much?

No. Surely that's impossible.

Or maybe it's the fact that I haven't been with anyone in a while. How long has it been? My brain is trying to put the puzzle pieces together. *Stacy.* Has it really been over a year since I spent that one night with her? And there wasn't anyone before her in a while either.

I brush my hand over my face, rubbing my chin, enjoying the scruff under my fingers. I barely ever let any facial hair grow, and it feels nice to not worry about something as simple as that. At least while I figure out my life.

I attempt to focus on the movie, but my attention is shot. My brain is busy thinking about Chloe, about wanting to touch her again.

With every additional brush of our fingers—accidental or not—I shift some more in my seat. Did someone turn up the heat in here? My heart pounds faster, and I close my eyes to inhale deeply, the same smell as always filling my nostrils but also something else. Or rather, someone else.

Just like so often before my races, I focus on my breath so I can zone out. Escape this overwhelming need to be closer to Chloe.

When the movie is finally done, my body is wound up tight. Why the fuck does this feel like the longest foreplay in history? And all of that from just a few innocent touches.

Maybe I'm losing my mind.

That must be it.

Even though my suddenly too-tight pants don't seem to agree with that.

When the credits roll, I stand up first before bending to get my water bottle, at the same time Chloe pushes to her feet too.

Which lands me right in her chest.

Those breasts. Are they as amazing as I remember them?

My dick strains against my zipper, getting way too excited.

I straighten up and almost manage to headbutt her.

Way to go. That's definitely not how you get in her pants.

What the fuck is even going on in my head right now?

Who said anything about getting into Chloe's pants?

That can only end in disaster, and who needs that?

I shake my head, ready to tell myself to shut it. "Shit, I'm sorry. You okay?"

She laughs, brushing small pieces of popcorn off her

clothes. "Yeah, no worries. It looks like we're clumsy number one and number two today."

I chuckle. "Yeah, something like that."

And then I stare at her as the lights slowly get brighter. Her purple ponytail is a little crooked, her eyes shiny. There's a slight flush to her face, and my eyes wander down to see if the flush extends to her chest.

Damn it, I forgot her shirt goes up to her collarbone. When my gaze ascends again, I pause at her mouth. Those lush lips that have brought me so much— *Stop*.

Of course, they part in that moment and her tongue darts out to swiftly lick over them.

Fuck me now.

Not literally.

I think.

Shit.

I'm screwed.

SEVENTEEN

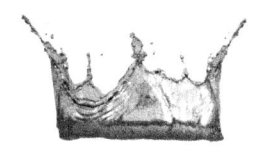

CHLOE

I don't think any other movie has ever felt this long, and I've watched this specific one a gazillion times before too. With Noah, of course.

But why does everything feel so different this time?

Is it the touches, the stolen glances, my own thoughts and wants? The longing that's been settling deep in my bones? It's been getting more intense with every minute I spend with him.

From the looks of it, I might need an extra minute in the restroom to calm down my flushed face. I run cold water over my hands and wrists, hoping it will cool me down. Extinguish that fire that's burning me up from the inside, and take care of the pulsing between my legs.

According to my body's reaction, watching a movie together at the theater is now some weird kind of foreplay. Even the air from the hand dryer feels like a caress as it blows over my sensitive skin.

And now you're officially losing your mind.

A snort escapes me as I shake my head at myself. I clearly

have issues. But, nothing a night in bed with my trusty vibrator can't take care of. Even though I can't help the images that have been flooding my mind. Noah's strong hands on my body and *him* taking care of things.

I've been fine by myself for a while now, somewhat happy even, but imagining Noah's body covering mine, of him pushing me over the edge instead is . . . bliss. And so unhelpful. Daydream-induced wet panties definitely won't solve my problem right now, that's for sure.

After a few calming breaths, I finally leave the restroom to find Noah waiting outside in the hallway. Leaning against the wall in all his handsome glory, searing a hole into my heart with his torching gaze.

My panties might get ruined tonight after all.

He pushes off the wall and walks over to me in long strides. "Are you ready to head home?"

It takes everything in me to not think about the definition of home and what I once thought it would mean for us at this point.

Instead, I push those thoughts away and nod. Even smile at him.

Fake it 'til you make it and all that.

My focus shifts back on his presence beside me. On the warmth that radiates from his body when we walk out into the breezy evening. The brush of his hand on mine when he reaches past me to open my car door for me. His breath on my face when he straightens back up and stands closer than before. So much closer.

By the time we leave the parking lot and head "home," all my senses have zeroed in on him again. He makes it easy, and it's a nice escape for me. It makes me forget about that dang competition for the publisher that still gives me trouble. It makes me forget about everything I want but can't have. It lets me be.

It might be self-destructive in the long run, but oddly enough, I'm still grateful for it.

Noah's fingers tap on mine. "You okay?"

I lean my head on the headrest and turn his way. "Yeah."

"Good."

"Thanks for today."

His gaze stays on the road, but one corner of his mouth lifts half an inch. "Always."

I repress the sigh, this snippet reminding me so much of when we were younger. When we were carefree and so in love. When I didn't get to wake up next to him nearly as often as I'd like because of course, our parents didn't agree with that.

Where would we be now if things had gone differently? Where would we be if things had gone as they should have gone? As we had planned them?

My insides churn, and I pull up my mental wall. Bring my thoughts back to my mural sessions at the hospital this week, to my time spent with my family and my friends. With Noah.

Noah, my friend.

My friend I'd also really like to see naked and do naughty things with.

But I shouldn't. Daydreaming is one thing but to be with him for real, I just . . . I can't. How would that even work? How would I explain—

"We're here." Noah unbuckles and gets out of the car, while I stay there, frozen in place.

I can't tell him what happened. That might make me a coward, but just thinking about telling him the truth—the whole story—makes me nauseous.

What I can do though, what I've perfected over the years, is to pretend. It's what I'm good at, and what works for me.

Carpe diem.

That's it.

I swing open the door—almost hitting Noah in the process who had come around the car to help me—and step out.

Look at this man.

What a damn miracle that life has brought us back together like this. It might not be in the way I'd once thought, but here we are nonetheless. And I like having him in my life.

So if he's willing to forgive me and be my friend, I'll be the best fucking friend he's ever had.

When I'm out of the car, there's a spark of something in the air, an electricity that wasn't there before, and I shiver.

Noah shuts the door behind me and locks the car before he puts his arm around me. "Cold?"

Cold? With him right there? Ha. Good one. I wish he could see the fire that's threatening to burn me alive from the inside whenever he's around.

Before I can respond, he pulls his arm back and I immediately miss the weight of it. And the heat.

We get to my front door, and I unlock it before turning back to face him.

He grimaces and scratches his neck. "Sorry about that, I didn't mean to—"

My gaze flicks from his glorious biceps to his eyes.

The way he looks at me so expectantly. It's mesmerizing.

The way he's so unsure about how he's supposed to navigate our reconnection, just like I am. It's endearing. The way he still ignites this instant lust in me whenever I catch a glimpse of him looking at me. It's maddening.

"Don't be sorry." I swallow. "Please."

There's been so much regret where we're involved. I don't want there to be any more.

All regret does is eat you from the inside while you try your damnedest to patch up the holes in your soul faster than new ones can form.

I don't know if it's my spinning mind, or my pleading words, but something snaps between us.

And then we're moving.

I'm in his arms.

His delicious lips are on mine.

The same ones I've dreamed of for so many years. Those dreams that gave me hope and destroyed me at the same time.

My soul infuses me with greed, and I open up for him, ready to take everything he gives me.

He groans into my mouth with the same fierceness he puts into pressing my body against the door.

My hands are in his hair, pulling him as close as possible, while his are under my butt. Holding me, squeezing me, tempting me.

One of my hands fumbles behind me until I find the doorknob. A few seconds later, we're inside, and the door is locked behind us.

"Bedroom. Upstairs," is all I get out before attacking his lips again.

When we make it to the bottom of the staircase, I slide down his body, and grab his large hand.

We don't talk as we rush up the stairs and walk into my bedroom. We don't have to. Being with him is like activating another part of myself without having to think about it.

Excitement and pleasure flood my body as he closes the distance between us in strong, confident strides. This man exudes sex appeal and strength with every step he takes. While his approach is slow, it's the opposite once he's within reach. Immediately, we grab one another, pulling hair and pulling on clothes as we unabashedly convey each other's desire and need.

I don't waste any time. Getting him undressed is my main focus. When he pulls his shirt over his head, I work at the button of his pants, unfastening it as quickly as I can before slipping a finger beneath the waistline fabric.

A guttural groan escapes him that makes my movements even more frantic.

I need to feel him. All of him. I need to know if it's as good as I remember or even better.

Now.

I pull on his pants and underwear like my life depends on it. He hisses when I finally succeed and make contact with hot, hard flesh.

His reaction is unexpected, and I revel in this mixture of old and new sensation. When he starts to pump into my hand, I bite his lip without thinking. He groans and pumps faster. I love it.

The heavy weight in my hand somehow contrasts with the soft skin, and when I move my hand again, he steps out of my reach, pointing behind me. "On the bed, now."

I take slow steps backward, watching him as he fumbles with the pockets of his pants until he finds his wallet and pulls out a condom. I bump into the edge of the mattress when he puts it on.

Then his sole focus is back on me, and the throbbing between my legs gets so insistent, I'm afraid I might spontaneously combust.

He closes the distance between us and picks me up like I weigh nothing, just to throw me on the bed. I shriek, but don't get a chance to figure out what's happening when his hands go to my pants. He undoes them, and pulls them down faster than I thought was possible, my underwear along with it.

When he looks at me from beneath my spread legs, my knees go weak.

"Are you ready to fly, little bird?"

The fluttery sensation in my chest is impossible to contain—his intensity and focus a major turn-on—and I nod.

How else do you react when you know your whole world is about to change?

EIGHTEEN

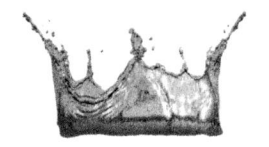

NOAH

The taste of her on my tongue has my dick flexing.

She tastes of sweetness, adventures, and an unabashed brazenness that is so fucking sexy, I have to double my efforts to not come before I'm inside her.

Has she always tasted like this?

I know I always enjoyed the sex we had, so why can't I recall how she used to taste?

What a tragedy.

Her inner muscles tighten around me when I push in a finger, then two, and I groan when she moves her hips up to rub against my hand.

Holy shit.

She definitely never did that before because I sure as hell would remember that.

The way her ass flexes with every push.

Using my shoulders, I push my way farther into her space, wanting to take over, wanting to be the one who makes her lose her mind.

When I latch on to her sensitive skin with my mouth, I don't just hear her moan but I feel it vibrating through her body. My eyes widen when her hands grab the sheets next to me before they find their way into my hair, pulling roughly at my strands.

Who is this little wildcat?

Spurred on by her behavior, my licks and nibbles get more intense too until her legs start to shake around me.

"Noah. Oh fuck." Her hips, her pelvis, lifts up as much as it can with me keeping her grounded as her orgasm rips through her so intensely, a small sob escapes her.

My movements turn gentle as I continue to watch her, continue to savor her, wanting to make sure she's okay. Needing to know she's more than okay.

When she gives me a small, lazy smile after a few deep inhales, something realigns in my chest. The drumming behind my breastbone echoes through my whole body before my dick takes over again.

Reminding me that he wants in on the action too, that *I* want to be inside this woman as soon as possible. Feeling her warmth all around me, having her vibrate around my hard length like it's the best she's ever had. Like *I* am the best she's ever had.

"I need you. Now." She claws at my shoulders, trying to get a hold of me so she can pull me toward her.

With the soft light coming from the bedside lamp, I revel in her neediness, straightening my spine at the lust swirling in her eyes. Wanting to take her. Needing her too.

I kiss my way up her stomach and push her shirt and bra up. I didn't even realize she's still wearing them. When I move my hand around her side to remove them, she grabs the back of my neck and holds me against her nipple, moaning loudly when I suck on it.

"Now, Noah." Her hips surge up, searching.

And who am I to deny her when I want her so badly?

We'll take it slower next time.

Caging her in with my elbows, I interlace our hands as I align our bodies, staring at her face so I don't miss a moment of her reaction. The small inhale of air when I first push inside, the pleasure-filled gasp when I press further, the widening of her eyes when I'm all the way inside of her. And the tight frown when I move and hit that one spot that is *her* spot.

Her breathing turns shaky as her eyes roll back in her head as I hit that spot over and over while trying to contain my impending release, which is threatening to overpower me at any moment.

The muscles in my back are tense, a slight sheen of sweat forming on my forehead from staying in control.

Chloe's legs wrap around my ass and we both moan when that position allows me to go deeper. When she keeps digging in her heels insistently, I pick up my pace, wanting to feel her come around me.

She lifts her hips to meet mine, our slick skin slapping against each other, and I know she's close too. Letting go of one of her hands, I push my arm under her ass to lift her lower half. The angle changes, and I know it's more intense for her this way too. Her body arches off the mattress, spurning me on. Her moans fill the room as I chase my own release.

A few pumps later, my whole body shudders, my tense muscles momentarily going weak before I collapse on Chloe.

After a few inhales, I roll to the side, not wanting to crush her.

And then I just lie there for a while, one of my hands still interlaced with Chloe's as I stare at the ceiling and listen to our still-rapid breathing.

Then, the whole situation crashes down on me.

I just had sex with Chloe.

Holy shit.

I just had sex with Chloe.

What have I done?

I was so caught up in the tension that had been building all day and wrapped itself around me that it was all I could see. All I could think about. All I wanted.

Now, the clouds have lifted, and I'm not sure what that means for us.

Does it have to mean anything for us?

Do I want it to mean anything? Fuck if I know.

When I glance over at her, my eyes wander over her face, trying to gather her response to all of this.

Her eyes are already on me, her gaze soft and sleepy. Satisfied. She blinks and turns sideways to face me. Next time, I'll make sure to have her naked from head to toe, so I can properly pay tribute to her gorgeous body.

It's still as beautiful as it used to be, even though she's gotten more muscular, yet more curvy at the same time. There's an opposing softness to her strength that fascinates me. What happened to the girl that used to eat donuts for breakfast and scoffed at me when I had to leave to work out?

This Chloe is different. And I really like what I'm seeing. Tasting. Touching.

When her hand comes up to move toward my face but

stops mid-way, I take it in mine to pull it to my face. Kissing her palm once before putting it down on the mattress.

"Time to take care of business." I lean forward to give her nose a quick kiss.

Something that's more of an old habit than anything else.

Why does our brain remember random things like this but not others?

"Be right back." I turn away from her and grab my boxers.

I walk to the open bathroom door and pull it closed behind me. After getting rid of the condom, I use the toilet, and wash my hands.

My gaze roams around the neatly organized place when I dry my hands. It's quite the opposite of her disorganized and messy bathroom she had as a teenager.

When I hang the towel back on the rack, my eyes land on the open mirror cabinet that's on the side of the bathroom. My brows furrow when I take a closer look, and I swallow hard while my brain makes sense of the contents in front of me.

My chest tightens as I push open the door all the way for a better look. A suffocating pressure builds inside my chest, and I have to steady myself on the counter as I take in the orange and white pill bottles. They're all filled to various degrees. Solid red pills, several different-sized white pills, and blue and red pills.

With a shaking hand, I grab one of the bottles and look at the label. *Chloe Williams.* Mechanically, I pick up every single one and check it. They all have her name on it and were just refilled last week.

What the fuck is going on?

Why does Chloe have so much medicine? None of the

prescription names sound familiar as I look at them, trying to figure this out.

How sick do you have to be to need this much medicine?

Once more, I grab the edge of the sink for balance, my nerves enjoying the hard material pushing into my palms. It's so much better than my other thoughts.

A glance in the mirror confirms that there's no way Chloe won't know right away something's up. My pained expression is visible from a mile away.

Shit . . . Chloe.

I grab one of the bottles again, reading the label once more, needing to make sure I didn't imagine this.

Why hasn't she said anything?

My feet carry me out of the bathroom before I know how to handle this situation, the medicine still clenched tightly in my fist.

Chloe is sitting on the bed, the blanket pulled up to her lap, her shirt back in place.

She gives me another one of her lazy, orgasm-induced smiles, and I stop dead in my tracks. I'm only a few feet away from the bed. Why does it feel like a punch in the face to see her like this? So happy and carefree?

When the turmoil inside me doesn't have an ounce of happiness left.

I see the exact moment she notices my expression and her smile drops. "What's wrong?"

My breathing is too erratic, too out-of-control for me to speak. I close my eyes and inhale deeply.

Maybe it's nothing bad. Maybe those are some new vitamins and minerals I haven't heard of.

When I open my eyes again, I wordlessly hold up the pill bottle in my hand.

Her mouth falls open, and one of her hands lifts to cover it, while she shakes her head.

I don't have the right to confront her about this. What we had, our incredible friendship so many years ago, that's when I had the right. But now? Now, after a decade away from her, I don't have that . . . permission. I used to know everything about her. And yet, she's almost a stranger, but not.

We stare at each other, and I want to know. I want to be the one she lets into her life. Perhaps that's stupid, but inside my heart, after spending so much time with her today, after being inside her, it's like we simply fit again. I think. *Hope.*

I also know two things with absolute certainty as I watch her fold her other arm against her stomach.

These aren't vitamins.

And I'm not going anywhere until I know what the fuck is going on.

NINETEEN

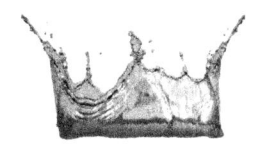

CHLOE

No. No, no, no.

Dread pools in my stomach like a dead weight, flooding my body with a wave of nausea so violent, I'm not convinced it won't have any long-lasting effects.

I stare at Noah, at that damn pill bottle in his hand as my own fingers and toes tingle and start to numb.

This can't be happening.

Not like this.

Not now.

I'm not ready.

My breathing speeds up, and I shiver.

"Chloe, tell me why the fuck you have all of those pill bottles."

My mind is running a mile a minute, and I can't focus on one thought.

Shit. Why was I so stupid and forgot about them? How could I have been so careless and invite him into my bedroom? And did I really just have sex with Noah? How did things just go so monumentally wrong?

I was planning on telling him about everything . . . eventually. This was definitely not how I had envisioned it though.

"How bad is it?" He takes a step closer.

How can I explain things to him right now? After he was just inside me and gave me one of the best orgasms of my life.

How am I supposed to deal with this?

"Chloe, damn it, talk to me." Noah lifts his arm, and throws the pill bottle on the bed. It bounces on the comforter several times before it comes to a stop right in front of me, the label facing upright.

Staring me straight in the face, like it's making fun of me. Like it's laughing at me.

Look what you got yourself into now.

My hand flies up to my chest to lie against my racing heart.

Then, a strange numbness overtakes my body. It's as if I'm present but not fully there, like I'm watching all of this through someone else's eyes, unable to control my body.

"Is it bad?" His voice cuts through my haze, and I shrug.

I don't know how to do this.

"Fuuuuuuuck." Noah grabs his hair into his clenched fists, pacing across the room.

I'm not sure why but somehow the sight of him like this pierces my heart. His actions are so opposing that I press my palm harder against my chest, to the point of pain. Unsure if I'm trying to protect myself from the pain that comes from loss or the pain that comes from love, as right now it all just hurts like someone sliced me open from the inside.

And then he's right in front of me.

I was so lost in my thoughts again, in my panic, that I didn't notice he had walked over to the bed.

The air of his irritation—his confusion—is still shadowing his face, his eyes darting over my face as if to make sure I'm all right. That I'm still okay. As if he fears I'm not.

And isn't that the real reason why my heart is in such a frenzy? Because what if he doesn't care? What if he walks out of here as if nothing happened? Not the sex, not anything else.

Even though I know we can't be together—we shouldn't be—I also don't want this to mean nothing to him.

I don't want to mean nothing to him.

That would hurt too much.

I want to keep up the illusion for as long as possible that we've always shared something special in our lives. A bond, a deep connection, that was just ours. An invisible string that somehow kept us connected over a decade despite our physical distance. Because isn't that what souls do with their mates?

His hands come up to my face, cupping my cheeks, holding me in place. Making me look straight into his cloudy eyes. His shaky thumbs brush across my skin as he breathes warm air into my face. "Baby, listen to me. I need you to tell me right now what's going on before I lose my fucking mind, okay?"

I swallow and press my lips together. The back of my eyes burn like they're on fire.

When I have my emotions under control—at least as much as possible in this situation—I give a quick nod.

"Okay, good." A rush of air escapes his lips, and he

caresses my cheeks one more time before letting his hands drop to the bed.

"I . . . the . . ." How am I going to tell him? Where to start?

One of his hands inches closer to mine on the covers, and the contact helps. It centers me.

You've got this. Just say it.

Once the words are out, they aren't yours anymore. They'll be his to process.

"So, the medicine . . ." I look at the ceiling and blink. I've talked about this a gazillion times, so why is this so hard with him?

"Yeah?" His thumb rubs over my knuckles. "What's it for?"

Deep breath. Three, two, one.

"My heart." I push out the words and stare at him.

Two words. They hold all the meaning in this world to me—my whole life—while to him they are still only two words. A few letters put together to name the core of our mortality.

His brows draw together and he stiffens. "What about your heart?"

Crap, I can't bring myself to just say it. The words are stuck in my throat, and I can't get them out. Seeing him like this has my gut clenching.

"Do you have high blood pressure? Is that what the medicine is for?"

"Two of them, yes."

His head keeps bobbing like a bobblehead. "Okay, okay." There's a pause and more intense staring that I can't seem to escape from. Like no way in hell will he miss even one single second of anything regarding me. "And what's all the other medicine for?"

My chin quivers. "Anti-infection and anti . . ."

"And anti what?"

My cheeks puff up before I blow out a breath. I repeat that several more times, trying so hard to keep my impending breakdown under control. "Anti . . . anti-rejection."

There. It's out.

I watch his face as he continues to stare at me, and I wonder if he's replaying our conversation so he can put the puzzle pieces together. Or attempt to.

"Anti-rejection . . . anti-rejection. What did Daisy mention about this bef . . ." And then there it is. Possibly some info his nurse-sister shared with him before, but something clicks. He shakes his head and rears back. "For an organ?"

A gasp escapes my mouth when he jumps up and begins to pace the room, his head tilted to the ceiling, his hands clasped behind his head.

And I let him. I give him the time he needs to work through this. Allow him to make a decision on how to handle it.

When he stops and looks at me, his gaze is so tormented I'm unable to draw in my next breath. For so long, this man's happiness kept me going. It fueled me, convincing me I made the right choice when I let him go. Seeing him like this hurts in so many ways that my insides feel stretched. Overdrawn to the point of excruciation. But isn't that exactly what I deserve after leaving him all those years ago, after removing myself from a situation where I'd never see his pain?

"How long ago?" His voice is so low I can barely make out his words.

"A while ago."

"Chloe." His hands are shaking so hard by his sides, he balls them into fists. "How. Fucking. Long. Ago?"

I curl my hands into the comforter to keep them from trembling. "Ten years ago."

"No. That can't be true. No, no, no." After one look at me—seeking confirmation once more—he turns and lets out a cry that I'd normally associate with a wounded animal. It's so haunting, I feel it all the way to my core. My whole body is shaking as I track his movements, unable to look away from him.

And then he slams his fist into the wall before falling to his knees.

I startle and freeze, before my body jumps into reaction mode. I throw back the blanket and rush to his side, dropping down next to him. "Oh my gosh, are you okay?"

I try to get a look at his hand but he pulls it back, his gaze fixated downward.

"I'm fine."

I press my lips together and sit down with my legs crossed. And then I wait.

He wasn't supposed to find out today, and definitely not this way. The least I can do is follow his lead. He deserves that.

When his head slowly lifts after a few minutes, his eyes are glassy, making my own water in response. He wordlessly shakes his head like he's still in denial. Then he pulls me onto his lap and holds me close. As close as anyone has ever held me in their life. Like his life depends on it.

I'm positive this must hurt his hand, but he doesn't complain.

I lace my hands around his neck and he slouches forward, adding his weight to mine.

My whole world slows down when he places his head on my chest. He doesn't move or say anything, but my heart stutters.

This man.

This moment. This gesture.

After a long time of utter stillness, he touches my hips and beckons me to stand up.

Once he stands in front of me, he takes my hand and leads me to the bed.

His hands go to my waist and he lifts me onto the mattress before grabbing the hem of my shirt. He lifts it only a couple inches before he stops, looking at me. Waiting.

We didn't get to the part where I was completely naked as we devoured each other. And I'd felt so . . . complete. But now . . .

"I need to . . . can I?" His eyebrows draw together in an anguished expression.

Since there's no way I can push even a single letter past the knot in my throat, I nod and lift my arms above my head.

Inch by inch Noah uncovers my skin alongside my weaknesses. But if there's one person in this world I want to see me completely the way I am, with all of my defects and imperfections, it's this man.

There's not an ounce of fear in my body over what he'll think of my scars. One of the things I've learned is that no matter how perfect or imperfect your body is from the outside, if the inside doesn't work, no amount of outer perfection will help, especially when it was all an illusion to begin with.

But I've also learned that my diagnosis has a severe impact not only on my present but also on my future. And that's what scares me the most. That's what stirs my decisions and what dictates how I live my life.

Having ripped away a life that I was once so sure of. What I once thought was an absolute, a sure thing, incapable of imagining a different scenario like the one I'm living now.

Noah tosses the shirt aside, and his hands settle on my bare thighs as he stares at my naked chest.

I straighten my spine and give him this moment. He deserves it. Heck, maybe we both deserve it.

I stay strong and upright even as I watch Noah's face fall, as the worry lines on his forehead deepen, and his breathing speeds up.

He blinks a few times before averting his gaze to the floor. But not before I see the pain in his eyes, the pure devastation before his lips press together and he covers his mouth with his trembling hand.

Then he climbs on the bed beside me, still avoiding my gaze. "Can we lie down for a bit?"

His voice cracks at the end, which unravels something inside my chest.

His emotions mix with my own, my memory of when I first found out and how I reacted, how my parents reacted. It was so similar, the shock on all of our faces. The paralyzing panic and inability to process the info properly, the unwillingness to accept any of it.

"Of course." I climb toward the top of the bed and lie

down on my back, holding my arms open toward him. "Come here."

And he does.

He lies down beside me and places his head right on the long scar on my chest that starts under my neck and goes all the way down to just past the end of the sternal bone under my breasts.

Right on the heart that beats for him like it knew him all along, like it loved him all along.

But seeing his reaction—which almost justifies leaving him—causes my second heart to shatter into a million pieces for Noah Winters as a single tear runs down my cheek.

TWENTY

NOAH

When I open my eyes, it's dark outside.

My cheek is still on Chloe's chest, the same way I lay down on her earlier after her confession.

I swallow hard, pushing all thoughts away about what Pandora's box we opened. I still have so many questions I want answered—*need* answered—but right now, I don't want to think about any of them. I just want to hold on to Chloe some more. To be with her.

The alarm clock on the nightstand confirms it's the middle of the night. Chloe must have turned off the light at some point, but since the curtains aren't drawn, there's enough moonlight coming through the windows to illuminate the room in a light glow.

It also allows me to see Chloe's body under me when I slowly raise myself. Her skin shimmers in the silvery light as my eyes move from her stomach to the breast that's closest to me. Staring at her perfect brown nipple that I want another taste of.

My dick stirs in my boxers, wanting another round. Not

having had enough of this woman yet.

After a deep inhale, my gaze wanders and stops in the middle of her chest.

My own chest restricts just like earlier, still incapable of understanding what the fuck happened to her. Unwilling to accept any of it.

But there's that scar.

When she said anti-rejection drugs earlier, and I put two and two together, I wanted to throw up. I wanted to revert back to being a child, throw my hands over my ears, and pretend none of this was happening.

A new heart. Fuck. Not only have I heard more than enough stories from Daisy about her work at the hospital over the years, but I've also attended my fair share of fundraisers and organ donations is always an important topic.

My gaze focuses back on the scar. It's lighter than most of the surrounding skin, only darker in a few spots. But it's long, and I have to close my eyes from the images penetrating my mind. Doctors cutting so much of her body open to get out the one piece of her that I once thought of as mine.

Why wasn't I there for her?

The sense of having failed her is so strong, I have to cover my mouth with my fist to keep myself from choking on these emotions.

All this time I thought she left me for a better life, not wanting me anymore because I wasn't good enough for her.

But now? Now, I don't know shit.

My mind keeps spinning, my thoughts buzzing so loud, that the urge returns to hold my ears shut.

Instead, my fingers reach out to touch her chest, to trace

the scar with featherlight touches, not wanting to wake her, yet unable to not feel her skin with mine.

A longing to please her, to make her—make both of us—forget about everything that just happened surges through me, literally propelling me forward.

Toward her body. Wanting to reunite with her again.

Because that's the one thing that's still right with us right now.

Our bodies. They still unify in a way I've never experienced with anyone else. Like we were meant for each other and no one else. The perfect match.

Her scar feels soft in the lighter spots, contrary to the rougher dark ones that still retain some smoothness. Her breast is right in front of my face, her chest still evenly rising and lowering.

My gaze is on her breast, that nipple silently taunting me, begging me. Unable to control myself, I latch on to her nub like it holds the sweetest nectar of them all.

Of course, this doesn't go unnoticed. Chloe's breathing hitches, and when I swirl my tongue around her taut peak, her eyes fly open.

Neither one of us says a word as I take my sweet time with one breast before moving over to the other, but not before kissing every single millimeter of her scar from the bottom all the way to the top.

When I reach her collarbone, I get sidetracked by her throat that's been working almost mechanically, entrancing me with its rhythm. I make my way up one smooth side, to her ear, down the curve of her jaw, until I finally get to her mouth.

I press my lips to the corners of hers and stay there for

one solemn moment. Just feeling her, breathing her in, letting this forlorn feeling of joy wash through me that she's actually here. Alive and well.

"I've missed you, Chloe." They're very simple words, but they describe my life well. I've missed this girl something fierce.

"I've missed you too, Noah. So, so much."

My thoughts want to run but I pause. *She came back to me.* I shut off my analytical brain. To enjoy her. All of her.

When I move an inch to the center of her lips, my tongue darts out to lick over her curved cupid's bow. The same one she used to complain about as a teenager, because it's always been pointier and not as round as she considered more beautiful.

I've always loved it exactly the way it is.

Her mouth opens at the action, just as I hoped.

When my mouth closes over hers in a deep kiss, her tongue comes out to play.

Sassy and adventurous just like she seems now. More confident, taking what it wants.

My dick twitches in approval, imagining a lot of other uses for that tongue and sweet mouth.

She gives as good as she gets, and even though this is a slowed-down, sweeter version of our earlier session, it doesn't lack an ounce of heat or passion.

My body is on autopilot at this point, crawling on top of her, lining up perfectly with her core that's still covered in her underwear.

We continue to kiss and dry-hump in earnest, something I haven't done since . . . well, since high school with this very woman.

Both of our breathing accelerates, and for a moment, fear grips my chest that I might actually come like this.

Chloe pulls back, rubbing her hot core against my dick like it's the best thing she's ever done in her life. And then her moan reverberates around the room as if it's meant for just that.

My balls tingle, and I slow my movements for both our sakes.

When she's calmed down, her eyes focus on me, her hand coming up to gently brush over my cheek and mouth, tracing my lips lazily until I snatch her finger and begin sucking on it.

Her eyes flare, the fire igniting to almost torturous levels.

Her head turns to the side. "Condoms are in the top drawer."

I nod and reach over, shaking thoughts away of why she'd have any at all.

Thirty seconds later, I pull off my boxers and sheath myself while she wriggles out of her underwear and tosses it across the room.

My mouth waters at the sight of her.

So open to me. So wet for me.

The pressure behind my breastbone builds.

Mine.

Before I can analyze that damn thought, she pushes against me. As impatient as before.

Instead of moving above her, I stay on my knees, and pull her toward me and my waiting erection.

When she's right in front of me, waiting, begging with her body, glistening for me, I take a steadying breath and push into her. Filling her, making both of us groan in relief at the reconnection.

Her breasts move with every thrust until she cups them. Playing with them, driving me insane. I let go of one of her legs and move my hand over her hip to her sensitive nub, watching her writhe under my touch, so on edge from the stimulation that my movements turn sloppy and out of sync.

When I feel her tighten around me, I lose my battle and come so hard that my vision goes blurry for a moment.

Our harsh breathing is the only noise in the room.

Why does the sound of that make my stomach feel all weird?

When Chloe scoots up the bed to grab some tissues, I slip off the bed and go through the same routine I went through earlier. Taking care of the condom, washing up, and putting my boxers back on.

This time, I keep my gaze straight, not looking at the medication.

I know I'll have to face reality at some point but not now. Later. Tomorrow.

After I get some more sleep with my woman in my arms.

My woman?

I scoff at myself. I'm simply falling into old patterns. A slip of the tongue.

When I slip back under the covers, Chloe faces me. Her shirt from earlier is back on, and I'm sure she's dressed under the covers too.

I mimic her sleep position, lying on my side facing her, with my hands in front of me.

We lie like this for a long time, just staring at each other. My mind is tired, still exhausted from the new revelation, satisfied after the sex, but also curious about what's going on in Chloe's head.

How does she feel about all of this?

The sex, the fact that I found out about her . . . what do you call it? Situation? Sickness? Condition?

"Were you going to tell me?" My voice is rough, and my throat dry as if I haven't had a sip of water in days.

But I have to know. The question has been on my mind ever since I found out, spinning in my brain like an angry tornado, causing damage I'm not sure I'll ever be able to repair.

Because fuck. This is Chloe.

With. A. New. Fucking. Heart.

She shrugs, and a gush of air whooshes out of my lungs at my exhale.

"I don't know. Probably at some point . . . I think." She closes her eyes, and I feel an odd sense of relief that she doesn't see me right now. And that I can't see her eyes right now either.

Why the hell wouldn't she tell me? Would I tell her if the roles were reversed?

Shit.

I don't know if I would.

Maybe it would depend on the intentions I had for her, for *us*.

Well, fuck.

I'm not sure I like where that thought leads either.

When she wordlessly turns around, I can't help myself and close the gap between us.

Did she just sniffle?

God. I know I wasn't given a choice to be with her, but she was my world. And I would have wanted to be there every step of every grueling moment. Yet somehow, this brave woman fought on her own. Is still fighting.

She's had years to accept this, yet here she cries. Selfishly, I want to be angry, hurt, sad . . . but that makes this all about me.

I cannot fathom how hard this is for her. This is her everyday.

I put my arm around her and pull her close, letting the comfort of her body aligning so perfectly with mine slowly soothe me to sleep.

TWENTY-ONE

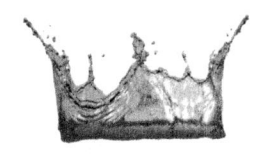

CHLOE

When I wake up the next morning, my brain is fuzzy. Until the events from last night slam into me. The sex. Goodness, the amazing sex.

Then Noah finding my medicine. My stomach clenches at the image that's stuck in my mind. Noah looking so broken, so helpless. Then more sex later in the middle of the night. More tender this time, making me feel cherished and complete.

The bed beside me is empty, and I roll onto my back to stare up at the ceiling for a few minutes. Then I close my eyes and place my left hand on my heart and my right on my stomach, focusing on each deep inhale and exhale. Trying to find my equilibrium. Needing it to get through whatever will happen next. To me. To Noah. To us.

Even though there isn't a future for us, I still know that I owe him more—he deserves to know how this happened.

And I was planning on telling him. Eventually.

My therapist used to say, "What happened is done and

can't be changed. How you will react to it, and what you'll make of it though, is up to you and will shape your future."

One of the most important pearls of wisdom I carry around with me as if it got imprinted on my new heart. She retired only a year after I received my transplant, and I had great therapists after her, but her impact has always been the most significant.

I know what the right thing to do is, but sadly, that doesn't eliminate the desire to flee, to pretend none of this happened.

Ten more deep breaths. That's what I give myself before I push back the covers and walk to the bathroom where thankfully, my morning brain takes over. Using the toilet, brushing my teeth, taking my medicine. It's been my routine for so long, I don't pause. I don't wonder. I just do.

When I gather my hair and twist it on top of my head, my gaze drifts to the small window. I lift the blinds and stare at my tiny backyard, if you can even call it that. More like a small patio area, but that's more than enough for me. I was lucky to snatch up a house I could afford in this neighborhood. It's a bit out of the price range I was looking at, but it works for now.

Like an invisible pull, I look to the patio where my beloved swing is. The main reason I go outside at all. And that's where he sits. On one side with his legs outstretched in front of him and his arms crossed over his chest, staring at the sky.

He didn't go home. Why does my heart react to that?

I try to get a read on his face, but he's too far away.

My fingers and toes tingle as I change into leggings, a T-shirt, and a big sweater and head downstairs. I forgo the rest of my morning routine of tea and breakfast, for now. The need to talk to Noah first overshadows everything else.

The sliding door closes quietly behind me as I make my way to the swing, without a word or a sound, not wanting to disturb this serene scene. The sun is still rising in the sky, barely able to cast its rays through the morning clouds.

The swing protests when I sit down but it came with the house, so I can't complain. I scrubbed it until it sparkled as much as it ever would. Plus, it's comfortable. Squeaky but comfortable.

We aren't high enough in the hills to have a view of the bay, but this little piece of lush greenery makes up for it. The quiet melody of the fountain soothes my nerves as I pull my feet up on the cushion and wrap my arms around them.

Minutes tick by as we sit like this with Noah keeping the movement going.

When I bite my lip so hard that I'm afraid I might have drawn blood, I close my eyes and take a calming breath.

You've got this. You will feel so much better once it's out there.

"Do you remember I told you my sickness got worse when we went to see my grandparents?" I don't wait for an answer and keep my gaze on the fountain. "It was shortly after we got to Los Angeles, and everyone thought I might have gotten pneumonia like my mom had a few weeks before. So my dad dragged me to the doctor. They did a bunch of tests and the X-rays showed that my heart was enlarged and that I had possible fluid around my lungs."

The swing stops for a moment before it resumes, and I use that time to swallow past the obstruction in my throat.

"You never told me about the heart stuff."

"I know." I lower my gaze. "It was all too much, and I didn't want to worry you. You had started your summer swim camp already, and I knew how much you were looking forward to it."

He exhales loudly but stays quiet.

"The next few weeks are a bit of a blur. They rushed me to the hospital where they specialize in cardiac care, which happens to be one of the best in the country. I was put on medications and more tests were done. I spent some time in the ICU and the cardiac unit, but was sent home when the medication seemed to work, even though they still couldn't diagnose me." I don't tell him how miserable I was, or that I missed him with my whole being and cried myself to sleep more nights than not.

"And you guys were staying with your grandparents?"

"Yeah. Grandpa wasn't the youngest anymore, and Grandma had just broken her hip. It was a bit of a mess. My parents didn't know what to do, but when things took a turn for the worse a week later, I was rushed back to the hospital with an abnormally high heartbeat. At that point, they were able to diagnose me with cardiomyopathy caused by myocarditis, a heart disease that can lead to heart failure."

I snort and glance over at him. "Can you believe it can be caused by a common cold?"

His eyes are closed, but I wait until he opens them and looks at me. I need to establish this connection with him, I need to know I didn't imagine it last night. When his glassy gaze finally locks with mine, time stops for a moment.

I don't want to go on, but I know he needs to know, even if he doesn't really want to.

His chest hitches when he opens his mouth. "Is that when you sent me that message?"

I'm lost in his gaze and can't look away even if I wanted to. But I know there's no way I can get any words out right now, so I nod.

And swallow. Hard. It takes me three times to finally succeed.

He scrubs a hand over his face. "I could have been there for you."

"I know."

"I would have *wanted* to be there for you."

My chin trembles. "I know."

"Fuck." He releases a heavy sigh and leans back again against the cushion, covering his face with his hands.

I'm glad for the short break because it allows me to get a grip on my emotions too. I've already shed more than enough tears over the last decade.

When he leans forward with his elbows on his knees, my stomach knots. I know this isn't easy for him. I knew back then it would break him right alongside me, and he would have dropped everything to be with me, which is exactly why I ended things. I couldn't do that to him. Not when he had such a great career—such a great life—ahead of him . . . when I couldn't even be sure I'd survive the following days or weeks.

"Did you get your transplant shortly after that?" His voice has lost its power, and I want to reach out to him but know he needs to get through this on his own terms. If he wants the contact, he'll initiate it.

How much should I tell him? I've already skipped a lot of

the gruesome details, so I don't see why I need to make this worse than it already is anyway.

"It took several months."

He turns his head to look at me. "And your heart was okay until then?"

Crap. Did he hear something in my voice? Why does he need to ask the questions I wanted to spare him the answers to?

He winces at my expression.

"I'm not going to lie and say it was a fun time, but it all worked out in the end. At least for the time being, and that's what I choose to focus on."

"I can understand that." He looks up at the sky that's a little brighter than when I first came down. "So, you're okay now?"

"Right now I am, yes."

"For how much longer?"

"I . . . I don't know."

The color drains from his face, and this time I can't help myself and reach out to place my hand on his back. I don't move it but want him to know I'm there. And as weird as it sounds, I want to be there for him, even when it's about me in the end.

Unlike him, I've had many years to come to grips with my diagnosis and life situation though.

And I know that everyone works through the onslaught of emotions differently. I've seen it with my friends and family, and myself. There's no right or wrong way to deal with the kind of pain and grief that comes from knowing that the chances of surviving this in the first place and then living for a long time are stacked against you.

But that's where I come in.

Because after overcoming the shock and going through my own phases of anger, grief, sadness, and depression, I came out on the other side ready to fight. Even if I couldn't have the life I always thought I'd have, I still wanted my life. I still wanted *me*.

Noah opens his mouth when his phone vibrates in his pocket.

He gets it out just as it stops and sighs in frustration when he looks at the screen. "Damn it, my sister's called a gazillion times."

"Call her back to make sure she's okay."

He gets up and steps to the far edge of the property. I don't know if he doesn't want me to hear their conversation, or if he wants to put some distance between us, but it's easy to tell he's tense.

When he comes back, his shoulders are drooping. "I'm sorry but I have to go. I forgot I promised my nephews I'd take them swimming this morning. My sister is going to drop them off soon on her way to work."

"No worries, I have a bunch of work to do anyway. We can talk more later if you want."

His eyebrows rise. "Yeah?"

"Of course." How could I say no to him? The look on his face, the concern, reminds me of what it used to be like when he looked at me. That he wanted to know when he'd next see me. It gives me . . . hope.

"Okay. Well, I better get going, then."

"Okay."

He shuffles his feet, and I clear my throat.

This must be the weirdest morning after ever.

Especially with our history and everything I just unloaded on him.

I just wish that spark of hope I can feel burning brightly in my chest would go away.

Because there's no future for Noah and me.

No matter how much I want it.

And no matter how much it will break this heart too in the process.

TWENTY-TWO

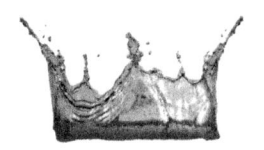

NOAH

My sister will be here in about twenty minutes, and I go through my morning routine as fast as I can, taking my toothbrush with me into the shower. The last thing I need is my sister telling me that I smell like sex.

Though I can't deny that I love the smell of Chloe on me.

Probably more than I should.

Because sex with her . . . holy shit. Talk about the best sex ever.

I could devour her all day long if that was possible.

And just like that, my mind gets away from me. Imagining her under me, on top of me, in front of me.

With those perfect breasts.

And that scar.

Fuck.

How is that possible?

My brain wants to push those thoughts away and focus on better things, on happier things. But what good would that do me?

It's not like I can escape reality. I don't have any personal experience with heart transplants or transplants in general. A quick Internet search this morning confirmed what I already knew. Anti-rejection drugs keep your body from rejecting your new organ. The thought alone that her body could decide to reject her new heart makes me sick.

But beyond that, I now also know about the lowered life expectancy, and that it lowers with every passing year. If that realization isn't enough to bring anyone to their knees, I don't know what is.

I try my hardest to keep the emotions at bay, to not let them in, but the pain slams straight into my chest anyway. And isn't that just ironic?

The look in her eyes when she told me she doesn't know how much longer she'll be okay. The almost casual way she talks about her own life.

I'm also not sure how honest she was about everything. I wouldn't put it past her to spare me some of the info, some of the details. To try and protect me again like she did back then. How could she do that to me, though? And to herself? To both of us?

My brain battles with my differing feelings, not sure what to focus on. Because shit, I'm mad. So fucking mad that she took away the chance for me to be there for her, no matter how good her intentions were. I loved her so damn much.

To know that she went through this by herself while I was moping around here, upset about our breakup. And then I channeled all my emotions into my swimming, keeping my eyes straight on the prize, on *my* future.

But the devastation keeps pushing at the anger, making me dizzy and numb.

When she left, when we said goodbye without knowing

our lives would change forever, she was my sunshine. The one person who could always make me laugh. My little bird.

To imagine her hooked up to monitors, her chest pried open to take out her heart because it had failed her. To know she could have died right then and there, and in all those years since from the consequences of that surgery.

Would I have known? If she had died, would I have been told? Surely her parents would have... Fuck. I was so angry that she'd broken up with me, but not for a minute did I imagine a world where she didn't live in it with me. Still longing for her no matter how livid and devastated I was.

I cover my mouth with my shaking hand, and the thoughts become too much, causing me to sway on my feet. The sorrow is so strong it brings me to my knees.

Why didn't I call more often? Why didn't I try harder to reach her after she broke things off? Shouldn't I have known that something was wrong? That she wouldn't just finish us and tell me that we should explore what else is out there?

The fact that she broke us to protect me and my fucking career still hits hard. The same career that hadn't even existed at that point, yet she'd already believed in it anyway.

A strangled sob escapes me as the water pours down over me, washing away the remnants of the one person I thought I'd lost forever.

My beautiful, selfless, brave, and irrationally stupid Chloe.

A surge of energy courses through me as I snap out of my puddle of misery because fuck it.

Fuck. It. All.

I'm here *now*, and I'm not going to give up easily.

Not when I know what really happened.

I wash up and get dressed in record time, zooming out of my house just when my sister pulls into my driveway. I hold up a finger so she knows I'll be right back.

And then I'm across the street.

Knocking on Chloe's door. Hammering on it when she doesn't open right away.

But then she does. Her wet hair is slicked back over her shoulders, her eyes wide and slightly red, her mouth forming the perfect O as she stares at me.

I step into her space and cup her cheeks in my hands. "Don't think for even a second that you can get rid of me this easily again, you hear me? Not a fucking chance."

And then I kiss her, taking everything she gives me, before spinning around to walk back across the street.

Past my gasping sister and the giggling boys in the back of her car.

Then I throw my bag in the car, usher the boys into mine, kiss my still-stupefied sister on the cheek, and reverse out of my driveway to go swimming with my nephews.

"Stop it, Uncle Noah."

"Never." I keep splashing Mason and Alex until they swim out of my reach.

The boys and I moved to the kids' pool after we swam a few rounds in the big one, or according to those two rascals, we were "competing," and they won. At six and eight, they're both amazing swimmers, enrolled in swim lessons as often as they can with my sister's work schedule.

I haven't been able to swim with them as much as I'd like,

but these random mornings with them have been good for me, especially now that I'm on my half-forced, half-needed break from my otherwise grueling training routine.

Even though it's been good for my mind to slow things down, I'm also itching to do something. I'm just still not sure what it is. Do I want to go back to my career and do another few years of it, participate in some more competitions and maybe another Olympic Games, or am I ready for a change in my life?

Chloe pops into my mind like she's been waiting right at the edge of it, which she probably has. This woman has turned my life upside down in more than just one way, never far away from my thoughts.

Making me question and reevaluate the last ten years of my life.

I know I can't change any of it, but I can't help all the what-if questions either that have been bombarding my brain.

"We're gonna go down the slide, okay?" Mason yells across the pool even though it's not that big.

I give him a thumbs-up. "Be careful. And remember, no running."

"Okay," they both yell as they get to the far end of the pool to climb out.

I make my way to the deeper section of the pool where the other end of the tunnel water slide is. It also allows me to keep an eye on the boys as they climb up the spiral ladder that leads to the top of the water slide.

"Hey, man. What are you doing here?"

I turn at the voice, watching Ryan and Jace make their way over to me. "Hey. I was wondering if you guys might be here today."

Loud squealing and splashing accompany them, making me smile.

It also makes my ribs squeeze, reminding me once more what I don't have in my life.

Ryan is wrestling Isabella, who we quickly noticed seems to take after Harper, just as wild and loud as her mom, while Tanner is happily kicking his feet on Jace's back.

"Where's my Izzy?" I hold out my arms toward Ryan and take the little wiggle ball from him, who gives me a toothy grin in return. "Hey, sweetie. Want to hang out with Uncle Noah? Your daddy is no fun, is he? He's way too old for that."

Ryan points his finger at me. "You're lucky you're holding her right now, or I'd show you old."

I laugh, which Izzy takes as her command to splash some more.

Jace stays a few feet away, pulling Tanner off him and giving him the kickboard they brought. That kid loves the water, they both do. But where Izzy gets excited, Tanner is more chill, more eager, and focused on learning how to be a great swimmer, wanting to be just like his dad.

After checking that Mason and Alex are still doing okay—it's almost their turn for the slide—I look at Jace. "Is it just you guys?"

He nods. "Yeah. Tanner doesn't have preschool today, and Em and Harper are shopping together for Izzy's birthday."

As if she knows we're talking about her, Izzy splashes harder and squeals.

Ryan blows out a loud breath. "Harper's going a bit overboard, but whatever makes her happy, right? It's not like Izzy will remember her first birthday."

Jace nods. "Seriously. Em went nuts for Tanner's fourth birthday last month, but he loved it."

I grin at the thought of that party. "The construction party was awesome. I've always wanted to eat a giant pile of dirt."

"That chocolate cake was dope," comes from Ryan.

We all chuckle, knowing how easily we can get excited over normal things after being on such rigorous training plans for so many years.

"Daddy, look." Tanner smiles widely as he gains some good speed in the water, the board stretched out in front of him, his little legs kicking up a storm in the back.

"Good job, buddy. Remember to tell Mommy later when we get home."

"Okay." He slows down as he gets closer to the edge before he turns around to come back to us.

Emilia and Jace had quite the start together when Jace hired her as a nanny for Tanner, the son he didn't know about until he turned up on his doorstep last year out of the blue. Thankfully they make the perfect team.

I turn to Jace. "Is Millie feeling better?"

He mutters a quiet curse. "Yes, thank goodness. It has gotten so much better since she started her second trimester."

"I'm glad."

"Uncle Noah, we're coming." When I look up to the top of the stairs, the boys are already gone.

Ryan holds up his hands, moving closer to the end of the slide where the kids are thrown out. "I've got the boys. You keep that little stinker for a few more minutes." He smiles at his daughter in my arms, who squeals and drools all over my hands.

"Incoming," Mason yells while he's still in the slide, and I chuckle as he flies out of the opening. Ryan is there when he breaks through the surface to pull him aside, just in time for Alex to follow suit.

The boys grin from ear to ear, bouncing in Ryan's arms with excitement, especially when they spot Jace, Tanner, and Izzy too.

We go back over to the shallow end that has a small kids' play area they all love.

Ryan takes Izzy from me when she reaches for him, but his gaze stays on me. "Have you figured out yet what you're going to do?"

And just like that my stomach hardens. All of the worry and uncertainty has been pushed aside for a while by everything Chloe. She's been a great distraction in that aspect. But it's never been far away, just waiting under the surface to find an opening to slip through.

I shake my head. "Not really." I try to keep my voice neutral. It's not my friends' fault that my life has been unraveling at the seams like someone's pulling at the strings, unknotting one thing after the other.

After sharing a look with Ryan, Jace drums on Tanner's board. "Do you have time this week to meet up? We wanted to talk to you about something if you're interested."

I nod, curious.

But before I have a chance to ask, Mason and Alex spray me with water, practically begging for a water fight. Foolish nephews. Let the fun begin.

TWENTY-THREE

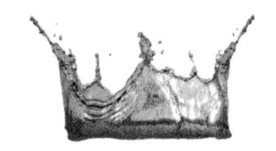

CHLOE

"I'm so sorry I'm late. Everyone and their neighbor was at the store for some reason, and the lines were atrocious." Eadie plops into the metal chair across from me and blows out a breath.

"No worries." I smile at her, always happy to see her. I made a few friends in Los Angeles but never got really close to anyone. First, there were my health issues, then my dad got sick not too long after I finally got better. My grandpa passed away in between too, and I was content to be with my family, help wherever I could, spend as much time together as possible, especially when everything was so uncertain.

And I honestly was just happy to be alive, while also mourning what I'd lost. Not just the people, but also the things I'd let go. The life I'd wanted so badly.

When I got my first job with a small publisher, I quickly figured out that throwing myself into my work was the perfect escape for me. It became my solace. And I had my uncles and Eadie to constantly message and video-chat with too. That was all I wanted, what I knew I could have, and that was enough for me. Mostly.

After rummaging through her purse, she pulls out her wallet and points at my tea. "Do you want another one? Or some food?"

I shake my head. "No, thanks. I just got a new one right before you came."

She nods. "Sounds good. I'll be right back."

"Okay." I pick up my pencil and turn to a new page in my drawing book. I already finished my work for today, putting the final touches to an adorable rhyming book for babies. Bringing these little characters to life, imagining what children might enjoy. I love it.

It's something that's always come easy to me. It doesn't matter if the words are easy, or the story isn't long, I always have a blast imagining the characters and coming up with the perfect illustrations for the stories.

Now, this competition from the big publisher, that's a totally different ball game. We're supposed to draw the illustrations for the first chapter of a major young adult novel. The series has been so successful that the publisher is planning on publishing all books as an illustrated collection as well.

I know the books inside out, having read them several times before I heard about the competition, but I still haven't had a good idea about how to bring the characters, the story, to life.

The story is about a girl who finds out she's the daughter of the biggest dragon trainers without even knowing that dragons exist. The story is amazing. Addicting. The character growth, the love story, the storytelling itself, it's all absolutely beautiful. Magical.

The first chapter begins with her in her normal life, having fun with her girlfriends, giggling over boys, moaning over her chores. And then she's kidnapped and told about her responsibilities. That her parents disappeared, and she's the key to finding them.

Talk about being pulled out of your normal life and thrust into a totally different world. Into a life you haven't planned for, and one you're so not ready for. I read the series for the first time during my recovery after surgery. In a way, I could relate. It also offered the perfect escape from everything else that was on my mind.

And every*one* else.

Specifically a certain someone.

My hand flies over the paper as I'm immersed in my own fantasy world, letting the pictures in my hand translate into real images on paper.

"Holy shit, that's fantastic." Eadie's voice pulls me out of my bubble.

When did she come back? And how long has she been standing right next to me, watching me draw?

She leans closer. "Oh, and quite . . . interesting, too."

"Uh, thanks." I blink a few times before my eyes truly focus on what's in front of me.

A colossal dragon, its wings spread wide as it soars through the sky. There are two people on its back, leaning low, clutching the dragon for dear life.

She walks around the table and sits down, setting her coffee and croissant on the table. She grins at me. "I guess I don't have to ask who's on your mind?"

"What do you mean?"

Leaning forward, she taps her finger on my paper.

My eyes widen when I take a closer look. I hadn't paid much attention to the people before because I was entranced by the majestic dragon. But shit, she's right.

On the back of that dang dragon is none other than me and Noah as teenagers.

Crap, how am I supposed to get out of this one?

I huff. "I . . . uh."

"Mm-hmm, that's what I thought." She pulls off a piece of her croissant and puts it in her mouth.

Eadie tilts her head to the side before putting her hand behind her ear. "I'm listening. How was lunch at your mom's and what happened with Noah afterward?"

My stomach flutters and my mouth goes dry. After taking a large gulp of my tea, and nearly scalding my tongue, I clear my throat. "Well, let's see. Lunch was a little weird but not as bad as I thought it might be. And then Noah and I went to the movies. You know that old movie theater we used to go to a lot? They're playing old movies now for a couple bucks."

"Oh yeah. I haven't been there in forever."

"It was nice."

"Nice, huh? Did you also make out when the movie theater got dark like you used to?"

Heat rushes up my neck and into my face. Not because she's right of course, because we didn't make out at the movie theater, but goodness did we make up for it at my place later on.

My muscle aches and pains are proof of that, a delicious reminder of how amazing our time together had been. At least, in bed.

Eadie's eyes glow as she rubs her hands together. "Oh, this is going to be good. Tell me everything."

I open my mouth just as the doorbell above the entrance door rings and a gush of wind blows into the cafe, followed by excited kids' chatter, and three men. The baby babbles a happy "Mama," when a blonde gets up from her chair on the other side of the cafe with a cheerful "There's my baby girl," and a "Hey, handsome," at the guy who's holding the baby.

The scene is so serene, so normal yet perfect, I try to tune out the rest before it gets too much. No need to torture myself.

Instead, I cross and uncross my legs, and try to force my brain back to my conversation with Eadie and how I'm going to tell her what happened. I mean, how do I even summarize everything that went down?

"Hey, Uncle Noah, isn't that the girl you kissed this morning?"

My insides freeze at the combination of Uncle Noah, girl, and kiss.

Because, what the hell?

The "ew" that follows and several people chuckling doesn't make it any better.

"Holy shit." Eadie gapes at me as I stop breathing.

Should I turn and confirm my suspicion or pretend I didn't hear anything? I can't decide which one would be worse.

My face, neck, and ears feel like they're on fire, and I have the urge to hide under the table.

Someone clears their throat. A little too close for my comfort.

I fidget and squirm in my seat before facing the inevitable, plastering on a big smile as I look up at Noah.

"Oh, hey there."

He smirks at me. "Hey."

Yeah, not awkward at all.

And damn it, why does he have to look so good? He's wearing sweatpants and a hoodie, with that dang hat on his head again. The sight shouldn't have a bout of lust shoot straight between my legs. But of course, it does.

He's still the only guy who does it for me like this.

Thanks so much, universe.

All these years I spent without him I thought it was a figment of my imagination, or I wrote it off as teenager hormones, but nope. It's definitely *him* my lady parts love to pieces.

He rubs the back of his neck. "Sorry about the boys."

A giggle pops out of my mouth, and the urge to hide comes back. The embarrassment just keeps piling up.

I wave my hand in front of me. "Kids."

Oh goodness, what is going on with me today? And where is that black hole that swallows people who make total asses of themselves?

We stare at each other until Eadie kicks me under the table.

I flinch and Noah frowns.

"You remember Eadie, right?" I point toward her and shoot her a look she doesn't see as she's occupied gazing at my Noah.

Whoa.

My Noah?

Definitely not mine.

No, nope.

"Wow, Eadie. Long time no see."

"You could say that." She gets up and they do a half hug.

Why didn't I get a hug?

Oh man, my inner goddess is in a mood today. Funny too after all those orgasms last night. You'd think she'd be blissfully happy, sleeping it off somewhere in a corner.

Before she can grumble any more, Noah turns my way and presses his soft lips to my forehead, lingering long enough for me to inhale his intoxicating fresh scent.

He's gone too soon for my liking, just as the two boys come running over to us.

The smaller one hides halfway behind Noah while the older one stops right in front of me. "Hi."

"Hi." I smile at him, which he returns.

"What's your name? I'm Alex, and this is my little brother, Mason." He jabs his thumb behind him. "And this is our uncle Noah. We just went swimming all morning, it was really fun. They have a water slide there, and a really cool play area. Mason and I are really good swimmers. We haven't been able to go swimming as often as we used to since our parents stopped being married, but our mom said maybe we can take more lessons again soon. Are you Uncle Noah's girlfriend?"

Noah chuckles and pulls him back in front of his body. "Whoa, buddy. That was a lot of information you just threw at Chloe."

He wrinkles his nose as he turns his head to look at Noah. "Her name is Chloe?" He wrinkles his nose and looks back at me. "My girlfriend from last year was Chloe too. We played together on the playground."

I want to squeeze him. How adorable. "She sounds nice."

He shrugs. "Yeah, she was pretty cool." Then he looks back at Noah again. "Can we get some food now? I'm really hungry."

Oh, the attention span of a child.

"Sure." Noah nods at his nephew before locking gazes with me. "It was good seeing you."

I do my best imitation of a bobblehead. "Yeah."

"I'm really hungry, Uncle Noah," Alex pipes up again, and I laugh.

"You better go and feed them."

"Yeah." His eyes widen for a moment before his hand disappears in his pocket and he pulls out his phone. After tapping on it a few times, he hands it to me. "Want to put your number in it?"

"Uh, sure." I type in my number and give it back to him.

How weird is it to not have the phone number of the man I've been working with at the hospital, took to lunch with my mom, went to the movie theater with, and had glorious sex with.

"Thanks. I'll send you a text, so you have my number too." He taps the screen a few times before putting the phone back in his pocket.

"Okay."

"Well, have fun."

"You too."

Noah does a little salute and he and the boys head to the counter.

My gaze stays on them, watching them interact. How Noah follows whatever Alex points at, and how he bends down to talk to Mason.

Just like earlier, I have to eventually avert my eyes. They stray over to the group of people he came with who are all staring at me before looking away quickly.

Were they watching us the whole time?

"Oh, for the love of I don't even know what," Eadie sighs and slaps her hand on her chest.

I put my chin on my hand. "I know."

"I've seen photos of him, and videos, of course. But shit, it's nothing to this." She tilts her head in the direction of where they stand. "This is like a wet dream come alive. But better."

"I know."

"Chloe Williams, you are in so much trouble."

"I know," I sigh, this giddy feeling in my stomach reminding me too much of my teenage years.

And all of a sudden, it's hard to remember why Noah and I can't be together.

It's like he's dousing me in some magical dust whenever he's around and I can't think straight.

All I want is to be with him.

And I'm not sure I'm able to resist him.

I'm screwed.

So very screwed.

TWENTY-FOUR

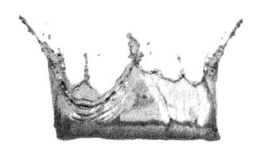

NOAH

Noah: Did you have a good time with Eadie yesterday?

Chloe: I did. It was nice to spend some time with her.

Noah: Good. Are you busy tonight? I thought maybe we could hang out?

Chloe: Sorry, I'm going over to my mom's.

Noah: No worries. Have fun.

I blow out a breath. I was really hoping to see her tonight.

There's still so much to talk about, especially after I've had some more time to process our past with different information. With the truth.

Do I feel like I have a right to be angry? Yes, especially when it comes to having choices taken away from me.

But is it worth holding a grudge against her after all this time? After everything she told me? After knowing what she's had to endure, what she's still dealing with on a daily basis? After not being able to help myself and googling the life expectancy of heart transplant patients and seeing that the number steadily declines with each year post surgery and how low the number is for a ten-year survival?

The answer is a big fucking no.

It doesn't make what she did back then right. But we were only fresh out of high school, and to be honest, I'm actually also amazed that she had the wisdom—the selflessness—to set me free as such. I know she loved me. I know she wanted a future with me. But she somehow let me go so I could achieve the goals I had been merely hoping I'd have a chance at.

Who has that amount of altruism at eighteen? *Chloe Williams.*

Punishing her for . . . being noble hardly seems right or fair. Despite my anger, I never stopped caring about her.

My phone vibrates in my hand.

Chloe: Maybe tomorrow after the hospital? You'll be there, right?

Noah: You bet.

Chloe: Okay. I left Crush for you to paint. You always liked him.

Noah: *Dude*. I just watched Nemo with my nephews a while ago, and they agreed that the turtles were super cool.

Chloe: Ha. I bet they did.

Noah: Yeah.

I lean my head against the headrest.

It hasn't been that long since I saw her. Less than twenty-four hours. A little longer than that since I touched her. So why do I have this insane urge to see her again?

Something bangs against the car window and my heart's ready to jump out of my chest. My head whips around and my gaze collides with Jace's.

"You all good in there?"

I shake my head at him. "Coming."

After grabbing my keys and pocketing my phone, I get out of the car and give my friend the stink-eye. "Seriously?"

"Sorry, dude. I wanted to make sure you're okay when you didn't come inside."

"I was texting."

"Oh yeah?" We make our way up the walkway, but his eyes stay on me. "With Chloe?"

"Why would you think that?"

Jace gives me a look.

I sigh. "Yeah."

"How are things going with her?"

What a loaded question. I don't even know how to answer it. "Uh, good I guess?"

He's quiet for a moment. "You said she's an old friend?"

"Yeah."

We walk into the living room where Ryan and Hunter are watching something on TV.

When they see us walking in, Ryan pushes the button on the remote and the screen turns black.

"Hey," Hunter complains.

Ryan nods his head in my direction, and Hunter's eyes go wide.

Jace didn't say anything about Hunter when he called to ask if I could meet up with him and Ryan so we could talk.

I nod my head at Hunter. "What are you doing here?"

He shrugs. "I thought I'd spend my break with you before I go back to the pool."

"Mmm."

Jace claps me on the shoulder. "What do you want to drink?"

"Water or a sports drink if you have it."

"You got it. Be right back."

I sit in the corner of the sectional and lean back into the cushions.

Jace comes back and throws a cold bottle at me.

"Thanks."

He sits down and they all look at me.

"What?"

Instead of talking, they all look at each other, until Hunter throws up his hands and looks at Ryan and Jace. "You're such pussies." He shakes his head at them before facing me. "They—we—wanted to know what's going on with you and Chloe."

I frown as Jace chuckles and Ryan rolls his eyes.

Hunter grins. "It doesn't happen often that your nephews call you out in public for kissing someone."

Oh yeah, that.

I was able to get away from an inquisition yesterday since all the kids were there, thank fuck. They're definitely not a prime audience for spilling the beans.

"Nothing's going on, really. She's an old friend."

"An old friend that you kiss?" This time it's Ryan, who has put a few extra ounces of disbelief in his voice.

I shrug. "I guess so."

Ryan's eyes narrow to slits. "Is she the one you dated in high school?"

Wrong direction. "Yeah."

He nods like that explains everything.

We're all silent for a few moments, and a weight settles on my chest, getting heavier with each passing second.

"She broke up with me via text message when she was visiting her grandma the summer we graduated. We were supposed to go to college together. She said her plans had changed and that we should see what else is out there. Separately."

I inhale deeply, trying to calm my racing heart. "She just told me this weekend that she broke things off because she got really sick and needed a heart transplant and didn't want to hold me and my career back. It's why she lied to me."

The words are out of my mouth at record speed, like someone else said them. But the weight on my chest also feels lighter.

I scratch my head and keep my gaze down, unable to look at my friends. That was the shortest summary of something so tragic and major in my life I've ever given.

Especially when I still haven't figured out how to deal with everything, or how things are going to continue from now on.

"Fuck, man." Jace blows out a loud breath.

"Is she okay?" Ryan asks while Hunter murmurs, "Holy shit."

"She is right now from what I understand." My chest heaves as I try to draw in enough oxygen.

The room is so quiet, you could hear a pin drop.

But what do you say after such a bomb has been dropped on you? I felt just as overwhelmed when Chloe told me. It's so much to take in, so many things your brain's trying to wrap its head around.

"There are always exceptions, of course, but when you look up the life expectancy of someone after a heart transplant—if they survive the first year after the surgery—the average is ten to twelve years." My voice is flat, the exact opposite of how I feel on the inside.

"How long ago did she get hers?" Ryan's deep voice cuts through the tension in the room.

"Ten years ago." I slump forward with my elbows on my knees and let my head hang low. This dreadful darkness is looming over me again, trying to swallow me every time I think about Chloe and her health. I know nothing can really make this better right now, but I still interlace my fingers behind my head to rub at my skin.

I haven't talked to anyone about this since I found out, and this is why. Because I can't handle it. The knowledge wants to destroy me.

The couch dips next to me, and a hand lands on my back, squeezing a couple times right over my shoulder blade.

"I don't know what to say." Jace's voice is quiet and a little ... shaky? "If something like this happened to Em, I'd lose my fucking mind."

"Yeah, me too." Ryan's always been the most somber in our group, which probably comes from him being older than the rest of us, but I've never heard his voice break like this.

"I'm so sorry, man." Hunter comes over to the other side of me. "I would've never guessed this by looking at her. She looks so normal and happy."

And isn't that just a kick in the balls? To have someone so positive and joyful fall apart on the inside? It's not fair. It's so not fucking fair.

Even though she just came back into my life, I can't imagine a world without a bright light like her. It's impossible. She doesn't deserve this. None of it.

The heat behind my eyelids turns up a notch, making my eyes burn hotter. Shit, I can't remember the last time I cried in front of people.

I bring my hands to my face and rub over my eyes.

The guys give me space, and I don't think there was a time I was more grateful for them.

We've been friends for so long now, being there for each other throughout our careers, celebrating each other's wins, and commiserating over our losses.

And to think I thought that was the most important thing in my life, to win, to be successful. All while she was literally fighting for her life, not even knowing how much longer she had to live.

Although, she still doesn't really have a clue, does she?

Could her body decide right now that it doesn't want her heart anymore? Or something else could go wrong with it?

"Babe?" The front door closes, and several pairs of footsteps come closer.

"Crap. Let me talk to Em. I'll be right back." Jace pats my back once and leaves my side.

I focus on breathing, inhaling and exhaling at a rhythm that blankets me in familiarity, calming me.

"Is there anything we can do?" Ryan's voice sounds more normal than before but he still keeps it quiet.

When I think I've got it all under control, I slowly raise my head and sit back. I still don't have it in me to look one of them in the eyes though. I can't see their pity and pain right now. It's too much. "I don't think so. I still only know the basics and what info I could find online. She's taking good care of herself as far as I know."

"That's good at least."

"Buddy, wait." Jace's voice comes closer, but it looks like he wasn't fast enough because a second later, Tanner runs into the living room and jumps on the couch between me and Ryan.

"Hey, guys." Cute Tanner, with his curls and his big smile.

Jace's son.

I want a son.

"Sorry." Jace comes to snatch Tanner who pretends to eat his dad.

I watch them like I've done so often before, and then my eyes land on Millie, Jace's wife, who's expecting their first child together. Her hand is clasped over her mouth, her eyes shiny as she looks straight at me.

Fuck.

I have to look away.

But the image of her is stuck in my head. But not of her sadness, but of her being pregnant, showing the first hints of a belly. The image morphs into something else, into *someone* else.

Chloe, a pregnant Chloe smiling at me, carrying my child.

I never wanted anything else in my life this badly.

And why the fuck did I have to work that out when the girl I've always seen in my future may not even live for the next two years? Fuck. My. Life.

TWENTY-FIVE

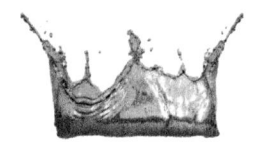

CHLOE

I haven't heard from Noah since our text messages yesterday. Why does that seem like such a long time ago?

The need to be with him is slowly creeping toward previous—and crazy—teenage levels. When you just want to be with the other one. To be their *person*. To want them to want you as badly as you want them. Day and night.

I told my mom last night what happened and she reminded me about what several therapists have told us before, both individually and together. First, when I went through my health issues, then when we were told about Dad's cancer and learned we'd lose him soon, and then when we lost him. *Many* therapy sessions over the years.

Grief is different for everyone, and we need to allow people to go through their own process. As long as it's in a healthy and safe way.

I dropped an enormous bomb on Noah, one he couldn't have seen coming from a mile away. And all of that right after we had amazing sex.

Talk about going from a high to a low.

It might take some time for him to come to terms with my situation. With everything that entails.

And I know that because my whole family has had to grieve several losses, something else Mom and I discussed. Not just my grandfather's death blackened those days all those years ago. My parents were grieving the possibility that their daughter would die before them. So many tears. So many moments of sheer agony. And then Mom and I again walked through a dark, dark time when Dad was diagnosed.

Part of me doesn't want to start the grieving process again with Noah, but I do want his friendship. I'd hate to lose him as a friend now that I just got him back.

Of course, I'm insanely attracted to him still, and I don't mind enjoying some physical benefits from our . . . friendship, but only if we can both handle it.

And isn't that the sore spot? Because I'm not sure we handle it, but then, I don't think I could deal with more either.

When it comes down to it, wasn't this exactly the reason why I lied to him back then? Because I didn't want to derail his life with my issues? Because he deserves everything he wants without being held back by me?

Are things better now for me? Yes, and no.

Ugh. All of this is ridiculously frustrating, and I let my feet hit the asphalt a little harder than necessary.

Normally going for a walk helps, but it doesn't seem to work today, which sucks. I really wanted to clear my head before I go to the hospital.

I stop and put my hands on my hips. Huffing and puffing about this won't make anything better. When the wind blows in my face, I close my eyes.

Trying to relax, trying to get rid of all this anxiety.

When I feel marginally better, I continue and turn into my street—our street—just as two cats race past me. At least one of them is letting out a terrible noise.

What on earth? The noise shrills through the air once more. Goodness, that doesn't sound normal. Are they okay, or is one of them in danger and needs help?

I run after them, across the street, where they disappear behind Noah's yard gate.

Dang it.

Should I let them be, or should I check on them?

I rattle on the gate, and of course, it's locked.

The noises that definitely sound like painful wails to me don't seem to have left Noah's yard. Shit.

Did one cat get the other one and is attacking it now in earnest?

Ugh. Somehow I just know I'll regret this, but I can't let a cat massacre happen on my watch.

So, with all the finesse I possess, I jump up to grab the top of the gate and try to pull myself up.

It takes me several tries to heave myself all the way to the top, but I eventually manage.

Mental note: Add more upper body exercises to my workout plan.

When I finally get to the top—with my stomach resting against the top of the gate—I rest for a moment to catch my breath.

"Mmm, Chloe?" Noah's voice comes from behind me, and I close my eyes.

Might as well die of mortification right up here.

My ass is probably right at his eye-level.

How embarrassing, seriously.

Then the cat noises sound again and I wiggle around, just to realize that I've somehow gotten my shirt stuck at the top.

What is this? The "make Chloe's life miserable" show? When all I wanted was to help.

"Hurry up and open the gate so we can check on the cats. It sounds like they're murdering each other."

He clears his throat. "Uh, you want me to open the gate while you're hanging on it?"

"I'm stuck," I mumble and huff.

"You're stuck? Let me help you down."

"Yes, please." It can't get worse than it already is, right?

"Okay. One sec. I'm going to grab you by your thighs and hold you up so you can let go at the top and get your shirt unstuck, yeah?"

"Sounds good."

Wrong.

Bad idea.

Bad, bad idea.

Because Noah does hold me by the thighs, exactly the way he said. What I didn't think about though is that the second I lean back to take care of my shirt, I push back my butt.

Yup, right in his freaking face.

This seems to be the day that keeps on giving.

I shake my head. "I'm so sorry."

He mumbles something that is completely muffled because, well, his face is pretty much pressed into my butt that is only covered by thin workout leggings.

Either he hasn't gotten the memo that I can't hear him, or he keeps doing it on purpose, but man, it tickles. Which makes me wiggle around more, probably pushing my behind even more in his face.

I chuckle. "Stop it, right now."

With one final yank, I finally get my shirt free, and the momentum of the movement almost makes us fall backwards like a bad circus act.

I try to steady myself on the fence to make it easier to slide down Noah's front this way, only to get stuck on a hard bump for a moment. And then I'm past it and land on the floor, Noah's hands immediately reach out to steady me.

"What did I just get stuck on? Did I hurt you? I'm so sorry." I turn around and look him up and down until my gaze gets stuck on the front of his jogging pants. And the very obvious bulge. Right there, in front of me. Like it's saluting me. "Oh . . . Wow . . . Mmm . . . Sorry."

Noah chuckles and puts a finger under my chin to tip it back. "Hey."

I blink up at him. Inhaling his fresh scent, noticing his wet hair. And then I blink again. "Hey."

His thumb brushes over my cheek before moving to my lips. "I've been wanting to do this ever since I left you yesterday."

And then his lips are on mine. Rough and demanding. He pushes against me and together we move backward until he has me pressed against the gate. I'm up on my toes, my fingers intertwined behind his neck, pulling on his short hair. His hard length hits the right spot between my legs, and I barely bite back a moan.

Holy crap, this is hot.

His mouth leaves mine and he moves over to my ear. "Are you wet for me?"

The words hit my sensitive ear, and I shiver.

Since when does he dirty talk?

If I wasn't wet before—which I totally was—I would have been now.

When I open my mouth to reply, a loud whistle sounds through the air, snapping me out of this hormone-induced trance. It's like someone dumped a bucket of cold water on me. Noah takes a step back, with his back still toward the street, and adjusts himself in his pants.

Damn it, even that is hot.

Why do I feel like my 14-year-old sex hormones just woke up?

I peek around him until I see Bessie and Agnes across the street. Waving, and grinning like two fools. I think Agnes might actually be fanning herself rather than waving.

Lifting my hand, I grin and hope it doesn't look like I'm constipated. "Hey, ladies."

"Well, hello there, Miss Chloe. And Noah?" Bessie grins like a Cheshire cat. Of course, she knows it's him.

Noah chuckles and slowly turns around. "Hey, Mrs. B."

Both ladies look left and right before they cross the street.

Agnes huffs when they get to us. "Did you see our cats by any chance? They took off earlier like the devil's after them, and we haven't been able to find either of the two."

Noah coughs awkwardly. "Chloe followed some cats to my house, so why don't we go to the backyard and check it out."

He pulls a set of keys out of his pocket and unlocks the gate, opening it wide. "After you, ladies."

Agnes and Bessie take the lead, and when I turn to follow them, Noah slaps my butt.

I yelp before glancing over my shoulder at him.

The urge to stick out my tongue at him like I've done so many times before is almost impossible to resist. Especially when he looks so carefree like he does right now. So normal, like yesterday didn't even happen.

I almost bump into Agnes when I round the corner, who has her hand over her mouth, while Bessie giggles next to her.

Noah comes up behind me—a little too close—and snickers. "Well, I guess we found your cats. Looks like they're busy though."

We all just stand there and stare at the scene a few feet in front of us. Just as the black and white cat that's on top thrusts once more before pulling back. Which results in the tabby cat jumping up from her position and attacking the other one. All while screeching at the top of her lungs.

Two seconds later, they sprint past us and out the gate again.

Our elderly neighbors go after them and we follow.

Noah shuts the gate behind us before coming over to where we stare down the street. "Do you want us to come with you?"

Bessie waves him off. "Nah, I bet they'll go back home. You know, now that they're done and all. We just wanted to make sure they didn't get run over during their crazies. But I'll let you know if we need your help, thank you."

They both wave as we watch them cross the street where Agnes turns around once more with a snicker. "You kids continue to enjoy your time together. Sorry for interrupting you earlier."

"We will, thanks. Have a good day, ladies." Noah smiles and waves back.

I hit him on the chest. "Oh my gosh, you're so bad. They probably think the worst of us."

"If by worst you mean how it feels to have a case of blue balls, they might be onto something."

I cover my face and bump against his chest, giggling. "Stop it."

"Only if you admit that your panties are wet."

I pull back and stare up at him. "Mmm . . . it's getting late. I better get ready to go to the hospital."

"Want to carpool?"

"Sure." I get my keys and bounce them against my leg. "Give me five minutes to get changed into my painting clothes."

"And to change your panties?" The crooked smile he gives me is killing me.

It also makes me want to jump him right here, right now.

I bite my lower lip and mumble a quick, "You wish," before I spin around and walk across the street.

Of course, I change my panties, because one thing's for sure: it will always be Noah Winter who my body wants.

TWENTY-SIX

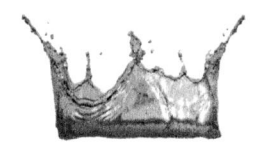

NOAH

"I think my arm is going to fall off soon." I put my paintbrush on the floor and stretch my upper body.

"Oh you poor baby. Is a little painting too much for big, old Noah?" Chloe pouts next to me, her eyes filled with mirth.

I love when she's playful.

"What?" Her voice does this little hitch thing it does when she's embarrassed or unsure about something. "Why are you staring at me like that?"

My mind goes back to our conversation, and I chew the inside of my cheek. "Just wondering what I should do with you for being so sassy." I lean closer. "For being so naughty."

I don't miss her sharp intake of breath, or the way a small shiver runs through her body.

I give her nose a kiss before picking my paintbrush back up and continuing to color in the animals she outlined so beautifully. If we can get some good work in over the weekend, especially if Hunter will help too, I think we might be able to finish up. The hardest work was definitely transferring Chloe's concept to the wall, and she did most of that by herself.

What we're doing now is mostly a glorified paint-by-numbers, or at least, that's what I'm doing. Chloe wrote down the paint numbers for me on the animals, so I know what paint to use and don't have to stop her every few minutes to help.

"What did you have in mind?" Her question throws me off.

"For what?"

"For a punishment." Her gaze stays on the wall in front of her, her paintbrush not once losing its spot.

And then her tongue darts out to wet her lips.

Little minx.

Oh . . . if she wants to play, we can play.

My paintbrush goes in the dark green once more before I continue my work on one of the smaller turtles. She added numbers for a whole bale of them for me. They look amazing, even though I've drawn outside the lines more than once already, but Chloe always comes to the rescue, right there to help with my mishaps.

"So you do want to get punished?" I finish with the green and clean my brush to continue with some brown, and next some red and yellow to fill in the patterns on the shell and the body of the turtles.

"That depends."

"On what?"

I can feel her eyes on me, but I stay strong, and don't look her way. "On what the punishment is and if I'll like it."

Fuck. I don't need a hard-on at the children's hospital. There aren't a lot of people left, but a few are still milling around for their late afternoon appointments. But no one needs to witness this disaster in the making if I can't get a handle on my dick soon.

Or someone's hands . . . or mouth.

Shit, what's wrong with me? This is so not helping.

Let's think about cute baby turtles. There's little Squirt right in front of me.

Couldn't get much more adorable than that.

I swallow repetitively before I clear my throat too. Pathetic. "Well, I guess you can find out later if you want."

"Oh yeah?"

"Sure." There. I sound totally nonchalant, like I don't have a care in the world. And there's definitely nothing to see here in this roped-off area, people. "Want to grab dinner when we're done?"

"I have lasagna at home."

The paintbrush almost falls out of my hand as I look at her. "*Your* lasagna?"

"Yup."

"Hell, yes." I'm only a decibel away from shouting it from the rooftops.

"Shush. Little ears." Chloe chuckles and swats her hand at me. "Plus, only special people like my family and friends are allowed to know about my lasagna."

Little ears? Fuck, she's cute.

She'll be the best mom one day. I've always known that.

But one thing at a time. I don't want to overwhelm her either and drive her away. Because did she just throw me in the friend category there with her little statement? Huh. Not ideal, but I can be her friend, with benefits—lots of them—until she's ready for the next step.

I give her a cocky grin because that's the kind of relationship we have. "We can Netflix and chill?"

She shakes her head and laughs. "Something like that, sure."

Awesome.

Chloe holds up her finger. "But only if we focus for the next hour now and paint."

"Deal." I hold out my pinky to her, and she stares at it for a moment before gingerly curling hers around mine.

"Deal." She gets her phone out of her pocket and plays around with it for a moment. "I'm going to listen to some music. I need all the help I can get to stay focused. Let me know if you need anything, okay?"

I nod and get working on my own painting. Sometimes, I peek over and watch her paint, all engrossed in not only her artistic skills but also how she moves her body to whatever music she's listening to. Until she looks at me and laughs before giving me a shoo motion with her hand.

She was right though, we do get a lot done during the next hour. And even though my painting lacks some skills, I also feel oddly accomplished.

After we clean our brushes and trays in the bathroom, we stow everything in the hallway closet and make our way to the elevator.

A man rushes toward us. "Chloe."

The same man I've seen her with before here at the hospital—where she'd kissed his cheek, or was it him kissing her?—and another time where he picked her up at the house.

"Hey." She goes up on her toes and hugs him. For a lot longer than you'd hug an acquaintance or normal friend. Hmm.

He gives her a peck on the cheek and looks at her. "You're all good?"

She smiles up at him. "Yup, all good."

"Great." He gives her shoulder a squeeze before his gaze moves to me. "Hey, Noah. It's been a while." He holds out his hand and I shake it. Dumbfounded.

Do I know this guy?

"Hey . . ." It couldn't be more obvious that I have no clue who he is.

"Oh my goodness, I'm so sorry." Chloe slaps a hand on her forehead. "Noah, do you remember my uncle Cody? He used to look a bit different. More hippie with longer hair and a beard."

"Thanks for that reminder." Cody laughs and elbows her in the side. "I'm glad Checco isn't here to witness that trip down his beloved 'fashion faux pas' memory lane, or I'd never hear the end of it. Again."

"He loves to tease you about it."

He lifts his hand in an "oh well" gesture. "I'm not saying he's wrong. That doesn't mean I want to hear about it all the time either though."

"Fair enough."

Then they both turn their attention to me again.

"I definitely didn't recognize you. Wow." I push my hand through my hair.

He shrugs. "I totally get it, no worries. How are things going? Congratulations on your athletic success. It's been a great ride for you."

"Thank you, I appreciate it."

The elevator arrives, and we head downstairs while Chloe updates him on the painting. And some competition I don't have a clue about. I need to remember to ask her about that later.

"I'm over there." Cody points to a car row over after we enter the parking lot. "Will you be at the bar on Friday?"

She chuckles. "Wouldn't miss it."

What's at the bar Friday? And what bar?

Even though so much seems to have happened between us, and things have started to feel so normal again, I only need a five-minute conversation with a third party to show me how little I know about her life.

Good thing we'll spend the next few hours together.

"It was good seeing you, Noah." Cody and I shake hands again before he turns to Chloe.

"Text Checco before he stands in front of your door unannounced."

"Will do." She leans up to kiss him on the cheek, and with a wave, he's gone.

Chloe turns to me. "Sorry, was that weird? I keep forgetting that things have changed."

I get my car keys and play with them in my hand. "No worries. But I have questions."

"Well, let's go home, then, and I might just answer some for you." With that, she turns and walks in the direction of where I parked earlier.

My hand shoots out and connects with her butt.

She gasps and looks at me over her shoulder. "First at the car gets dibs tonight for dessert."

And then she's off, leaving me standing there like a total idiot.

When I finally get my feet moving, she's already several

rows ahead of me, zig-zagging her way through them like she does this for a living.

Her laughter flows through the air, and my heart bounces happily behind my ribs. The heavy weight on my chest momentarily lifted.

With a smile on my face, I reach my car where she's bent over, with her hands on her knees, trying to catch her breath.

Fuck. The weight is back tenfold, all the air sucked out of my lungs when panic takes over, and I come to a stop in front of her. "Are you okay?"

She looks up at me and grins. "That was fun."

I squeeze my eyes shut and force the breath out of my mouth. "Shit. You scared the crap out of me."

"I'm sorry." Her hand lands on my chest. "I keep forgetting that you just found out. It takes a bit to get used to everything."

She puts her head next to her hand on my chest, and I put my arms around her.

If I hold her a little too tight, she doesn't let on.

Inhaling her sweet scent that's mixed with the remnants of old paint smell on her clothes, I kiss the top of her head.

Like I've done so many times in my life.

Like I haven't done in so long but want to do for a lot longer.

TWENTY-SEVEN

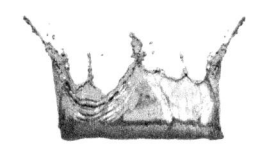

CHLOE

"This is exactly what I needed." Noah puts his plate on the coffee table with a quiet *thud* before leaning back and patting his stomach. "Still the best damn lasagna ever."

Since my portion was a lot smaller than his, my plate's already on the table. "Thank you."

It feels so dang good to just sit next to him and enjoy a meal, especially after the scare I gave him earlier in the hospital parking lot. The laughter got stuck in my throat as he was rushing toward me, his face pale as a white sheet.

I keep forgetting that he still frightens so easily.

Of course, I freak out too when I don't feel well, but at least that doesn't happen often anymore.

There are a gazillion people with health issues—both mentally and physically—and a lot of times, life throws you a curveball and kinda leaves you stranded at the side of the road without a way home. So you make the best of it. You keep on fighting and get used to your new normal. And then you keep going. Rinse and repeat.

Which of course means different things to everyone.

This, right here, is pretty perfect for me.

I've read stories about people who use this second chance and completely change their life. They travel the world, change their career, or do other extreme things.

When everything happened, I was still so young, unsure of what my life would bring me, what life would have been like if I hadn't gotten sick. Besides Noah, of course.

It definitely helped me cement my choice of getting a degree in fine arts though, something I haven't regretted for a second. It was one hundred percent the right choice. It's helped me with my journey and has brought me joy when there was so much darkness.

Noah stands up and walks to the painting that hangs above the other couch. "Did you paint that?"

I nod and move next to him. "It's one of my favorites."

We stare at the two figures sitting in the rain. The boy has his arm around her shoulder as she rests her head on his shoulder.

A soothing wave washes over me, like always when I look at this piece. "I sketched this when I was at the hospital before I got my transplant. I didn't have the best time, and I missed you so much. Drawing us like this, pretending that you were there and held me . . . it helped, I guess."

"I would've been there had I known. In a second. I wouldn't have left your side. Ever." His jaw is so tight, he barely gets the words through his lips.

"I know. I really do. Everything in my life was so uncertain at that point, and there was nothing I could do except hope for a donor heart to become available. But it wasn't like that for you. Your life was different. I knew you'd go far, have the incredible career you always wanted and dreamed of. The one you deserved. And you got it. I'm so proud of you."

"Don't say that." He stares down at his empty hands, and I grab one of them to give it a squeeze.

"It's true though. You achieved so much, and I was always rooting for you."

"I was so mad at you."

"I know. I'm really sorry. It was the hardest thing I ever had to do." My vision blurs, and I blink a few times to clear it. "But we're here now, and that's what's important to me. It wasn't planned, but I'm happy we're close again. I've missed this. I've missed *you*. More than I ever thought I could miss anyone."

Noah doesn't say a word. He pulls me against him and kisses me. It's nothing like the kisses we've shared so far. This one is so soft, so gentle, I can feel it seeping into my body. And it hurts. So much.

Everything with us is a mixture of happiness and pain that can reach an intensity at times that's too much to take.

But after all the misery, after all the pain Noah had to go through, I owe him this. I owe him kisses that pierce my soul and leave a permanent mark. Right next to all the other ones he's left there before.

Because if there's one thing about Noah and me, it's that we were never meant to be apart. Life didn't make that decision for us, I did. And for the rest of my life, I will equally hate and be proud of myself for making it.

After a few more pain-filled—yet beautiful—kisses, he pulls back and puts his forehead against mine. "I never stopped missing you. Throughout my career, I always imagined your face in the stands. Cheering me on, knowing I made you proud."

"You did?"

He nods just as the kitchen timer beeps.

I lean into him to seal my lips with his once more before stepping away. "Dessert time."

He does his adoring half-snort, half-huff thing that always makes me want to squish his cheeks and kiss him senseless.

I pick up the plates from the coffee table and put them into the sink in the kitchen before checking on the apple crisp in the oven. The corners of my mouth tug up when I look at it. "Perfect."

After getting it out and putting it on top of the stove, I turn around and find Noah putting the dishes in the dishwasher. *After* washing each plate off under the faucet. "You still do that, huh?"

He doesn't look at me but his cheeks lift. "I can see you're still *not* doing it."

I press my lips together before answering. "And I still haven't broken a dishwasher either."

He pushes the dishwasher door closed and leans against the kitchen counter. "Lucky duck."

I sigh. "Yeah."

We stare at each other in silence until he lifts his chin in my direction. "Do we have a few minutes before we can eat it?"

A million questions float through my mind. *Why are you asking? Do you want to eat me first?* Those two might just be on repeat too. So I keep my mouth shut and nod instead.

"Great." He pushes off the counter, his tall, lean body towering over mine. "Want to show me more of your work?"

"My . . . work?"

"Yeah. Only if you want to, of course. I looked up some of your books online, but I bet they look a lot better when they're printed."

Oh, that sweet, sweet man.

"Sure." I make a waving motion with my hand to follow me and walk through the living room, past the front door, and to the small hallway that's off to one side with my office and a bathroom.

When I walk inside, an immediate calm washes over me at the sight of my garden out the window. It offers great light, and the same sense of pride and happiness overcomes me whenever I see my workspace. It's my element, the time when I most feel like myself. "There you go."

My drafting table, my desk, my drawing pads—both paper and digital—my bookshelves filled with books I love, and books I've illustrated.

"So this is where you create your magic?" Noah walks around, stopping at the bookshelves, pulling out books and flipping through them. Smiling. Laughing. Seeing him enjoy my work makes my chest thump to a happy beat.

When he makes his way back to my desk, he picks up a stray piece of paper.

Looking at it, leaning closer, inspecting it more.

"Holy shit, is that . . . is that *us*?" He turns the paper around like I don't already know what he's talking about.

Of course, I had that drawing lying on my desk, because I've been staring at it when I'm supposed to be working.

But surprisingly, it has helped me make progress with the drafts for my submission. I changed the looks of the characters to match them with the description of the characters. Shorter than Noah and me, darker skin and unruly black curls for the girl, and olive skin for the boy with wavy brown hair.

And I have to say, these are some of my favorite drawings I've ever done. For some strange reason, it was easier for me to picture this abstract world when I imagined it with Noah and me.

"It's for a young adult illustration competition I'm going to enter. Not the drawing with us of course, but the theme is the same."

"You'll do amazing. These are great."

"Thanks."

He puts the paper back down and looks around the room as if it's a magical place. Would it be very inappropriate to kiss him? Because that's honestly all I can think about right now.

That undeniable heat is creeping up my face again. "I wouldn't call it magic, but yes, this is where I sit most of the week to work."

"And you love it?"

Why does his gaze have to be so intense? "Yes."

"Good." He looks like he wants to say more. "Do you . . . do you mind if I take a picture of it?"

To say his question takes me by surprise is an understatement, but it also makes me all warm and fuzzy on the inside. "Of course."

"Thanks." He gets out his phone and positions it over the paper. When he's done, and satisfied, his phone vibrates in his hand. He reads whatever is on the screen. When he looks up, he studies me. "Feel like going to a kids' birthday party with me on Sunday?"

I gulp.

"Ryan and Harper's baby girl turns one and they're throwing her a party." When I don't say anything, he continues, "Never mind, I know it's crazy. You don't have to go with me, no worries."

"No, it's okay. I'd love to come with you," I blurt out, not sure I really mean it. Even though I've been curious to meet Noah's friends and their kids. To see who he's been around all these years when I wasn't around. "But only if you come to the Parrot Lounge with me on Friday."

"The Parrot Lounge?" His eyebrows shoot up.

"Yup. My uncle Francesco's tiki bar. Have you been there?"

His eyebrows shoot up. "Oh that's his? I haven't been there yet, but I've heard interesting things about it."

"Well"—I'm ready to defend my uncle and his bar—"it *is* an interesting place with interesting people."

"Deal."

"Deal."

He types on his phone and puts it away.

And then he's in my personal space, his hand going to the back of my neck and pulling me to him. "And now I want my dessert."

I hum my approval and he whisks me off to the living room couch.

An hour—and multiple orgasms—later, we sit naked under the blanket with reheated apple crisp on our laps, laughing at something on the TV.

I haven't had any of . . . *this*.

Sometimes that makes me angry, which is where I go in my head when I think about what I missed out on. A boyfriend, someone who loved me so deeply. Nights filled with food, great conversation, amazing sex, and . . . love. No sadness. No limitations.

Nights like this is what I've yearned for and missed.

Because it can't get any more perfect than this.

TWENTY-EIGHT

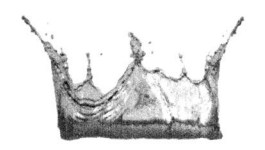

NOAH

THE PARROT LOUNGE IS PACKED WHEN WE GET THERE Friday night. Chloe leads the way, and I keep my hand on her lower back as we make our way through the crowd.

When we make it to the far side of the bar, I'm glad there's an empty spot.

I put my arm around Chloe's waist and lean close to her ear. "Why are there so many people here?"

Chloe smirks. "Rosa is on tonight. She always draws a big crowd."

Before I have a chance to ask who the heck Rosa is and why she draws a crowd, someone taps the microphone near the stage. "Welcome to Drag Night."

The whole bar erupts in cheers and hoots, and Chloe chuckles when I look at her with wide eyes.

She mouths "Surprise," and I want to kiss the damn smile off her face, so I do.

This was supposed to be a quick, mostly chaste, kiss, but fuck, she's intoxicating. The way her tongue plays with mine, the way she nibbles on my lips. If I don't find the willpower to pull back soon, this night will end with blue balls for me.

"Hey, kids. I thought that was you, Chlo, but I couldn't tell for sure with all the . . . you know, face-sucking and all." The guy on the other side of the bar is older than us, but it's impossible to tell by how much. The dim lighting isn't helping either. He also looks strangely familiar.

"Hey." Chloe untangles herself from me and chuckles before leaning over the small partition to give him a hug. Then she turns around, with one arm still around the man's waist. "You remember Francesco? He's now officially my uncle on paper too."

Now the whole Checco comment Cody made the other day at the hospital makes a lot more sense.

"That's awesome, congrats." Then I hold out my hand to him. "Good to see you again."

"Oh, the pleasure is all mine, Noah." His handshake is strong, his expression amused. "And thank you. I'm glad you were able to make it out here with Chloe tonight."

"I didn't tell him." Chloe leans into his chest and chuckles.

Francesco's eyes glimmer. "Oh boy. Well, you're in for a treat. The house is always packed when Lady Rosa is in the house. She's the best in all of Northern California."

Chloe nods. "She really is amazing. I've seen countless videos of her over the years, but it's nothing compared to seeing her live."

Someone calls Francesco's name and he lets go of Chloe after kissing her cheek. "I've got to go, but I'll send someone over to take care of you, okay?" Then he turns to me and winks. "Enjoy the show, Noah."

And then he's off, and a guy on the side of the stage announces Lady Rosa. The crowd goes wild once more as an Amazonian walks onto the stage, taking her place in the middle of it. Everything is quiet for a moment until the music almost explodes around us and the Weather Girls' *It's Raining Men* starts playing.

One song turns into another, then a few more, and I have to admit that even though I've never seen a drag show before, this is entertaining as hell. Chloe has one hell of a time too, dancing in the small space in front of me and taking big gulps of her water in between.

When the waiter came over with a large glass of something sparkling for her—complete with an umbrella and a bright pink loop straw—she told me that this is her uncle's way of being supportive and taking good care of her. Cody joined us a few songs ago, and it's been a fun evening.

Once Lady Rosa is done, the whole place calms down, and the music switches to background music again.

When Chloe leaves for the bathroom, Cody studies me quietly.

I can't help but chuckle at his obvious perusal. "What?"

He takes a sip of his drink and smiles. "Sorry, I guess all bets are off when it comes to this girl. She's been through a lot, and the last thing any of us want to see is her getting hurt even more."

I hold up my hands. "I couldn't agree more. She told me about what she went through and about her dad. I can't even imagine what she's gone through. And how she's still this happy person. It's . . . amazing."

"That's Chloe for you."

"Very true."

"But I'm glad she told you. That's a good thing."

I purse my lips and nod. It's situations like these where that anger, and a bit of jealousy float to the surface over everyone knowing what was going on with her, but me. Everyone important in her life, but *me*.

Chloe chooses that moment to return, as usual, with a smile on her face, followed by a yawn she barely manages to hide behind her hand.

"Looks like someone's ready for bed." Cody smiles at her.

At that, she yawns again and grins. "I sure feel like it."

"Let's get you home, then." I get up from the barstool and finish my water. I'm used to not drinking because of my usually very strict swimming routine, so it's not a biggie, but I also wanted to support Chloe and allow her to have a fun night out.

We say goodbye to Cody and Francesco, who comes over when he sees we're getting ready to leave, and then we're off into the cool night. We took an Uber earlier because Chloe said parking will be a pain tonight—which I'm guessing is due to Lady Rosa—so I called for another ride when Chloe came back from the bathroom, and thankfully, one was close by.

We slip into the back of the waiting car and have a quiet ride back home with our fingers intertwined and Chloe's head on my shoulder.

By the time we arrive, Chloe's passed out. She doesn't wake up when I thank the driver, or when I not-so-gently get her out of the car. This girl has always been a deep sleeper. I walk up her driveway and to her front door but realize that I obviously don't have her keys, and I don't want to wake her up either.

I turn around to take her to my place when I remember

her medicine. Does she still need to take it tonight? Can something happen if she doesn't take it on time?

Fuck. I thought I knew so much after googling the shit out of heart transplant surgery, patients, and life after heart transplant surgery.

"Chloe." I talk quietly, not wanting to freak her out. Of course, nothing. "Chloe." A little louder. "Little bird." Her breath hitches. "Little bird." Louder again, and this time, I nudge her nose with mine too.

She stirs in my arms and slowly, very slowly, opens her eyes to give me a lazy smile. "Hey."

"Hey, gorgeous. Where are your keys?"

"Purse."

"Can you stand?"

"Mmm."

I put her down but hold on to her by the arms while half of her arm disappears in her purse.

After a minute, she pulls it back out with her keys dangling between two fingers. "Jackpot."

"Well, there had to be something good in that monstrous bag." I poke her side and she leans away from me.

"Stop it. You know I'm ticklish."

"Oh, I know." I pull her body flush to mine and stare into her eyes. Her porch light is dim, but bright enough to see her dilated pupils. "There isn't a thing I've forgotten about you, Chloe."

She inhales sharply before blinking furiously. "I know what you mean."

I swallow, the late evening air cold enough to bite at the tip of my ears. "Let's get you inside. I don't want you to get sick."

"Okay."

I watch her fumble with the door lock long enough to want to take over, but then she gets it.

When she turns around in the open doorway, I look at her. Deeply. The slightly droopy eyelids. The small hint of dark circles under her eyes.

Fuck. I read about how important sleep is for someone like her, and here I've been keeping her up at night when we're together. And so often, when we're not, we're texting or on the phone until late.

She's rubbing at her eyebrow. "Are you . . . are you coming inside?"

Damn it. I hate that she seems so uncertain. Doesn't she know how much I want her? How much it physically hurts me to not be with her every possible minute?

Two more steps and I close the distance between us, cupping her face into my palms. "Not tonight. I want you to get a good sleep. When I see you next, I want those dark circles under your eyes gone, okay?"

She nods and yawns.

When I press my lips to hers, it's easy to tell by the lack of pressure how tired she really is.

She wipes at her eyes. "You said you're going swimming tomorrow morning, right?"

"Yeah. I don't want to get too out of it."

"Makes total sense. So, I'll see you at the hospital later, then?"

"Yup. I'll be there as soon as I'm done with my training."

"Sounds good."

I lean in to give her a chaste goodnight kiss before sending her off to bed, but either she's hornier when she's tired, or someone's just woken up. Her hands disappear into my back pockets, and she pulls me to her like a woman on a mission, a moan slipping past her delicious lips.

My earlier hard-on comes back with a vengeance, and I know I need to take care of that before I have a chance of getting some sleep.

As much as it pains me to do, I end our kiss and take a step back, still holding on to one of her hands. She groans in protest, and I chuckle. "I know, babe."

Her gaze snaps to mine, her eyes smoldering with heat. Out of reflex, I rub my thumb over her wrist, just to freeze when I feel the raised skin under my finger pad. "Sorry."

"It's okay."

My gaze is fixated on her tattoo, on the birds mid-flight that look so peaceful and free. "We never . . . we've never talked about it again."

"I know." Her swallow is audible in the quiet night. "Do you want to know?"

I nod and somehow find the strength to look at her. She's more alert than before, her eyes bright and awake.

"It happened about a year after I got my transplant. It had been a long year and a half since I'd gotten sick. Things happened so quickly, and the time after the transplant surgery was no walk in the park. It wasn't an instant fix. The surgery itself and all the medicine was hard on my body, I had a lot of side effects, which meant a lot of experimentation with medicine dosages and different mixes. One night in my bedroom, I just felt so overwhelmed and cut my wrist."

To imagine her doing this feels like a punch straight to the gut.

Her shoulders lift. "I don't even know what I expected, or

what I wanted to happen. I just wanted for things to be easier."

"I'm so sorry, Chlo. So fucking sorry." I pull her to me, not sure how to ever let her go again.

But a few minutes later, she's the one pushing me away. "Now, let's both get some sleep. You have to be fit in the morning. And someone told me I look like a zombie, so I better haul my ass to bed too."

She's smiling, but there's strain behind that smile that she can't hide fully. For Chloe to have become so desperately unhappy that she tried to take her own life . . . that she didn't want to live anymore . . .

It takes every ounce of self-control to not shudder.

Without a doubt, there are levels of grief. Sometimes, I can spot glimpses of Chloe's until she covers it up with a lighthearted comment or shrug.

But not only did she survive, she's thriving.

After one more kiss, I finally peel myself off her, even though it's so much harder after hearing that brief but poignant story.

Leaving this woman is hard.

Leaving her after everything I know, is extra hard.

Leaving a piece of my heart with her might be the easiest of them all.

TWENTY-NINE

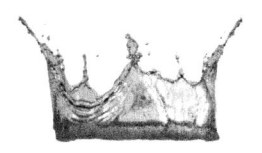

CHLOE

"Stop it. You look beautiful." Noah puts his hand on my thigh and squeezes as he drives down a street that's lined with lush green trees on both sides. "Everyone will love you."

Why did I say yes to going to a kids' birthday party again? Oh yeah, because I'm a sucker for this man. How could I forget?

Noah told me all about his friends, the other "kings of the water" as the press loves to call these four. Ryan and Jace, who I've briefly seen when I met with Eadie at the cafe but quickly avoided eye contact when Noah's nephew exposed us. Hunter I know from the hospital, even though he hasn't been able to help as much after the first week due to some unexpected commitments with one of his sponsors.

Noah said his sister will be there with her boys too. Let's hope they won't blurt out anything else about us. I met Daisy a few times when we were dating, but since she's four years older, she was already at college when Noah and I met.

It helps to have this info about them, to at least feel slightly prepared and calm my nerves.

Noah parks on the side of the road behind a black truck and comes over to my side to help me out of the car, even though I'm fully capable of doing so, of course. Instead of stepping aside so we can head up the walkway, he crowds me and pushes me against the car.

His head dips as he stares into my eyes. "You okay?"

"Yeah. Just a bit nervous."

He nods. He knows this.

I've always been this way. Wanting to be social, loving the idea of being around people, but then easily getting overwhelmed when I'm in the midst of it all. Mostly, I'm actually enjoying myself and have a blast, but then I feel exhausted afterward.

Sometimes, that makes me feel like a lunatic. Like my brain can't decide if it wants to be an introvert or extrovert. An introverted extrovert. Yikes.

Noah leans closer until his warm lips touch mine and he begins to suck on my lower lip. The hint of mint chocolate he ate on the drive over is still fresh, buzzing on my tongue when I touch his.

Way too soon he pulls back, resting his forehead on mine.

"What was that for?" I'm thankful for the car behind me. My legs are wobbly from that searing kiss.

"I could hear you thinking from all the way over here."

"Sorry."

"Don't apologize. I just don't like it when you're so in knots over stuff." His lips press against my forehead in a featherlight kiss before he takes a step back.

I frown at him, liking him in my space. Wanting him back in my space.

Maybe I can talk him into staying out here? Yeah, because that wouldn't be awkward at all if someone saw us.

He chuckles at my expression. "Don't look at me like that. But this is a kids' party. Probably one of the worst moments to have a hard-on."

I flinch. "Okay, I'm good. Sorry. Let's do this."

It's not that being around kids is anything new. I mean, I illustrate children's books. Have been to lots of signings over the years and participated in reading programs at local charities and libraries. I should be okay, then, right?

I mean, what's the worst that could happen? That Noah's friends don't like me?

Noah grabs Izzy's birthday present from the trunk—a super cool wooden stool with her name as a puzzle-piece of sorts in the middle—and we make our way up to the front door that's decorated with tiny felt donuts stickers.

The door opens before we can knock and a handsome guy greets us.

"Hey, Noah."

"Hey, Zane. How's it going?" They give each other one of those shoulder-thumping half hugs that for some reason always make me want to snort.

"Good, you? I heard you're retiring?

Noah lifts a shoulder. "Yeah, maybe. Not sure yet."

Zane nods as if he completely understands before his eyes travel over to me, and his smile gets wider. He's clearly way younger than us, but he's adorable with his light-brown hair and brown eyes.

Noah puts his arm around my waist and pulls me to him.

"Zane, this is Chloe. Chloe, this is Zane, Ryan's *little* brother. He studies at Hawkins University."

"Oh, hi. It's so nice to meet you." I shake hands with him, seeing the similarities between him and his much older brother. Noah showed me some pictures on his phone when he told me about his friends. He took this bringing-me-up-to-date project seriously.

"You too." He gives me one more smile before looking at Noah and wagging his eyebrows a couple times.

Noah shakes his head and laughs before elbowing Zane in the ribs when we walk inside.

Zane leads us through the house and out the patio door, and I stop.

"Wow." I'm not even sure where to look first.

The pastel tassels and balloons everywhere, the "donut bar" where donuts hang on wooden hooks, the impressive pink cake that's surrounded by miniature donuts and covered in sprinkles.

"Harper really pulled through, huh?" Noah looks at Zane, and they both chuckle.

Zane says something under his breath that sounds a lot like pussy-whipped.

"Watch it, dude." Noah smacks him over the back of the head. "You're just jealous."

Zane snorts. "Yeah, sure."

I pinch my lips together to keep from laughing. We all know that Harper is closer to Zane's age than Ryan's—and beautiful and funny—so I wouldn't be surprised if Zane had a crush on her at some point.

"Speaking of the devil." Noah tilts his chin toward the

blonde that's walking toward us, with a wobbling baby on the ground in front of her.

With a death grip on both of her mom's hands, the sweet girl walks toward us on unsteady feet in an adorable "one" shirt—with the o in the shape of a donut, of course—and a pink tutu. Her eyes are set on Noah, who's crouched down, his smile mirroring the adorable girl's toothy one.

"Look at you, Izzy." He holds his arms open and she happily walks into his embrace after letting go of her mom's hands. He stands up with her on his hip and tickles her stomach. "Such a good birthday girl. You'll be running around in no time."

Harper laughs. "I'm not sure I'm ready for that yet."

Noah raises his eyebrows at her. "Well, it looks like you were ready to throw a party at least."

She flinches. "A bit too much, huh? Ryan wanted to rein me in but look at all of this stuff. It's just too cute."

Her husband walks up beside her—the two of them eloped on their babymoon, much to everyone's dismay—and pulls her to his side. "There wasn't a chance in the world to stop you from this craziness."

He winks at her before turning toward me. "Hey, Chloe. We haven't officially met. I'm Ryan, and this is Harper and Izzy."

"It's so nice to meet you guys." We all shake hands, and somehow I end up with my finger clutched in Izzy's hands, who's still happily chilling in Noah's arms.

The girl squeals and babbles, drool running down her chin. I smile at her, copying her noises, because how could I not? She's absolutely adorable.

The euphoric butterflies in my stomach turn into knots, a

ball of sadness and devastation twisting my insides like a fist is trying to bury itself deep within my rib cage.

Her big beautiful eyes, her long lashes, her cute button nose, her perfect doll lips and plump cheeks, her easy smile, the soft tendrils around her face.

I'll never have that.

Until now, I was able to bear it. I *had* accepted it.

That I'd never have this. That I'd never have a sweet angel like Izzy stare up into my eyes and call me mama.

But seeing her in Noah's arms like he was meant for this role as a dad, while still holding on to my hand . . . it's too much.

My heart can't handle this picture.

I can't handle it.

Pressure blooms behind my rib cage from forgetting to breathe, while my skin is starting to feel clammy, buzzing from top to bottom like it's losing circulation. Which it is.

Do not faint, Chloe. Especially not in front of all these people.

"I . . . I, I'm sorry. I need to sit down for a moment." I pull my fingers out of Izzy's grip and step away from the group, unable to look at any of them but sure all of their gazes are on me.

Way to ruin a baby's birthday party by being dramatic.

I thought I could get through this, but I guess I'm not as strong as I thought.

After half-stumbling back inside, I plop onto the couch and put my head between my knees. Not two seconds later, rushed footsteps come closer, and a big hand lands gently on my back. Rubbing soft circles.

"You okay? What happened?" Noah's voice is calm except for the small crack at the end of the sentence.

"I'm okay. Maybe it's just the heat and the nerves." It is exceptionally hot today, so it's sound reasoning.

"Can I get you anything?"

"Maybe some water?"

"You got it. I'll be right back."

There's a light pressure on the back of my head. Did Noah just kiss that spot?

And then his footsteps echo through the house, more noise coming from farther away, before he's back. The couch dips next to me, and he holds something cold against the outside of my knee. Goodness, it feels good.

I turn my head slowly and peek at the full cup in his hand. "Thank you."

My throat feels as dry as it sounds, and I take as many small sips as I can comfortably manage while propping myself up on my knee with my elbow.

Noah brushes my hair away from my face. "Do you—"

"Uncle Noah." Two boys run across the room toward us, a small dark puppy hot on their heels.

Alex and Mason.

Mason points at the dog as if there was any way to not notice the fluffy bundle that's currently trying to jump up my leg. "Look, look. That's Brutus. Isn't he so cool? I really want a dog too, but Mom said we can't have one until we're older. Can you talk to her? We really want one."

"Yeah." Alex's head bobs in an excited nod. "Please?"

I wish I could buy them five.

Noah shakes his head. "Sorry, guys, but this is between you and your mom."

They both groan and look at me as if they're only just noticing me.

Mason stands up a little straighter, a small smile back on his face. "Can *you* tell our mom she should let us have a dog? I mean, you're Uncle Noah's girlfriend, right? I bet she'll listen to you."

Thank goodness I drank my water before these two cuties came over, or I'm sure I would have choked on it. "I . . . uh."

Noah shakes his head. "Come on, guys. You know that's not okay to ask. Your mom is the boss and the only one who can make decisions like this."

They both let their head hang. "Sorry."

Meanwhile, Brutus has taken a liking to me, still jumping up my leg and licking at my hand with an enthusiasm only a puppy can muster.

But goodness, I'd take him if I could. I have no idea what kind of dog he is, but he's all soft fur and big dark eyes.

"Were you allowed to take Brutus out of his room?" Noah's met with silence when the boys look anywhere but him.

Busted.

They shake their heads. With a resigned huff, they turn around and head toward a hallway that's off to the side.

Mason pats his leg. "Come on, Brutus."

After one more lick to my hand, and a tiny yelp, the fluffball turns around and runs after the boys.

"Those two." Noah brushes a hand over his face. "I'd better make sure they behave now. Will you be okay for a couple minutes?"

Our gazes meet and I swallow. He's so close. Almost too close after what just happened. Like my heart needs some space right now between us to function better. To get a breather, so I can clear my head.

"Actually, I need to use the bathroom if you could point me in the right direction." I hold up my slobber-coated hand. "Need to wash off these germs and all."

He closes his eyes for a moment. "Damn it, I read about animals and transplant patients but didn't even think about it just now. I'm so sorry."

"No worries. I just want to make sure I can wash it off."

"Of course. Are you okay to stand up and walk?"

"Yeah, I'm good now, thanks."

"Okay. Then follow me."

And I do, because frankly, I'd pretty much follow this man everywhere.

Which is still a problem, because while I know what we're both in for, he still doesn't know all of it.

And while he deserves the whole truth, I'm not sure I'm strong enough to tell him.

THIRTY

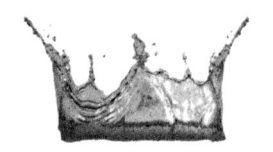

NOAH

One thing is abundantly clear. Something's bothering Chloe, but I have no idea what.

When she suddenly turned pale and had to sit down, worry slammed into me so hard, I slumped down next to her. Panic followed, and all I wanted to do was haul her out of here to get her checked out by a doctor.

But of course, she wouldn't have any of it.

That's Chloe. Stubborn.

And I clamped my unsettling emotions down hard so she wouldn't see them.

Of course, after we took that break inside, she said she was fine and is now happily chatting away with Millie, Harper, and my sister on the other side of the backyard where they set up a pink stand with drinks. She's smiling, laughing. But whenever she thinks no one's watching, I see how the happy facade slips.

Am I obsessed with her? Pretty much, yes.

After the history we have, and after seeing how she's turned into this strong, independent woman and reacquainting myself with her. How could I not be? Reconnecting with her fascinating mind. Relearning every curve of her perfect body.

"Hey, man." Ryan snaps his fingers in front of my face. "You okay?"

Begrudgingly, I pull my gaze away from the woman who has my stomach in knots and face the birthday girl's dad. Dang it, I'm one rude ass, sitting here with my friends and ignoring them. Especially since they wanted to talk to me about something important.

"Yeah, sorry." I hold Ryan's gaze, even as his brows pull together tightly. "Just distracted."

"No worries." Jace shakes his head. "You've had a lot going on lately, and we can talk about our offer another time."

This time, I shake my head. "No, I'm good. You already wanted to talk to me last time and it didn't work out, so hit me."

I can give my best friends a few minutes of sole focus. It's already bad enough I haven't been around a lot lately.

Ryan nods. "You're still not sure what you want to do going forward, right?"

Easy answer. "Nope. Not a clue."

I haven't even really had a lot of time to think about things. Chloe has fully infiltrated my life and brain.

Even though I've been wondering lately if she ever actually left?

My thoughts wander again, but I push them aside for now.

Jace shifts in his patio chair, stretching his arms above his head before leaning forward and fixing me with a serious gaze. "We want you with us."

I blink. My mind going utterly blank for a moment.

They want me? With them? "For your swim school?"

They both nod in unison.

"Seriously?"

Ryan cracks a smile. "Of course. Why are you acting so surprised?"

I shrug. "I don't know."

Jace pops a piece of donut in his mouth before washing it down with water. "You love swimming and you're good with kids."

He's got a point.

Ryan and Jace's plan to open a swim school close by is still fairly new, but I know they've already been able to rustle up some reputable sponsors. It will take a while to get a new aquatic center built that offers more than the local one does.

My brain's on fire, imagining what life would be like with a coaching future. Would I like it? Sharing my knowledge with the young ones and making them better swimmers? "And the plan is still to use the current aquatic club for lessons until the new building is done?"

Ryan's head dips in a quick nod. "Yeah. We just got all the details finalized after we figured out a schedule that works for everyone. But we need more people to help. You're clearly at the top of that list."

"Thanks." My thoughts wander back to Chloe.

I take in all the info. Weigh the pros and cons in my head. Am I ready to give up my own career? I definitely had a good run. A really good run. And coaching would also allow me to be more flexible with my time. To be able to spend more time with my family. And with Chloe. To use the time she has left.

Fuck. *Don't think about that.*

She's okay for now. Strong and healthy. Taking good care of herself.

Unable to help myself, my gaze flickers over to *her*. Now playing with the kids on the lawn. Her ponytail swinging around as she chases Tanner, who's become a carbon copy of Jace in so many ways. With his blue eyes, his easy attitude, and affinity for water.

Ryan clears his throat. "We know you have a lot going on, so take your time. We still have a long road ahead of us until we can offer the whole schedule anyway. We'll need a lot more hands on deck for that. Until then, we'll rotate with the classes and different ages. See what works best for all of us."

Jace tilts his head toward our women. *Our* women—like Chloe's already a part of the group. "Em and Harper have been helping too, making suggestions about classes that can be more than just a sport for kids. Something that can help them, either with their health, or to get them off the streets. Offer them an alternative. We're in contact with local charities and organizations to see what we can come up with together."

My chin dips in approval. "I like that."

Hunter drops down next to me on the two-seater. "Hey, man, is Chloe okay? Daisy said she didn't feel well earlier."

That's Hunter. Dropping in at a party and cutting straight to the case. "How do you—"

"I ran into Daisy inside when I got here." He looks away from me to the other guys and holds out his fist for them to bump. "Sorry for being late. That dang campaign will be the end of me. How many ways can you possibly hold a sports drink toward the camera for it to look good?"

I stare at him as he lets it all out, because that's Hunter.

He's not a quiet guy. Sometimes he drives us all crazy with his antics, but he's a part of us and always will be.

"Anyway." He faces me again. "So she's okay? She looks like she's having a blast."

"Yeah." We both look in the direction where Chloe is sitting in the grass with Izzy, blowing bubbles for her and being rewarded with delighted squeals. "Just a dizzy spell I guess. She ate something and said she was better."

"That's good."

My gaze is still on Chloe. She's so good with Izzy, and all the other kids too. Exactly how I always pictured she'd be as a mom.

"What's going on with you two anyway?" Another thing Hunter doesn't do: beat around the bush. Ever.

I let out a long breath. "I don't know, man."

"You can barely keep your eyes off her. I think you do know."

"Smart-ass." I punch him in the shoulder and we all chuckle. "And you can hardly blame me."

"Never said that."

I'm quiet after that, still watching Chloe with the kids, while the others chitchat around me.

I can't get over how easy and right this feels. My friends never excluded me, but there have been many times lately when I've felt like the odd man. But not today.

"Did you have fun?" I click in my seat belt and look at Chloe, who's overtaken by a yawn.

A soft chuckle raises the corners of her mouth. "I did. But those kids wore me out."

"Yeah. Kids are no joke. Whenever Daisy works and I have the boys for the day, I'm exhausted by the time she picks them up. I don't know how she does it. Being a single mom must be super tough."

"She seems to be doing well though. Happy. I talked to her for a bit." Chloe finally buckles in too, and I start the car.

"I saw." I maneuver us out of Ryan and Harper's neighborhood. "You were really good with the kids."

She mumbles a quiet, "Thanks."

Is it too early to talk about kids with her? I don't know why but I have this sudden urge to go after everything I want with her. Maybe it's because there's this constant feeling in the back of my head that time's running against us.

Or is she not feeling well? Now that she's not at the party anymore, is she letting her mask drop fully like I saw inklings of earlier?

"You okay?" I look over to her when we're at a red light.

"Yeah." She clears her throat. "Just tired."

But I can't help notice the slumped posture, or the fact that she seems to be avoiding me by staring out the window. I don't think she's lying, she's tired, but I have this gnawing feeling in my stomach that there's something more happening.

When we get to our street, and I park in my driveway, she unbuckles and reaches for the door as soon as I shift the car into park. "I better head to bed. Thanks for taking me. That was fun. Have a good night."

And then she jumps out of the car like something's chasing her.

Does she really think I'd just let her go like that? What sort of lame goodbye was that?

"Chloe, wait."

She turns around but keeps walking backward, already in her driveway. She shakes her head and waves her hands around in front of her. "I have to go, sorry."

What the fuck is going on? And did her eyes look shiny?

I go after her in quick strides. I need to know what the hell is happening.

I need to make sure the knots in my stomach are from confusion, and the bad vibe they give off is wrong.

Because nothing bad can happen with Chloe.

Nothing bad can happen with us.

I don't know if I could take that.

Not now when our future is only just starting.

THIRTY-ONE

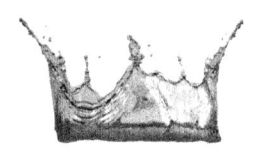

CHLOE

What the hell was I thinking?

Meeting Noah's friends was nerve-wracking enough. There's never a meet-the-friends situation where your head isn't spinning. Are you somehow lacking in his friends' eyes? Do you measure up to who they think Noah deserves? Or do you get a big, fat thumbs-down?

Especially if they know how much hurt I caused him.

Gosh, I remember it like it was yesterday. Typing out that message, telling him we would be better off to live separate from each other . . . to pursue our dreams independent of each other. I could barely see the phone screen by the time I pressed send.

After getting my diagnosis, I was fairly numb. I didn't cry much then, but what tore me apart was knowing that deep, deep inside me I had to let Noah go. That I couldn't distract him.

He was destined for greatness, and I didn't know if I'd live to age twenty.

I hated myself. I hated life.

And now? Have I just done the same thing again? Given him hope when there may not be a reason to have any?

I take the steps two at a time, the urge to do something I should have done a while ago pushing me. My brain can't focus on anything else right now. I don't even know what just came out of my mouth when I all but ran away from Noah and left him standing in his driveway.

Today pushed me over an edge I shouldn't even have come close to. The edge where I ignored one warning sign after the other when it comes to Noah.

Don't let him come too close.
There's no future for the two of you.
He deserves better than you.
You can't destroy his dreams.
He deserves the life he's always dreamed of, and you can't give it to him.

And I can't.

I really fucking can't give him the future he wants so desperately. His dream future.

I still can't.

The fact that none of this is my fault doesn't really make it any better either—or easier. Quite the opposite. It makes me mad. So damn angry.

Yes, I guess it's one of those things that I have to place into the category of "Life sucks and isn't always fair," but that still doesn't change how I feel about it. Regardless, that's what it boils down to.

But just because my life veered off the path I thought it was going to be on—the way my therapist liked to phrase it instead of my usage of "my life is ruined"—doesn't mean I need to pull others down with me.

I know I probably shouldn't have let things go as far as they did with Noah, but I couldn't help being drawn in by him.

By his presence and his addictive personality. His bewitching sense of humor and his captivating looks. And of course, his seductive bedroom skills.

I've never been able to resist this man. Not then, and certainly not now.

In my closet, I sink to the floor and push boxes away that I still haven't unpacked. Things I don't need right now but don't want to get rid of either.

My focus is on the box in the very back, my memories box, as I like to call it. The one I have mixed feelings about because it equally fills me with happiness and sadness.

In less than a minute, I create chaos all around me. The boxes I pushed away to make room are strewn around me, while half of the contents of my memory box are laid out in front of me.

So many family photos. Gosh, my dad. My fingers brush over his face.

Most of them are from better days, when he was still healthy. When his skin didn't have a gray, sickly tone to it, when he was still at a healthy weight.

I keep down the small sob that wants to escape as I grab the photo we took a day before he passed away. He was barely coherent anymore, but it was one of those rare moments where he smiled at me, where the recognition and love lit his eyes and turned him into the man who—together with my mom—made me into the person I am today, even if it was only fleeting.

Somehow, my mom captured that moment. I'd like to

believe it was fate. A *being at the right place at the right time* moment.

I can't even remember how many tears I've shed over that memory. Over the significance those few seconds allowed me to capture.

I loved him with all my heart, but he's always with me. Always has been. He's the reason I was able to get through the last decade, and also why I've reconnected with another piece of my heart.

No matter how much I miss him every second of every day, I can't help but smile now each time I think of him. How could I not for the way he enriched my life and still does?

My fingers are on the go again, rummaging through the eclectic shrine of my past. Pushing aside little knickknacks and random memorabilia, everything from jewelry to spelling bee prizes, until I get to a beige wooden box at the bottom.

I last opened this box shortly after we moved to San Diego, when I tried to say goodbye to my former life. A farewell to the life before my prognosis and a welcome to the start of my second chance at life when I received my donor heart.

Holding it now, why does it feel more like a Pandora's box than anything else?

Am I really ready to look at these things?

Do I really want to, knowing what's inside?

Deep breath. One, two, three.

Before I can chicken out, I open the lid, and exhale loudly.

My eyes are glued to more photos. Some with my family, some with Eadie, but most of them with Noah.

Kissing, laughing, being silly together.

Dates, dates, and more dates. Proms. Birthdays. Holidays.

We did almost everything together.

My hands dig all the way to the bottom, to the picture I know is waiting for me there.

You have to tell him the truth. The whole truth. He deserves to know.

He does.

Gosh, I know he does.

But my heart.

It hurts, and it's going to hurt even more than it already does.

Tomorrow. I'll do it tomorrow.

I can't right now when I feel this tender.

A noise behind me makes me whip my head around, a sharp pain shooting through the bottom of my neck at the quick movement. And then my throat closes at Noah standing there.

No. No. No.

Dread fills my body, tightening around my organs with such ferocity that I almost buckle over.

"What . . . what are you doing here?" My breath whooshes out with my words, both unsteady.

He pushes his hands into his pockets, a wary expression on his face as he takes in the chaos around me. "Sorry for coming after you, but you told me where the extra key is, and I was worried and wanted to make sure you're okay."

I nod, my throat too dry to get out a single word right now.

Shit. I didn't think he'd notice and come after me.

My hand is shaking so hard, I almost drop the picture in my hand.

The picture.

Panic has me clutch it to my chest, as I try to rack my brain for what to say.

But it doesn't feel like enough time to think of anything. To find the right words that will allow me to tell him this piece of the story.

My legs are wobbly, and my stomach churns. Maybe I can get him out of here somehow? Away from all of this stuff I don't want him to see.

"What's going on, Chloe?"

"I . . . I." My cheeks puff out when I release a nervous breath. "Do you still want kids?"

Why the hell did that just come out of my mouth? What on earth is wrong with me?

He studies me for a moment, the confusion clear on his face. Maybe he's also wondering if I short-circuited a fuse, because I'm certainly entertaining that option.

But then he nods, and a faint smile appears on his face. Followed by a shimmer of hope. "Yeah, of course. Nothing has changed for me."

I close my eyes for a moment and dip my head once. "Of course."

Shit. Shit. Shit.

"You too, right?" There's an edge to his voice now. Not anger, but something else. Maybe uncertainty?

"Well, yes, but also no." I meet his gaze again.

There's nothing to be ashamed of, Chloe.

Absolutely nothing.

You didn't do anything wrong.

Not a single thing.

He brushes a hand through his hair. "I'm not sure I understand. Do you want to have kids or not?"

Just say it. "I'd love to have kids more than anything, but I won't have any. Not with everything going on. I just can't."

There. It's out now.

At my answer, he stumbles back a step, almost banging into the closet door. With wide eyes, he looks at me. His gaze is so intense, it feels like he's trying to pull the thoughts out of my brain by sheer will.

"I . . . I don't think I follow." He's still shaking his head in denial.

Out of pure reflex, I take a step closer, reaching for him, the need to comfort him overriding any other brain function.

Noah's hand shoots out, grabbing my wrist. The one where my hand is holding the photo.

"Chloe. What the hell is this?"

I swallow the bile rising in my throat. "An ultrasound."

"Yours?"

I nod.

"You're . . . you're pregnant?" That hopeful glint is back in his eyes.

I don't even feel like I'm really present right now. My muscles feel weak, and I'm wondering if it would be better to sit down before I collapse.

All I manage is a shake of my head.

His eyebrows pinch together, and every last ounce of happiness is sucked out of his face? "So, you're not pregnant?"

Another shake of my head. My breathing accelerates, and I count breaths before I begin to hyperventilate.

"You . . . you were pregnant before?" His voice is so quiet I barely hear it.

This time, I nod.

As much as this whole situation makes my skin tingle with discomfort, I can't look away from him. Our locked gazes might be the only thing that keeps me upright right now.

He blinks a few times, not breaking our eye contact either. "So you had a baby?"

This whole situation is so similar to when he discovered my pills in the bathroom.

I'm blindsided. Unprepared. Paralyzed.

Incapable of uttering more than a random word.

Maybe it would have been better to tell him everything back then, but I just couldn't. This whole kids topic has always been one of the hardest parts about my condition.

Having your dream future go up in a cloud of nothing because your body suddenly decides it doesn't want to function properly anymore wasn't easy to accept. Without a doubt, it was the hardest part.

Yes, I wanted to live, and I'm beyond grateful that I got another chance, yet I'm still mourning the future I lost too.

Because isn't that what we live for? For our futures?

We build our dream future based on what we deem important to us, our must-haves and most-importants, and then we work our butts off to get all of those things.

That's all great and dandy until life decides to slap you in the face and yells, "Surprise, not anymore."

A tug at my hand brings me back to reality.

Noah's widened gaze burns into mine. "When was this?"

I'm sure he already knows because everything leads back to us. It always does. We're linked in so many ways.

"It was . . . it was a few weeks after I left."

He takes a few shaky breaths, looking at the photo between us. The ultrasound. The one proof that we once created something magical together that neither of us ever got to experience and that we never will. At least, not together. "No, that's impossible."

I sniffle and rub at my eyes. "They discovered my pregnancy when they did a bunch of tests at the hospital. But it was already too late at that point. They couldn't find a heartbeat, and I miscarried a few days later."

Noah raises my hand so he can take a closer look at the ultrasound. At the little blip that never got to be more.

Then he presses his fist to his mouth and turns away. "I . . . this is just . . . I can't." A loud exhale follows. "I have to go."

And just like that, he leaves the closet and my room, and a minute later, the front door closes.

I finally give in to my body and drop to the floor, collapsing in a heap of emotions that are too strong for me to endure right now. Too complex to tear apart. Too painful to even look at.

The man I'm still in love with just walked out on me after finding out the secret I wasn't sure I ever wanted to share with him.

My life imploded back then. My heart was already in tatters—literally and figuratively—and the losses just kept coming. My future. Noah. And then the part of him that I'd never meet.

I'd already let him go, and there was no reason to bring

him into that mire of sadness. I mean, look at how he got back up after heartbreak and succeeded.

No, I did the right thing back then, even though I still have words yelling inside of my head saying he had a right to know.

But the despair in his eyes a moment ago makes me think this might have been too much for Noah to handle. Not just back then but also now.

And I'm not sure he'll ever find his way back to me.

THIRTY-TWO

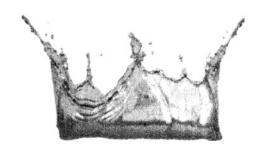

NOAH

Hushed voices in front of the bedroom door wake me up.

"What do you want me to do? Short of putting on a show for him, I've tried everything I can think of. He doesn't want to talk to anyone. As far as I know, he only leaves his house to get food, to hit the gym, or go to the pool."

Why is Hunter at my house?

Oh, that's right. He's conveniently been "passing out" on my couch since I got drunk as fuck after Chloe's revelation and butt-dialed Ryan, who came over with the other guys. The next day, they—and my sister who had miraculously shown up too—made me spill the beans, so I broke down and told them. I had almost been a dad.

The last time I checked, it was only Hunter here though. So who's he talking to?

"What kind of show are we talking about?" Of course, it's my sister.

There's some mumbling and laughter.

What the hell are they doing?

Can't they at least take this conversation somewhere else? Hunter was right. I don't want to talk to anyone . . . on purpose. All I want is to be left alone. To work out as much as I can, so all I manage to do is fall into bed and pass out.

This is my way of dealing with things. Of grieving something I thought I would or could have had. Something that was a mirage all along instead of the reality I spun it into.

But it was already too late at that point. I miscarried a few days later.

But where does that leave me?

I'm still not ready to think about it. About any of it.

Does that make me stubborn and maybe a little childish? Sure.

But I don't give a fuck.

After I left Chloe's house, I felt like someone had pulled the rug out from under me, right before jumping me, and punching me in the face a few times for good measure.

So, mission avoidance was born and has been in full-on mode ever since.

I have to say I'm pretty good at it too.

Exercising until I pass out is a pretty foolproof tactic. After I got over my hangover of the year, that is.

My phone beeps and I grab it. It's not like I'm not awake anyway thanks to those two dorks not-so-whispering in front of my door.

Mom: Hey, sweetie, I hope things are still going well on your side of the world. Sorry you haven't heard a lot from us in the last few weeks, but the connection out here in the rural areas isn't very good. We're still

planning on coming home next month, and I'll let you know as soon as we know the details. Give your sister and my two boys a hug. We love you.

My parents. Currently spending a lot of their retirement time in rural areas all over the world, this time in Africa. Helping others to have a better life. People who have so much less than we do, people who have so much less than *I* do. If that isn't like a kick in the gut, I don't know what is.

Can I be grateful for the life I have, for the possibilities I was given, and I've worked hard for, while also grieving something that was important to me?

A knock on the door pulls me out of my thoughts.

I swing my legs out of bed and pull a T-shirt over my head. "Come in."

The door opens and Daisy pokes her head in. "Hey."

"Hey." I look at her, the resemblance to my dad so evident in her features, where I look more like my mom. "Did you draw the shorter stick?"

"Huh?"

"Sounded like you guys were whispering about who has to come talk to me."

Her cheeks turn pink and she swallows half of her laugh. "We didn't. I came by because I wanted to talk to you."

I pick up my phone and show it to her.

She reads the message and sighs. "Awesome. It will be nice to have them back, for a while at least until they're off on their next mission."

I nod. I don't say what I know we both think. That it would be nice to have them here on a regular basis, but we both know it's just the way it is. It's their life, and they're happy doing what they're doing.

Daisy sits down in the armchair by the window, so I sit on the edge of the bed.

Her gaze is intense as she looks at me. "How are you feeling?"

I shrug. "Fine."

She nods. I'm pretty sure she expected that answer. "Can we talk about what's going on?"

"I don't know if there's a point. It's not like I can change anything about the situation."

"Shit, I hate this." She tilts her head back and looks at the ceiling for a moment. "Listen, I know this sucks. Gosh, my heart is hurting for both of you, so very much, but I know how much she means to you, so I'm just going to say it, okay? I think giving up on her will be the greatest mistake you can make."

Unable to be still, I push off the mattress and pace the length of the room.

Daisy turns in her chair so she can still see me. "I know I wasn't around much the first time, but I still know how much you loved her. It was evident every time we saw each other or even talked on the phone. And I don't think that has changed. The way you talk about her, the way you look at her . . . it's like she hung the moon. And she looks at you the same way."

I pause for a moment at her words before pacing some more. Up and down. Back and forth. The movement helps, but it also doesn't. "I don't know what to do."

"Well, what do you want? When you think about Chloe and your history, what do you want?"

I rub my hands over my face. Roughly. Wanting to pull

my hair out. "Her, of course. But, at the same time, I don't know how to get over the fact that we won't have any children. It sucks."

"I know."

I stop pacing and look at her. "I mean, regardless of how things turned out with Daniel and you, would it have been easy for you to accept that you couldn't have kids?"

She shakes her head before I even say the last word. "No. But of course, it's extra hard for me to imagine my life without the boys now that I have them." She stares at her hands. "It would feel empty to me, but then I don't know if Daniel was ever to me what Chloe is to you either. What both of you are to each other."

Damn it, she's got a point. Daisy and Daniel were an okay couple, but they never seemed crazy into each other. Whereas Chloe and I always used to be joined by the hip as my mom liked to call it.

"I don't even know if Daniel and I would have gotten married—or stayed together—if I hadn't gotten pregnant. We did the right thing, or rather what we thought was the right thing, which, of course, turned out to have been the wrong thing. But as I said before, I can't regret my time with him because he gave me the boys."

"Yeah." The word leaves my mouth on a heavy breath because shit, I'm not sure if what my sister said just made it worse or better.

No matter how much I don't want to think about Chloe dying at some point—possibly in the near future—the thought keeps popping into my head like a snake ready to strike. Filling my mind with images I'd rather not think about. Ever.

It would be a sad place—the saddest—and my heart

would surrender to the darkness that inevitably would come with her passing. I'd be like a flower without water, slowly wilting until the last particles of me were carried away in the wind, leaving nothing left.

Daisy clears her throat, her eyes slightly shiny when I look at her. "What do you see when you imagine your future? I know you've always wanted a family of your own, but sadly, we know that things don't always work out the way we want them to."

What do I see when I imagine my future?

Easy.

I see Chloe.

I doubt that will ever change.

"Chloe." Her name flows through my lips with wonder, like the miracle she is. She's been so strong, walking down a path that has caused her immense pain and sorrow, leading her straight back to me. And I . . . I don't fucking know where up and down, or left and right is anymore.

"What are you scared of?" Daisy's voice is quiet, like she knows she's treading hazardous waters.

I snort, too exhausted mentally to keep up any shields anymore. "What am I not afraid of when it comes to Chloe?"

She leans forward in her chair, trying to keep eye contact with me. "You know that's okay, right? We're all afraid of things. All of us. Especially where our hearts are concerned. We're all shaped by our experiences, and sometimes, it's the experiences that we know will shape us in the future, that we're most afraid of. And that's okay. It's normal. It's part of being human."

"Fuck."

There's a knock on the door, and Hunter pokes his head

in the door. "Sorry, guys. Daisy, it's three o'clock."

My sister nods and jumps up. "Thanks for keeping an eye on the time for me." She gives Hunter a smile before walking over to me. "I have to pick up the boys from school. But can I ask you to consider this from a different angle? What if you and Chloe were married and were trying to start a family. If you found out then that you weren't able to conceive naturally, would you leave her?"

"Fuck. No, Daisy. I'm not that kind of man. I wouldn't—"

I wouldn't leave her.

Never.

Fuck.

Yet the minute I find out we can't have kids, I walked out on her. *Shit. Shit. Shit.* As if she hasn't lost enough . . . and *I* walk away.

Maybe she was right to shut us down all those years ago. Because look at how I handled this. And I'm not a fucking kid anymore. I hang my head. Ashamed.

The kindness in Daisy's eyes suddenly feels like a punch in the face. I'm not sure I deserve it, but she offers it anyway. "But I'm here if you need me, okay? Always."

I nod.

She wraps her arms around me and squeezes tightly. "You've got this. Whatever you decide to do, you've got this. I believe in you."

"Thanks." The word barely makes it past my scratchy throat, but I mean it. Daisy has always loved to take care of me. Me being four years younger didn't often make us ideal partners for playing, but she was still a protective older sister, always there when I needed her, especially when our parents weren't.

After one more squeeze to my arm, she heads toward the door where she talks to Hunter, but I'm already zoned out again. My thoughts go back to Chloe, wondering what she's doing right now?

Is she still working, or already done for today? Has she gotten any further in the competition? Has she been taking good care of herself? Getting some good sleep? That's what kills me the most. I don't just want her for the grand future I had always envisioned for us. I want her for the little things, the everyday stuff, and everything in between.

With this woman, I want it all.

And that's exactly what I can't have.

So, the question is, will what I *can* have be enough?

Or maybe more importantly, would I be able to live without having her in my life at all?

I pick up my phone and pull up her contact, looking at the photo I took of her when she thought I wasn't watching. We were outside, catching the last sun rays of the day, when Chloe tilted her head toward the sky with a serene smile on her face. So damn beautiful.

Would I be able to live my life without her, to move on and chase my perfect future the way I had envisioned it without knowing if that would ever become reality?

But if it wasn't with Chloe, would it be perfect? She nearly died . . . without me. She lost her grandfather . . . without me. Fuck, she even lost her dad. Again . . . without me. All because she loved me so much that she sacrificed her own happiness, her own planned-out perfect future, for *me*. Doesn't that mean that the question is, what can I . . . what *will* I sacrifice for her?

Because is there really a guarantee for anything in life?

THIRTY-THREE

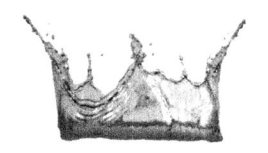

CHLOE

"How you're doing, Scribbles?"

I peek at Cody when he sits down next to me on my mom's porch swing. She loved mine so much that she bought one too. Apparently, she also thought I needed a babysitter while she's running some errands. Not that I'd ever be mad about seeing one of my favorite people.

Without replying, I lean my head on his shoulder, and close my eyes. His arm envelops me into a side hug, and I sink into the embrace. In my current emotional state, being held can go two ways. Either I cherish the contact and feel marginally better, or I break down like a baby.

Weirdly enough, I feel like both right now.

Neither one of us says a word as Cody gently pushes us back and forth.

"You were still pretty young when I came out of the closet. Back then, things weren't as well accepted as they are now, not that it's always perfect today . . . I was scared shitless. Absolutely shitless. I thought I'd fooled everyone, especially my family, and that this will come as the biggest shock in their lives."

I'd heard pieces of this story before, but we never sat down and talked about it like this.

"My parents grinned like lunatics when I told them. They were actually proud of me. Which, to be honest, confused me even more. Somehow, I was still coming to terms with being gay. Not the actual fact that I was—there was never a doubt about that—but more so what it meant for my life, for my future. In a strange way, I was relieved that the cat was out of the bag, but I was also grieving."

That gets my attention, and I peek up at him through my lashes, studying his profile as his gaze settles on something far away.

He swallows loudly. "I was terrified of how much pain this new life would cause me, yet I was also sad that I'd never have a family in the traditional sense. Sometimes, it's easy to forget how recent gay rights for marriage and adoption are. Things ended up differently for Checco anyway, and it was our decision to not have any children, but back then, I grieved what I wouldn't have regardless."

"It hurts so much." I close my eyes, shutting out the blurry world around me.

Cody's arm pulls me closer. "I know, sweetie. You've gone through so much, and you've had to accept and overcome losses that I can't even begin to imagine. If I had a magic wand, I'd give you everything you could possibly wish for."

"After my diagnosis, I thought I didn't deserve a new normal, that it wasn't fair to drag someone down with me." A tear rolls down my cheek, soaking into my uncle's shirt.

SECOND DIVE

"You deserve a beautiful life, even if things didn't turn out the way they should have. Don't let fear win, it will only lead to regrets. I want you to be happy, to find your person, your solace, who makes you wake up with a smile. Stand your ground and live the life you've been given. In every aspect. And don't think for even a second that you'd ever drag anyone down. We're all honored and beyond grateful to have you in our lives. Always."

"Noah's always been a handsome guy." My mom's voice startles me, and it's pure luck I don't draw a line straight across my drawing pad with my pencil. A flock of birds leaves the comforts of one of her trees in her backyard and shoots for the sky. Apparently, I'm not the only one my mom startled.

"Yeah." My fingers lightly brush across the page, across Noah's face.

Ever since Cody left earlier, my mind has been focused on Noah even more than it already had before. On every possible detail my brain could fabricate.

The way his hair has grown longer in the past few weeks, bringing back more of the waves he had when I first met him. Or his intense eyes that stare back at me from the page like they know me to a fault. And that devilish mouth. Oh, the things it can do.

My heart speeds up in my chest. A little faster than normal—even though my resting heart rate has been higher since my heart transplant—because that's what it does when it comes to Noah. Even when I only think of him.

Everything's more. Everything's heightened. My mind

loves to think about him, dream about him around the clock. Remember him at night when I'm by myself, when the sheets are too cold, when sleep is too restless by myself.

But that's what my life will be like now, won't it? Just like I had initially expected it to be . . . before I let myself fall down the rabbit hole of everything Noah. Before I let myself forget my own advice and ignored the nagging voice that *this won't end well. That this can't go anywhere.*

I won't take something this monumental away from him and his life. I didn't want to back then, and I don't want to now. Even though letting go of him a second time is a lot harder than the first time. And since he hasn't contacted me since he found out that I won't have any children, I guess it's pretty clear where he stands on this whole issue.

This time, he's done with me *too.*

And it hurts. So damn much.

But it also confirms that I did the right thing. He's had the chance to move on, to create his perfect future, so why hasn't he?

At least this break has been good for my productivity since work has been my way to get through the days that have felt longer than ever before. I was able to finish my sample for the young adult illustrated book competition.

My phone buzzes next to me on the table. It's in clear view for my mom to see since she's still standing right behind me, her hand on my shoulder both loving and reassuring.

"Speak of the devil." Her hand tightens in a quick squeeze before she walks around to sit down in the chair opposite me. When I don't pick up my phone immediately, her eyebrows rise. "Are you going to ignore him?"

My shoulders rise and fall. "I've turned into a quiet

hermit, either hiding at my house or at my mom's. Fantastic. But I can't handle any people right now, especially not any super awkward run-ins with Noah. It's too soon. Way too soon.

She gives me a long look before she claps her hands once and stands back up. "Go get your stuff. We're going somewhere."

I moan like the petulant adult-child I feel like right now.

All the while, my phone keeps begging me to see what Noah sent. His first message, and my body and mind are in overdrive. Unable to decide which way to go; excited or scared. Or maybe a little bit of both?

I want to talk to him so badly, but at the same time, won't that only make things worse?

What if he messaged to tell me that he found something of mine and wants me to pick it up? Or something equally impersonal and distant. And *final*.

My mom squats in front of my Adirondack chair. "I'll meet you at the front door in five minutes, okay?"

I nod and she heads inside, but not before calling, "Read his message, sweetie."

With a loud groan, I sink into the chair and close my eyes.

Should I read his text or not? I'm not sure what possible outcome is worse. But I know it will drive me crazy either way. After another deep breath, I close the drawing pad on my lap and place the pencil on it before grabbing my phone from the table.

Noah: Hey. Can we talk?

Seriously? That's it? Couldn't he have been a bit more

specific about the whys of wanting to talk? Is this a good can we talk, or a bad one?

I groan and close my eyes. I need to think about this some more.

"Come on, Chloe." My mom's voice is getting more insistent, so I gather my things and head inside.

After a quick bathroom break, I join my mom in the entryway. "Where are we going?"

"You'll see." My mom looks adorable with her short, dark bob and her new favorite cat-eye sunglasses that she's convinced will make her hip. I don't know what I'd do without her. This woman has gone through so much and still greets every day with a smile. She's my personal unicorn.

I try to channel some of her spark and link my arm through hers. "All right. Let's do this."

We hop in my car and Mom directs me to an area that's all too familiar.

When we get to the small strip mall—with *the* old movie theater in the back of the parking lot—I park in front of the smoothie place my mom directs me to.

Mom unbuckles and looks at me over the middle console. "Let's get a yummy drink and soak up a few more of the sun's rays."

Five minutes later, we get comfortable at a table outside. I definitely need to remember this place. They have a ton of super healthy options, and my tropical green smoothie is delicious.

My mom puts her red berry concoction on the table and points at the movie theater. "That's the place you and Noah used to go to a lot, isn't it?"

"Yeah."

She lets out a heavy sigh, but when I look at her, a small smile graces her face. "Did I ever tell you that I met your dad at that movie theater for the first time?"

My eyes widen. "What? I thought you guys met at school?"

"Well, we went to the same school, but we'd never talked. I don't know why. So for me, this movie theater is where our love story began. We bumped into each other, and I just knew."

She's quiet for a moment, lost in thought. "I still remember when David tried to put his arm around me during the movie by being all nonchalant about it. Like I wouldn't notice he's yawning and stretching before ending with one arm behind me. His awkwardness made him even more endearing."

My mom's laugh gets us a few stares from other patrons, but I couldn't care less. I live to see her this happy. It fills my bucket endlessly. No matter if it's supposed to be like this or not, but I think it takes someone special to live the way my mom does. To live in the moment and mostly thrive on the happy memories. To let positivity overshadow the negativity so it's unable to eat you alive. I wish we all could have that ability. It would do humanity some good.

Her hand moves across the table to grab mine. "I know things aren't easy for you, and I'm not even going to pretend like I know what it's like to be in your shoes, because I don't. Just like you promised your dad to not have any regrets in your life if you can help it, I want you to promise *me* something too."

I swallow and nod, not sure if I'm ready for whatever's going to come out of my mom's mouth next.

She squeezes my hand. "Don't let fear rule your life. Go after what you want, or who you want. You've gone through enough hardship already, and I want you to live your life to the fullest. To experience everything you want to experience. You deserve it so much."

The tightness in my throat squeezes before I force my way past it, my words barely making it out in a whisper. "What if it's not the right thing to do though? I don't want to screw up anyone's life."

We both know what—or rather who—we're talking about.

My mom leans closer across the bistro table. "Oh, sweetheart, I don't think you'll screw up anyone's life. And even if you do, then you can at least say you've tried. Only if you reach for the stars, will you be able to achieve true happiness. And if you fail, you'll be that much wiser because of that escapade. Some things will come with an expiration date, but that doesn't mean you shouldn't experience them in the first place."

My eyes burn with unshed tears, this whole conversation hitting home way too hard. Which is probably the reason for it. My mom has always given me the time to work through my issues, waiting until I'm willing to actually *hear* what she has to say when she eventually talks things through with me.

I try to hide my sniffle, but it's pointless. "It feels selfish to want those things."

"Why don't you let him make that decision?" My mom's voice is firm, and I can see the conviction of her words on her face. "Maybe he wants you to be selfish because he wants *you*."

A tiny speck of hope flutters in my chest, and it feels so

good that I don't have it in me to douse it. Is there a chance that my mom might be right? That I'm enough? Just me?

She clears her throat. "Let me tell you one thing. If I knew back then what I know now, I wouldn't have changed a thing. You and your dad are the highlights of my life, always have been and always will be. Would another life have been easier? Possibly. But it wouldn't have given me either of you, which sounds pretty lame to me."

An unsteady breath leaves my mouth as I listen to the woman I admire the most in my life.

"I'd choose you and your dad every single time, something I told your dad a million times, especially when he felt sorry for 'putting me through the wringer' as he always liked to call it. I *wanted* to be there. For him, but also for myself. Both of you have made me a better person. I've found myself because of the path I chose despite the heartache we've gone through, or maybe because of it. You are worth it. So very much."

A single tear slips down my cheek at the memory of my dad, and what both of us—and my mom—have gone through.

She pushes her chair back and finishes her smoothie. "I'll go use the restroom quickly. Maybe there's someone you'd like to message back?" She leaves with a wink.

There's so much to think about, yet nothing at all. It's never been about what I want, but rather about what I'm afraid of Noah might *not* want.

Me.

Despite my fear—or maybe because of it—I get my phone out of my pocket and open Noah's message.

Maybe it is time to show fear who the boss is.

THIRTY-FOUR

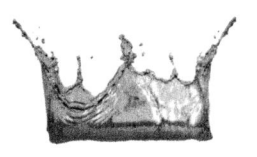

NOAH

The nightmare clings to me like a leech.

Chloe's lifeless body lying on the floor, not responding to anything. Her skin drained of all color and ice cold. Her heart not beating anymore.

I draw in a sharp breath, willing my tense muscles to relax.

My brow and neck are covered in sweat and my chest feels like someone placed a weight on it. My head is fuzzy, my mind still halfway clinging to that damn dream while the other half is trying to shake off this intense terror before it sucks me into its hole.

I grab my phone and unlock the screen. Maybe Chloe sent another message and I missed it? But nope, the one she sent yesterday is still the most recent one.

Chloe: I'll be busy the next couple days, but we can get together on Thursday if you want.

That's still two days away. Depending on when we meet,

more than forty-eight hours.

Shit. That's two fucking days too long.

The rhythm of my heartbeat whooshes in my ears as I get up and head to the bathroom. The gray tiles, gray countertop, and black cabinets match my dark mood.

I turn on the shower and flinch when I get a good look at myself in the mirror. I look like I was put through the wringer, which perfectly portrays how I feel on the inside. The pain in my chest still hasn't subsided from my dream.

When the water is hot, I step under the spray and close my eyes. Trying to will the damn images away that my brain keeps playing like a montage.

I won't even attempt to psycho-analyze this shit.

All I want is to see Chloe. To make sure she's okay with my own two eyes.

Before I lose my mind.

After toweling off and getting dressed, I send her a quick message.

Noah: You okay?

And then I wait, and wait some more. There's no response, no read tag either. Fuck waiting. I call her, but the call goes to voicemail right away.

Damn it.

Instead of going to the gym like I planned, I grab my keys and walk across the street. Chloe's house looks empty but I try knocking anyway. *Nothing.*

When I try her phone again, it goes straight to voicemail again.

With a heavy sigh, I run back inside to grab my wallet, a

protein bar, and a drink before I go to my car, slamming the door a bit too loudly. But I just don't care anymore. I *need* to see her.

After trying her phone unsuccessfully one more time, I let my head fall back on the headrest.

I could try her uncle at the Parrot Lounge but I doubt anyone would be there this early. That leaves . . . her mom.

I can't really describe it, but the urgency to get to Chloe isn't just about wanting to apologize. Whether it's leftover fear from the dream or adrenaline, I'm consumed by the need to be with her. Now.

So, I head to her mom's, hoping she won't turn me away after I walked out on Chloe when the truth was too hard to bear. But not anymore. I'm coming, Chloe.

When I pull up in front of the house, a couple of cars are in the driveway. I scan the street, hoping I missed Chloe's car somehow, but it's nowhere in sight.

It takes a few knocks until the door opens.

It's not Chloe's mom though but one of her uncles. Francesco.

"Oh hey, Noah."

"Hey."

Francesco leans against the doorframe and eyes me. Since I can't read his mood at all, I have no clue if he knows what happened between Chloe and me or not, or how he feels about it.

Someone calls his name, and a few seconds later, both Chloe's uncle Cody and her mom are there too. All three of them are staring at me.

"Everything okay, Noah?" Chloe's mom looks me over with a concerned look on her face.

I nod.

Cody frowns. "Are you sure? You look a little pale."

I rub my hand against my neck. "Yeah, just tired. Sorry to drop by like this, but do you know where Chloe is? I really need to talk to her and her phone goes straight to voicemail."

They share a look but no one says a word.

What the hell is going on?

"Is she okay?" I swallow, my Adam's apple stuck in my throat. When no one answers immediately, my heart sinks. "Please."

"She is." Chloe's mom takes a step closer, her gaze boring into mine. Chloe looks so much like her. It feels oddly comforting right now. "She might not be happy with me for telling you this, but she's at the hospital for her yearly heart checkup. The reception seems to be a bit spotty there."

"She's at the hospital?"

All three nod.

She never said a word about it.

Why are they all here though? "Did she go by herself?"

I don't know why that's the second thing that pops into my mind, but seeing that her closest family is standing right in front of me, I'm a bit confused. And shocked.

I can't imagine what a yearly checkup for someone like Chloe would be like. What if something's wrong?

Chloe's mom nods. "She always wants to go alone. I think we just add to her nerves. She also wants to spare me more hospital visits, even though she should know that it doesn't matter to me. But she insists. And we're all about making this time of the year easier for her. So we get together and wait for her to get back when she's done. At least on the first day."

I don't know what to say, so I just stare at them like a total loon. "It's more than one day of exams?"

Her mom nods. "It's two days. They have to perform a lot of different tests."

Chloe: I'll be busy the next couple days, but we can get together on Thursday if you want.

That's what she meant when she texted me she'll be busy? Shit. My stomach churns at the thought of having people prod at me for two days.

Cody waves his hand. "Do you want to come inside?"

I shake my head before I even realize I've made a decision. "I need to see her. Can you tell me where to find her? I'd really appreciate it."

There's no way I could sit down somewhere right now and wait to see her, especially now that I know where she's at and more importantly, what she's doing there. Alone. Why didn't she say anything? More than an "I'll be busy the next couple days."

Maybe because the last time you saw her, you left her standing in that closet and left?

Shit.

I don't know if it's the desperation in my voice, or whatever they see on my face, but after a moment, Chloe's mom nods. "One second. I'll write it down for you."

"Thank you." The tension doesn't leave my body at her response—nothing will help with that until I see Chloe's okay—but a small weight falls off my shoulders and they slouch.

A few minutes later, Chloe's mom comes back with a

piece of paper and hands it to me. "I wrote the info on there, as well as my phone number."

"Thank you. I'll keep you updated if I can." I give them a nod before turning around and speed-walking back to my car.

They're all still in the doorway when I hit the gas and I lift a hand in their direction.

My thoughts are spinning, wondering what it's like for Chloe during those two days. Does she fear that the doctors might find something? Is that why she goes alone so no one can witness it?

When I finally pull into the parking lot of the hospital outpatient building, I park as fast as I can and run. By the time I make it to the fifth floor, I have no clue where I parked or if I locked the car. Who would?

I try not to cringe at the different appointments, hospital levels, and stations that are listed on the paper. And Chloe has even more tests tomorrow? A shudder ricochets through my body, and I flinch at the sensation. This is all a lot to take in.

When I finally get closer to the other side of the building, where Chloe's supposed to have her next appointment, it feels like time slows down when I spot her dark hair. The purple tint has washed out, but it still helps pick her out of a crowd.

But she isn't alone. She smiles at a nurse who's holding a door to the side open for her.

"Chloe."

People stare at me, but all sense of embarrassment has left my mind.

My focus is on one thing and one thing only.

Chloe.

Making sure she's okay. Begging her to talk to me.

A family steps in front of me, making their way to another nurse waiting for them at a different door.

Shit.

They cut into my line of vision, and when they finally move along, Chloe is gone. The door closed behind her and the nurse.

After taking a few deep breaths, I go to the nurses' desk, but, like I expected, they tell me to wait for her.

Fuck.

That was so close.

Did she hear me? Did she *see* me?

What if she did and doesn't want to see me?

I guess I'll find out when she gets back because I'm not going anywhere.

Not anymore.

Nothing really made sense until Chloe came back into my life. Not at the charity dinner or at the hospital the first time, but at the movie theater. Then in her bed. Holding her close. Just being with her.

I'd given my all to the sport I've loved, but I don't need to keep achieving medals. I don't want to anymore.

What I need is to move forward.

I'm ready to take the reins back into my hands and go for what I want. To get out of the rut and go after what's most important.

Loving Chloe.

Swimming will always be a major part of me, which is why Jace and Ryan's offer couldn't have come at a better time.

But first, there's someone else who deserves the

truth. I pull up the contact and put the phone to my ear.

"Noah. You're alive."

I chuckle. "Hey, Coach."

"I thought you forgot about me."

"I could never."

Silence fills the line between us. I called without a plan, with absolutely no clue what to say when I pressed the call button, but I knew I had to call him anyway. I probably should have a while ago.

Coach heaves a heavy sigh. "You're done with swimming, aren't you?"

I scrub my face with my free hand at his question. The answer forms in my mind right away, equal amounts of elation and sorrow coursing through me at the truth of it. "Yeah, I think I am."

"All right, son. All right . . . I can't say I'm not glum about it, but I kinda figured."

"Sorry, Coach." It sucks ass to know that I'm disappointing him while I'm also doing something good for myself. "It just feels right."

"Everyone's time is up eventually. Do you already know what you're gonna do?"

"I . . . I . . . actually, Ryan and Jace were asking me to join them."

Another pause.

Since when can stretches of silence feel so heavy?

Coach clears his throat. "You'll do great."

"You think so?"

He chuckles. "I don't think so, I know so."

"What? How?"

"Because you've been doing it for years. Maybe not consciously, but nonetheless."

"I have?"

"Yup. You've been training with my college kids for a long time now. Not only are they studying your every move, but also listen to any piece of advice you've ever given them."

The door to the exam rooms opens, but still no Chloe. "Huh. I never noticed."

"It comes naturally to you, which will make you an even better instructor. I can't wait to see what stars you'll be raising."

"Thanks, Coach."

"Always, Noah." There's a commotion in the background but the sounds are muffled for a moment. "Sorry, kid, but I've gotta go. But let's catch up soon. Don't be a stranger."

My chest expands on a deep breath. "Deal."

We say our goodbyes and I end the call, feeling like a weight has been lifted off my shoulders.

After staring at the wall for a few minutes, I fire up a quick group text to Ryan and Jace. **Count me in.**

Ryan: Yes, dude.

Jace: Hell, yeah.

Ryan: Everything okay with you and Chloe?

Noah: At the hospital to talk to her. She's here for her annual exam.

Ryan: Good luck.

Jace: She's an amazing woman. Let us know how things go, or if you need anything. Em says to tell her hi.

Noah: Will do. Thanks.

Another thing that's off my back now, and everything falls into place.

My future. My personal life and my career.

Now I only have to convince Chloe of it too.

THIRTY-FIVE

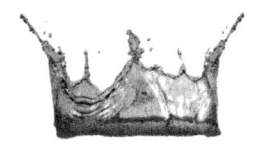

CHLOE

Once the door closes behind us, the nurse leads me to a small station where she takes my height, weight, and temperature. When we get to the exam room, she checks my pulse, oxygen, and blood pressure.

All the while, my brain is mostly off in la-la land, focused on the illusion that I just heard Noah call my name in the waiting area. But when I looked around, it was the same as always. No Noah in sight.

It's normal for me to be stressed to no end during my annual exam though, so I welcome the distraction. Even if it's only wishful thinking that Noah would magically pop up at the right time in the one place I dread the most every year.

Today, I've been extra tense and nervous because it's my first time at this hospital. New doctors. New nurses. But so far, everyone's been nothing but kind.

Even though nothing can diminish the feeling of dread during this time of year. A general dislike for hospital visits mixed with an unhealthy dose of fear that something is wrong with me. It's a toxic combination that leaves me with restless nights leading up to the appointments.

And it's why I always come alone. I can't put my mom through this level of stress. She's gone through enough. Maybe at a later point when losing Dad isn't so raw ... As for my wonderful uncles, I could never bring their relentless joy into this place. They think I'm so strong, and I don't want them to think of me in any other way.

Going alone is now my norm, and most likely my future. For however long I get.

Thankfully, the doctor comes in and saves me from spiraling any deeper with my thoughts. Sweet relief floods me when he tells me that my labs look good. Mostly. Only a few adjustments with my medication are necessary, which is pretty standard.

Shortly after, he sends me off to get my echocardiogram and chest X-ray done. At least, I will be done for today after that. The first day is always easier than the second day, but I don't want to think about that yet. For now, I'm trying to focus on the fact that my labs are normal—normal enough.

I push open the door to get back to the waiting area and turn right to head to the elevators.

"Chloe."

I stop, almost colliding with another woman.

My pulse races as I turn around and come face to face with the man who owns my heart.

"Hey." Noah's gaze roams over me from head to toe. I'm dressed for comfort in leggings, a T-shirt, and a big cardigan. The last thing I need during a nerve-wracking time like this is to worry about the way I look, or to feel uncomfortable.

"Hey." My voice sounds just as breathy as I feel, and I

brush a strand of hair out of my face that escaped my messy bun.

What are you doing here?

My mind is going into overdrive but the words don't come out of my mouth.

Noah's here at the hospital. Why is he at the hospital?

"How did you know where I was?" My brain doesn't know which way to go, and I squeeze my fingers to keep from fidgeting.

Which feeling should take the lead? Nervousness? Elation? Uncertainty? My thoughts hop around like someone hijacked them.

But loudest of all is my heart, reacting to the sight of this gorgeous man. Even though it stumbles a little at the sight of the dark circles under his eyes, the slight ashy undertone to his skin. Has he been sick?

"I had to see you. I needed to see you're okay."

I nod, even though that wasn't really an answer to my question. Actually, it doesn't explain anything.

As if realizing the same, he says, "Sorry. I begged your mom to tell me where you were."

Of course, she told him. She knows how I feel about him and that I was planning on talking to him. But here? Usually, I have this time to myself because I don't want to drag anyone down with my nerves and restlessness. Plus, who wants to be at the hospital anyway?

The corners of my mouth tip up. "She's always had a soft spot for you."

"Thank goodness. It helps to know she's in my corner, especially when I screw things up with her daughter."

My phone starts playing a soft melody in my purse. I get

it out and swipe the screen to silence it. After closing the short distance to the elevator, I push the call button. "I have to get to my next appointment. Can we talk later?"

"Sorry, of course."

The elevator doors open, and I step inside. Noah gets in beside me. My head snaps up at him. "What are you doing?"

"Going to your next appointment with you." He says it in such a matter-of-fact voice that I can only blink at him for a few seconds.

"You can't come to the appointments with me."

A small frown appears on his forehead. "I'll wait in the waiting area, then."

"Why?" I'm so used to doing this by myself that having him here throws me off-balance. Even more so after the way we parted last time.

The elevator doors open on the second floor, and our conversation dies as I make my way to the correct station.

After checking in at the desk, I join Noah on one of the two-seaters.

He turns sideways and props his arm up on the back. "Listen, about last week. You totally caught me off guard, and I obviously didn't handle it well."

I swallow and nod. "I should've told you sooner, but I . . . I don't know. I just couldn't."

"It's not an easy topic to throw out there."

"It isn't."

"You've gone through a lot. Your life, your whole future, so much has changed."

My throat clogs up, and the back of my eyes heat up. "I know."

We're in a public place, amidst a ton of people, and the

last thing I need right now is to have a breakdown. This day is already tough enough without that.

"I'm sorry I just left you like that. I . . . I—"

"Chloe Williams?"

My head snaps up as I look toward the waiting nurse. "I have to go."

Noah's gaze is intense as he stares at me. "I'll be here when you get back."

"You really don't have to do that."

"But I want to."

The nurse calls my name again, and I raise my hand like I'm at school, before heading toward the older woman who reminds me a bit of my grandmother when she was younger.

Before I slip past the nurse, I glance back over my shoulder. Noah's eyes are on me, and his burning gaze follows me long after the automatic door closes behind me.

The echocardiogram takes almost an hour, and I'm glad when I'm finally dressed again, even though the test itself is a rather comfortable test.

But my mind is focused on the pressing urgency radiating through my body, the anticipation of seeing Noah again. To figure out why he's here and what he wants. To see *if* he stayed.

Unless he only came to apologize? No, that would be silly, right? He could have waited a few more days for that.

When I walk out into the waiting area, I immediately spot Noah. He got comfortable in an oversized chair in the corner. Since he hasn't spotted me yet, I make my way over to him, admiring his handsome profile.

His face is turned toward the top-to-bottom window and

the hazy day outside, his gaze settled somewhere in the distance.

When I stop next to him, he turns his head, and wordlessly takes my hand to kiss it.

"Everything okay?" His sole focus is on me, and I'm momentarily stunned into silence.

His gentle gesture, the fact that he's here—that he *wants* to be here—and he's asking me about my test is . . . overwhelming. And a million other things.

Is it strange that it doesn't feel weird to have him ask me that? When I expected it to feel odd and out of place, when I couldn't imagine him in this part of my life, and now he's here, and it's just so . . . normal.

"I think so. They will give me a call in the next couple of days with the official results, but it didn't seem like anything was raising red flags."

"I'm glad." Noah gets up and looms over me. After a moment of hesitation, he pulls me toward him. "You only have the chest X-ray left for today, right?"

I nod into his chest, reveling in the soft rhythm of his heartbeat under my ear. How strange a thing a heart is. So soft and breakable, yet so strong. Pulling us through the toughest times, yet failing us under dire circumstances. A total oxymoron on so many levels.

I stiffen for a moment in his arms, a desperation breaching my system like I've never experienced before.

What if I want to own his heart on all levels like he does mine?

My *heart* wants to own his, it always has. So much so that my love for this man seamlessly switched from one heart to the next. Without a hitch, without losing an ounce of love for him. That's how pure, how true, my love for him has always been.

His breath blows in soft waves over my hair before his lips brush against my temple. "Let's get you to your next appointment, okay?"

I nod and we make our way to the correct station on the lower level.

Noah never lets go of my hand, until my name is called by yet another nurse. Thankfully, this is the quickest test of them all, and I'm back out in less than half an hour.

This time, Noah's gaze finds me right away when I walk toward him. His face is more relaxed than it was when he first got here, even though the dark circles under his eyes are still pronounced.

Without overthinking it, my hand goes up to trace the shadows. "You look like you could use some good rest."

"Yeah. But not until we've talked."

I stare up at him, mesmerized by the mix of adoration and something else in his gaze. Determination? He certainly showed up here today like a man on a mission.

Does he . . . Could he . . . Could *we* . . .

Desperation claws at me, wanting to know what he wants to talk about. But first . . . my mom. She's probably in knots at this point, waiting for an update.

"Do you mind if we stop by my mom's first before we talk?"

"Of course not. I was counting on that anyway."

As we head to the parking lot, I send my mom a quick update, and tell her that we're on our way.

I'm still nervous about my procedure tomorrow, but I try

to focus on what calms me, going through some of the mindfulness exercises my therapist gave me a few years ago.

What's weird? Normally, the nerves would be difficult to budge, but with Noah's arm around me, I feel . . . safe and protected. Held.

I feel like I can breathe again.

THIRTY-SIX

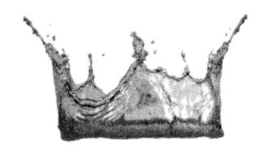

NOAH

I don't let Chloe out of my sight the whole time we're at her mom's place. She seems her usual self, smiling and laughing with everyone, that bit of vulnerability and nerves I saw earlier at the hospital wiped clean, or at the very least, hidden.

All I want to do is wrap her in my arms and never let go. As if she knows I'm thinking about her, her eyes flicker up to look at me.

A few minutes later, a yawn escapes her.

Chloe's mom tilts her head to the side and studies her. "You should probably go home and get some sleep. You have a long day ahead of you tomorrow."

Chloe groans. "I know. My least favorite part."

I want to talk to her more about tomorrow, and everything else.

When I have her to myself.

"Let's get you home." I stand up and walk to Chloe.

Since Chloe drove herself to the hospital this morning, we're here with both cars. The faster I can get her home, the faster we can talk.

Even though I have so much to say, I have no idea what to actually tell her. No words seem enough for the enormous shift that has happened inside of me. For the epiphany that's taken over my body and mind, consuming me so much, there's little room for anything else.

When another yawn ripples through her, her mom laughs and gives her a tight hug before sending us off. Her uncles already left a while ago, so it's just been the three of us.

I'm home first. Parking in my garage before marching straight over to Chloe's house just as she pulls into her driveway. She gets out of her car and looks at me, a small smile gracing her beautiful face.

I know she needs to go to bed, but I can't leave her yet.

Being with her is my top priority, it's that simple.

The uncertainty around her life and health has made that need for her even stronger.

Chloe chuckles. "Why are you staring at me like that?"

I take a step toward her. Then another.

When I stand right in front of her, I put my finger under her chin and tilt it until I can see the darkening sky reflect in her eyes. "Why shouldn't I look at you like that?"

"Uh."

I nod toward her door. "Let's get you inside and to bed, okay?"

She swallows.

"Do you want me to leave?" I search her eyes, needing to know this is okay for her.

I exhale loudly when she shakes her head.

Once we're inside, she goes through her routine.

Changing into her pajamas, taking her medicine, washing her face, and brushing her teeth.

We're both quiet through the whole process. I'm not sure if it's our fear that feeds the silence or our hope. Sometimes, hope is almost worse than fear because the fall can be so much more dangerous.

When Chloe walks out of the bathroom and plays with the hem of her shirt, I beckon her over to where I sit on the edge of the bed.

I take one of her hands in mine and play with her fingers. "You okay?"

"Yeah. Just a long day."

I rub my thumb over the smooth skin of her hand. "And tomorrow you have your angiogram, right?"

I've caught bits and pieces about the procedure and read a quick summary about it online. Apparently, they inject contrast dye into an artery in the leg via a thin, flexible tube so they can see the veins and arteries on an X-ray. Sounds pretty grueling to me. I'm glad Chloe only has to do this once a year.

On the other side, I can't help but be grateful for all of these procedures, medications, and tests—no matter how uncomfortable they sound—because they allow her to be here. Where I can touch her, see her, where I can be with her.

"Thankfully, I don't feel it because of the local anesthesia. It's just a long day. Having to lie flat on my back for four to six hours at the hospital so the groin entry side can heal is more annoying than anything, but a necessary evil. Usually, I just read a book while I wait."

"I can come and keep you company once you're done if you'd like?"

She looks up from where she was staring at our hands. "Why would you want to do that?"

I blow out a breath. This isn't really going according to plan. "We can do this another time. You need to get some sleep."

"I'm fine." She disentangles my hand and stands up, her nervous energy cascading around her like an invisible force. "Don't get me wrong, I love that you're here, that you dropped by today, but I need to know what this is—what we are—or I'll go crazy. I've had enough sleepless nights as it is."

Shit.

"I'm here because I don't want to miss another moment with you."

Her little gasp urges me on to continue. "I can't pretend the whole kids thing wasn't a total kick to the balls because it was. It still is. It hurts, and I'm sure it'll hurt for a long time, if not forever. But missing out on you—on *us*—would hurt even more. I don't know if I would survive that."

Unshed tears shimmer in her eyes as she hangs on my every word.

I stand up and step in front of her. Close enough to feel her breath on my skin, to be able to cup her face in my hands and stare into her eyes. "When I imagine my future, all I can see is you. It's always been you, little bird. Always."

The first tear rolls down her cheek, and I wipe it away.

But I'm not done yet. "I want to wake up next to you, and I want to fall asleep with you in my arms."

She nods, her lips pressed into a pout. "I want that too . . . so much."

The pads of my thumbs are wet from her tears as I lean down to touch her forehead with mine. "You and me, baby."

Her head moves against mine in a nod before her body catches up with us again and she yawns.

"Okay, bedtime. Now."

She wipes at her eyes and smiles at me. "Will you stay?"

"Of course." I lean in to kiss her gently. "I meant it when I said I don't want to waste another second with you."

"I feel the same way."

"Thank fuck." This time, our kiss is deeper, and I indulge in it. In the feel of her soft lips on mine, the minty flavor of her toothpaste still on her tongue. Her hands as they dig into my waist. The way she pushes her body against mine.

And that's when I pull the brakes. Begrudgingly.

I could fill buckets with the frustration I'm feeling over not having my way with her right now when all I want to do is strip her naked and bury myself deep within her. So deep that she can still feel me next week. Right after I'd taste every inch of her magnificent body that I've missed so much. Lick her. Nibble on her.

But her health is more important. To get rid of those dark circles under her eyes higher on my priority list than my raging hard-on. Even though he'd like to disagree with that.

After one more lengthy kiss, I finally pull back and allow the words to flow out of my mouth. "I love you."

Her hands bite into my sides. "I love *you*."

Another gentle kiss before I pull her into my arms and hold her tight. Ready to fight for this woman, to fight *alongside* her. Because her struggles are mine, and I'll try my damnedest to bring her as much happiness as I can. She deserves every single bit of it.

I lead her to the bed and pull the covers back. "Hop in, I'll be right back."

After a quick bathroom break and shedding most of my clothes except for my boxers, I climb in next to her.

"Come here." I pull her into my side like I've done so many times before.

But this time it feels different. More substantial, more significant.

My brain is busy putting puzzle pieces together in my mind. Shifting things around until I can see it all clearly.

My life. My future. My friends and my family. My new career as a coach. And Chloe. The woman I plan to marry, even though I know we don't need a piece of paper to prove that we belong together. Our hearts made that decision for us a long time ago.

She wiggles in my arms, trying to get closer, to get more comfortable. When I start brushing my fingers lightly over her back, she finally stills. *Some things never change*, which isn't always a bad thing.

I lie there for a while, listening to Chloe's breathing slow down.

Wishing I could protect her from what she's dealing with now and will face in the future. But isn't that what life is all about? What love is all about? To find that special someone and make their life better? To be their equal and protector. To help them ease their pain and lift their spirits and get through the tough times side by side.

I want to be all that.

I will be everything for her.

Even if she's snoring straight into my ear.

THIRTY-SEVEN

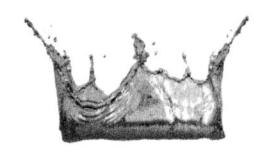

CHLOE

IF NOAH WON'T TOUCH ME SOON, I WILL LOSE MY freaking mind.

Waking up to him every morning since my exams last week has been absolutely amazing, yet torturous when my body wants so much more than just being held. Okay, we've made out a few times, but Noah always stops before it can get any further. My incision site has healed, leaving only a small bruise and new skin in its wake.

But nope, Noah insists that he wants to be safe, not wanting to risk hurting me.

So, it's time to take matters into my own hands, so to speak.

When I woke up a few minutes ago, Noah was splayed on his back next to me, the blanket low on his stomach. I mean, it's like he's presenting himself on a silver platter to me. That gorgeous chest I want to feast on, those muscular arms I want wrapped around me. And then all the goodies that are still hiding under the blanket.

Heat shoots through my body and lands firmly between my thighs.

Oh screw this.

Channeling every ounce of ninja power I possess, I push my hand under the blanket and slowly make my way over to his side. I'm strung so tight that I have to bite my lip to keep from groaning when I feel the soft material of his boxers underneath my fingertips.

Sooo close.

"Chloe, what are you doing?" Noah's voice is deep and gruff, filled with sleep.

I love it.

Who knew what a turn-on that would be too?

My body is lighting up like a Christmas tree, and I'm not even embarrassed by the fact that I was caught with my hand almost in his pants.

It's his fault really. How am I supposed to stay sane when he snuggles up to me every single night, his body setting mine on fire? Just to be doused with the equivalent of cold water every time I try to make a move.

"It's been almost a week." I sound whiny, but I don't even care. I want him, like yesterday.

We're finally together, for good, spending as much time together as possible. And I'm happy, so incredibly happy . . . and horny. But that's clearly a different beast to tackle. And tackle it, I will.

"The doctors said I'm okay. The test results were all good." I send Noah a glare that hopefully conveys how frustrated I am.

"I know. And I couldn't be more thrilled." He rolls on top of me, his morning erection greeting me hungrily. It's also pressing on the exact spot I need it so badly. After pressing a soft kiss on my lips, he lifts himself off me again. "Go get ready, baby. I have a surprise for you."

"You do?"

He nods and waggles his eyebrows.

"Wait. Is this a sex-related surprise?"

After staring at me like I've just grown a third eye, he laughs and shakes his head at me. "No, it's not. Now go."

I pout like the sex-starved woman I feel like and throw the blanket back, fully planning on taking care of things myself when I'm in the shower. Two strong hands grab me by the waist and haul me back against Noah's hard body.

A shiver ripples through me as I feel his breath on my neck. When his teeth catch my earlobe and bite gently, I'm about ready to dissolve into a puddle of pure lust.

He pulls back after one more kiss to my neck. "I'll be right there too."

After a slap on my butt, I walk to the bathroom in a daze. Using the toilet and brushing my teeth on autopilot while the shower warms up.

My clothes are in a small heap by my feet as I step into the shower. Less than a minute later, the bathroom door opens. Since the shower partition isn't glass though, I can only hear him moving around.

When he pulls the shower curtain back a few minutes later and steps into the shower with me, my heart skips a beat.

"Hey, little bird."

My mouth opens but nothing comes out as I stare up at him.

He takes a step toward me, and my breath quickens. I crave his touch so much that I automatically sway toward him. When his hands land on my hips and he comes closer, I'm more than ready to combust.

"I . . . I thought you had a surprise for me?" My eyes bore into his, unable to look away for even a moment.

He chuckles, clearly enjoying that he's got me so obviously worked up. "I do, but I never said we have to hurry up. We have plenty of time until we have to leave."

"Oh."

"Which comes in handy since it seems like we have a problem we need to take care of first."

I swallow. "We do?"

"Uh-huh."

"Mmm." Desire spreads through me like a wildfire. Hot and ready to destroy if it's not being taken care of.

"What are we going to do about that?" He lifts a hand and brushes his fingertips across my cheek and down my neck. Between my breasts and over my stomach. Stopping right on the curve of my hip, and moving around to my butt. "I love your ass."

With a quick pull, we're flush against each other. Our wet skin hot and burning between us. His hard length presses against my stomach in a way that's both exciting and agonizing. When he starts moving against me, I close my eyes from the delicious friction.

And then he leans down to kiss me. *Really* kiss me. With a desperation that borders on pain, but there's also wonder. Did I really get lucky and got the man back I've loved for most of my life? The one I let go so he can achieve his dreams while I was never truly capable of letting him go? Imagining him by my side makes my eyes burn.

The urgency between us grows—our kisses becoming

sloppier—as his hand moves between us, rubbing me, filling me until I come so hard, I see stars and cling to his arms for dear life.

"Holy shit."

Noah chuckles. "You can say that again. I almost came from watching you."

Heat rushes up my neck.

"So hot." Noah tilts my chin so he can capture my mouth, sucking on my lower lip before biting it and sending a surge of electricity straight to between my legs.

What the heck? How does my body have any energy left after that crazy orgasm?

We shift around so Noah shields me from the water while I'm leaning against the wall. His lips don't leave mine until he makes a slow descent down my throat, kissing down my scar before cupping one breast and taking my nipple into his mouth. Another moan escapes my throat. This man is like a miracle worker with my body, knowing exactly what gets me going.

And thank goodness we had our safe sex talk, where he demanded to be tested, so he can show me he's clean—I did the same—and I told him that I have an IUD, so we're good to have sex without a barrier between us. Because that's how I want things between us, without a barrier in every aspect of life.

And right now, I want him inside of me.

After pulling his face to mine, I plunge my tongue into his mouth. Noah growls in response and lifts me up with his hands on my butt. When he finally pushes inside, I gasp at the divine feeling. His pace is relentless, the desperation noticeable in his movements, and I love it. Knowing that he lets himself go like this with me is an incredible turn-on.

When I feel him swell inside of me, I'm right on the edge with him. A few more thrusts and I'm done for, another exquisite orgasm trembling through my body as he pulsates inside of me.

Noah leans his forehead against mine as we both try to steady our ragged breathing.

He steals a soft kiss from my lips before studying me. "Do you think you can stand?"

I chuckle. "I'm not sure but I can try."

He slowly puts me down, not letting go of me.

I never want him to let go of me.

Because I can, I step forward and wrap my arms around him, hugging him hard.

Noah returns the gesture and engulfs me with his strong arms. He rests his head on mine and plants a gentle kiss on my forehead. "I love you so much."

"I love you so much too." I squeeze him tighter, knowing exactly how he feels. Being with him, hearing his heartbeat under my ear, it feels like a gift. That it was worth going through everything I did, that all the decisions I made were the right ones, no matter how painful they were. Because I'm here—alive—with Noah.

A shudder runs through me when the water gets colder, and we step apart to adjust the temperature before we wash up. Even though I keep getting distracted by Noah in all his nakedness right in front of me. How is anyone supposed to focus with all that sexiness on display?

Noah taps my nose with his finger and laughs. "I'll leave so you can finish up in peace."

I nod, my eyes dropping to his firm butt when he steps out of the shower.

"Remember I have a surprise for you."

"Okay."

I have absolutely no clue what kind of surprise he could possibly have for me. The way I look at it, I already got the best surprise, the best present, by having him back in my life. And by having his love when I thought I'd never be on the receiving end of something so monumental ever again.

I'm exactly where I want to be, and I'm not planning on going anywhere.

THIRTY-EIGHT

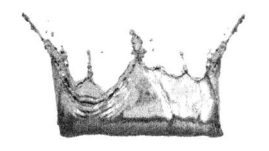

NOAH

Surprising Chloe might be my new favorite thing.

She's been this energetic and nervous bouncy ball next to me, and it's been a blast to watch.

When I turn into the parking lot at the hospital, she looks at me. "My surprise is at the hospital?"

The confused look on her face is adorable, and all I want to do is pull her into my arms, and kiss her senseless. But that would lead to other things, because I can't get enough of this woman. If it was up to me, we'd be spending the next week locked in the bedroom. Which really isn't the right thing to think about because it makes my dick move behind my zipper.

And just like that, my mind is all too happy to jump back to the shower we took earlier. The sex. Her hands and mouth on me, the moment I sank deep inside of her. Completely bare. It felt even more intense than before, now that we both know where we stand with each other. Now that we know this is it. For real this time, and forever. She's mine, always has been, always will be.

Focus.

"Yup." I grin at her and hop out of the car once I'm parked. When I make it to her door, she's still in her seat. "Come on, lazy butt."

She huffs and gets out but doesn't complain when I pull her close. Unable to help myself, I dip my head and give her a kiss. What I didn't expect, is her reluctance to let go of me as she nibbles on my bottom lip instead. My hands wander down her back until I reach her ass. After giving it a firm squeeze, I pull her pelvis as close to mine as possible. We both groan in response and pull apart when a car drives by close to us.

Talk about an inappropriate location for a public display of affection like this.

The last thing I need is us getting banned from the grounds by security.

But it's incredibly hard to stay away from her—pun totally not intended.

Chloe's blush is creeping up her neck and face. "Oops."

I laugh and sling my arm over her shoulders. She fits perfectly, something I've always enjoyed. We get into the elevator, and I push the button for the third floor. Chloe frowns but stays quiet, definitely more relaxed now after our make-out session than before.

When the doors open, I take her hand and pull her after me.

The group of people in front of us turns and yells, "Surprise."

Chloe gasps next to me, her free hand flying to her mouth.

Thank goodness the outpatient clinic is closed on

weekends or this probably wouldn't have been possible. Thankfully, we've had some great staff helping us pull this off.

Chloe's mom and uncles, Eadie, my sister, as well as most of my—now our—friends are smiling at us before they step aside to allow Chloe a good look at the wall behind them. The wall that showcases her beautiful mural, her beautiful *finished* mural.

My stomach is tight in knots, maybe a little nervous she'll be mad that we finished it, that *I* set all of this in motion. Maybe I overstepped after all and should have left it alone?

But when she was supposed to rest after her procedure, all she wanted to do was get up because she needed to finish the mural. With me leaving her hanging, and Hunter being occupied too, things haven't quite gone as fast as she'd hoped, and I wanted to take the weight off her shoulders. Make up for the delay I was partially responsible for.

With everyone's help, we got the task done in no time, especially since Chloe did all of the major work anyway by drawing and outlining everything in the first place. All we had to do was color it in.

"You did all of this?" Chloe's big eyes are on me, her fingernails biting into my arm.

"Everyone helped." I face her, needing to make sure this was okay. "Are you mad?"

Her eyes widen even more. "Mad? How could I be mad about this? I think this is the nicest thing anyone's ever done for me. Thank you so much."

"Anything for you. We all wanted to help and thought we could celebrate you today. Everyone's so happy all of your tests went well." My throat clogs up and I pinch my lips together.

She goes up on her toes and gives me a tight hug before walking over to say hi to everyone and to look at the work we did. I stand back and take in the scene in front of me. Chloe laughing and receiving hugs. My friends showing her what we did, and Chloe oohing and aahing over all of it, and throwing a thumbs-up in my direction that makes me laugh.

Hard to believe that this is my life.

That she's finally mine—again.

Am I scared shitless about our outlook on life together and what role her health will play in it? Hell, yes.

But I can't let that fear run my life. Just the thought of having to let her go—or not having her at all like my nightmare depicted so brutally—is unimaginable to me. It makes my insides churn so much that I'm afraid I might never recover from the repercussions of going down that path, even if it was only theoretical.

I'd go through all the pain again, all the loneliness in the last decade, if it brought me to this point where I know it was all worth it. Things might not always work out the first time around, but if they're meant to be, life will make a full circle, and throw you right back into it. All you need to do is hang on, and for the ride to take you where you're supposed to go.

When the whole group leaves the hospital a short while later, I can't stop staring at Chloe's beautiful smile. All of the work this last week, sneaking away from her to go painting at the hospital without her knowing anything about it, was so worth it.

Chloe's excited we're moving the party to the Parrot Lounge, and the whole drive over, she's either squeezing my hand or my leg, telling me how beautiful the mural looked. There's so much awe in her gaze, so much radiance I'm not sure I'll ever be able to fully comprehend what it means to be in her shoes.

But what I can—and will—do is to be right beside her, the whole entire time.

When I get out of the car, Chloe's phone rings and she answers it while I walk around the car and wait on the sidewalk, watching her through the car window. That's the reason why I don't miss a single second of her expression shifting. From wary to friendly, to confused, and then absolute elation.

The smile on her face is so wide, I grin like a damn fool myself, even though I have no clue what's going on.

Chloe nods, and nods some more, words flying out of her mouth until she finally ends the call, gets out of the car and jumps into my arms with a shriek.

"I did it. I got the deal." Her words are muffled because she buried her face halfway into my neck, but they're clear enough for me to understand.

I lean back so I can see her face. "The young adult book deal?"

She nods, her eyes shining, her smile bright.

"Fuck, yes. I knew you'd get it. Your illustrations were killer. They would have been idiots not to pick you."

She laughs and smashes her lips to mine. "I love you so much."

Our teeth clash while we're acting out another inappropriate PDA moment but I couldn't care less. Telling her I love her doesn't feel enough sometimes, and I rather enjoy showing her how much she means to me. And it makes Chloe happy which in turn, makes me happy.

It's what I live for, what I've waited for a whole decade.

I spin her around, eliciting a few more squeals from the woman I love.

I'm not a hundred percent sure what our future will hold for us, but for now there's only one thing that's important, to have her right where she belongs.

With me, in my arms.

EPILOGUE

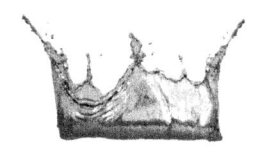

NOAH

Two years later

I OPEN THE PASSENGER DOOR OF MY TRUCK AND THROW my duffel bag on the seat, stealing a quick glance at the list I made for today, even though I've got it memorized.

1. Pick up food from Chloe's favorite vegan restaurant.
2. Stop by the flower store to buy flowers for Chloe.
3. Obtain documents from Mrs. Schuster.

Number three gets a huge mental checkmark since I already did that before my training this morning. Now I only need to make a couple stops for the food and flowers, and I'm good to go.

I'm just about to open my door to hop in, when quick, small footsteps slap across the asphalt.

"Coach. Hey, Coach. Wait for me."

I watch Timmy—who hates his real name Timothy—run

toward me, his mom several feet behind him. He's one of the little ones I teach a few times a week, and my grin spreads as I crouch down to meet him.

He's seven but a bit on the smaller side for his age. That doesn't keep him from carrying his huge blue duffel with all of his swim stuff though. In fact, he insists.

"What's up, buddy?"

He stops in front of me, starting to talk before he even caught his breath.

Mix that with his two upper front teeth missing, and I don't understand a word.

"Slow down, Timmy. I didn't quite catch that."

He gulps in huge breaths of air until his breathing slows down and then tries again. "Can we do some more diving next week for the rings in the deep water? I really liked that. I got almost all of the rings you threw in. My mom said I did a really great job."

His mom finally makes her way up to us and chuckles. "Sorry, Noah. He was so excited about it and took off when he saw you."

"It's no problem at all." I focus back on Timmy. "I bet we can do that if we have some time left at the end of our lesson. I'm sure we can talk Mr. Ryan into it too for the open swimming class on Sunday. If you can make it."

Shit. Maybe I shouldn't have said that without talking to his mom first.

"Awesome." He gives me a happy smile, and I stand up and ruffle his hair.

"You did great today. All the hard work is paying off."

"Thanks."

He gives me a high five before we say goodbye, and I

make my way out of the parking lot of the new aquatic center —the Majestic Aquatic Center, to be exact. Since we couldn't name it Kings of The Water aquatic center, we named it the next best thing. Thank goodness we had our women help us with their fantastic thesaurus skills.

This way, Hunter can join us too when he retires and feels like it. Especially now that he's settled down too.

Thankfully, the pit stops at the stores are quick, because I'm ready to spend the rest of the day with Chloe, preferably in bed, and in our birthday suits.

When I park in the garage of our home we moved into last year, I take a deep breath. It's a big day today. So much to be grateful for, so much to celebrate.

After taking care of my duffel bag, I place the food on the kitchen counter, still holding on to the flowers and the envelope as I go in search of my wife.

I take the stairs two at a time, walking past several closed bedroom doors until I'm at our master bedroom. Chloe did most of the interior decorating and everything looks amazing. The rooms are kept neutral with a few color accents.

And there she is. On the bed. In some skimpy lingerie— her almost-naked ass begging for my hands—completely distracted by her pencil and drawing pad.

Fuck, she's sexy. A pure vision of a goddess.

My goddess.

When I cross the threshold, her head snaps up. "Ah, dang it. I didn't hear you come home. I'm so sorry."

I chuckle, my gaze roaming over her body as she puts her supplies on the nightstand. "Why? Did you have something special planned?"

Her hand does a quick sweep alongside her body, and I

lick my lips. "I thought I was going to strike a special pose for you in all of this glory?"

"I like it." And how could I not? It's a few scraps of black fabric that beautifully wrap up some of her gorgeous assets.

"Thanks." She pushes her newly dyed purple hair out of her face and points her finger toward my hand. "Are those for me?"

I nod and hand her the blue iris bouquet. When I went to her mom last year to tell her about my plan to ask Chloe to marry me, she told me to get some blue iris. Chloe was over the moon, smiling and crying until she finally put me out of my misery and said yes. Then she told me the flowers mean hope, something we both have plenty of for our future.

Chloe smells the bouquet, inhaling deeply with her eyes closed. "They're beautiful. Thank you."

"*You're* beautiful. Happy anniversary, babe."

She gives me one of her breathtaking smiles. "Happy anniversary."

I sit down on the edge of the bed next to her and lean her way to capture her lips in one hell of a kiss. It's deep and slow until one of her hands grabs a fistful of my shirt to pull me closer. A chuckle escapes my mouth as I pull back to look at her.

"I've got something else." I wiggle the envelope between us, watching her excited expression turn wary.

"What is it?"

"Why don't you open it to find out?"

Chloe doesn't need to be asked twice. She takes the envelope from me and lifts the flap so she can pull out the stack of papers. I watch her as her eyes move over the words, page by page, as she goes through a myriad of expressions, her face an open book on how much the content affects her.

When she gets to the last page, she sniffles, and looks at me with shiny eyes. "Is this for real?"

I nod, swallowing past the thickness in my throat at seeing her so emotional and also feeling the full impact of what those papers mean to us.

"Oh my gosh." She tosses the papers on the nightstand before throwing herself at me. "I can't believe we're officially foster parents."

"I know."

She's only a couple of inches away from my face, and I'm fascinated by the spark in her eyes. "Wow."

"Yeah. Wow."

We've been talking about children for a while now, not about having any ourselves, because I respect Chloe's decision in that aspect and understand her reasoning.

But once we decided we're interested in fostering, we saw a psychologist, which was incredibly helpful for us individually and as a couple. We grieved together that we'd never have our own biological child, because that shit hurts. For both of us.

I especially had to see that the choice was our choice and not just Chloe's. In grieving, we learned to love each other more, and our marriage has become even stronger.

We grew up . . . together.

Ready for the next step in our life.

We also decided to foster teenagers instead of younger children, because Chloe's fear of not being around to see them grow up was too much for either of us to handle or disregard.

They're also close to our hearts due to the charity work we both have done at the hospital, and also at the pool now. It won't always be easy, but what good thing ever is?

We stare at each other in silence, knowing what a big change this will be for us. But we both want to try and see where this road leads us.

"I'm so excited." Her words are barely a whisper, her warm breath fanning over my mouth.

"Me too." My hands move down the smooth material on her back until I have both ass cheeks in my hands. "I think that means it's time to celebrate."

The slow smile on her face is so damn sexy, I have to sneak another kiss first.

When she pulls back a few minutes later, I nod my head away from the bed. "Now stand up, so I can take a good look at you. I'm ready for the pose."

"Yes, sir." She laughs and climbs off the bed.

Fuck, if that doesn't make me even harder than I already am.

She spins around in a slow circle before she stops right in front of me, dragging her fingers lazily up her body before cupping her breasts through the fabric.

Little minx.

"I want you." She never breaks eye contact as her hands move away from her body and make their way up my legs at a torturous speed.

"I'm yours. Always." I snatch her by the waist and haul her on top of me.

She giggles, her hair falling like a curtain around us when we fall back onto the mattress. "I love you."

I nudge her nose. "And I love you, little bird."

AUTHOR NOTE

Thank you so much for reading my words! ♥

I hope you enjoyed Noah and Chloe's story. If you'd like to read the free bonus scene to see how their future looks like together, please visit my website www.jasminmiller.com.

Thank you for all your help in spreading the word and telling a friend. I appreciate each and every one of you, and I hope you'll consider leaving a review on Amazon or your favorite review site.

I'd love to keep in touch, so join us in my Facebook group, Jasmin Miller's Awesome Peeps, and get exclusive giveaways and sneak peaks of future books. And to be sure you don't miss any releases, subscribe to my newsletter on my website.

ACKNOWLEDGMENTS

Where do I even begin with Noah and Chloe? This story was the first out of all the Kings Of The Water books that popped into my mind, the bathroom/medication scene to be specific. From there on, it developed, changed, but eventually morphed into the story it is now. It was so important to me to get these emotions right, to make sure the feelings looked as profound on paper as they did in my head. I fell in love with these two souls a long time ago and hope I did their story justice.

As always, a lot of work goes into writing a book, and I would be lost without my support team.

Foremost, my husband. Always. The man who makes it possible for me to chase this dream, who supports me, so I can get the scrambled mess out of my head and form it into actual stories. My little ones are also total champs. Not only do they share me with my book characters, but they also cheer me on. My heart belongs to you four. Always and forever.

Suze and Alicia. I can't decide what's bigger: my love for you, or my gratitude for being there for me whenever I need you. Thank you for all the help, guidance, honesty, and love you guys show me. This journey would be incredibly lonely without you two.

Kristen, Stephie, Megan, and Christina. Thank you so much for all the help with Second Dive. Having your eyes on the story helped a ton, and I'm so grateful for you and your feedback. You're rock stars.

Lynn and Courtney. Thanks a bunch for being my personal story highlighters. I appreciate you and your help so much.

Marion, thanks for everything you do. Not only do you polish up my baby so it can shine, but you also throw lots of encouragement my way. All while making me a better writer. It means so much.

Judy, your final touch always makes me smile. Thank you for making sure I don't embarrass myself with about 38473827 too many dashes and missing commas.

Najla, thank you so much for another stunning cover. I'm obsessed with your work.

My amazing ARC and promo teams. Thank you for showing up, and for the endless love and support you always show me. It makes me all warm and fuzzy on the inside. As always, there's so much to thank you for. First, you actually want to read my stories, which means more to me than I could ever tell you. Then you review them, send me wonderful messages about them, take gorgeous photos of the books, and spread the love. You make me smile and so happy. Thank you!!!!

Awesome Peeps, I love having such a fantastic group of people who are always there to support me and to cheer me on. I can laugh and cry with you, play silly games, do strange polls, or whatever else we feel like. You guys are absolutely magnificent.

My readers. You own a piece of my heart and my endless gratitude. Thank you for picking up my books. Thank you for reading them and loving them. Thank you for telling a friend, and for leaving a review. Thank you for connecting with me. You're marvelous.

♥♥♥

ABOUT THE AUTHOR

Jasmin Miller is a professional lover of books and cake (preferably together) as well as a fangirl extraordinaire. She loves to read and write about anything romantic and never misses a chance to swoon over characters. Originally from Germany, she now lives in the western US with her husband and three little humans that keep her busy day and night.

If you liked *Second Dive* and would like to know more about her and her books, please sign up for her newsletter on her website. She'd love to connect with you.

www.jasminmiller.com
jasminmillerbooks@gmail.com
Facebook.com/jasminmillerwrites
Instagram.com/jasminmiller
Twitter.com/JasminMiller_
Facebook.com/groups/jasminmillerpeeps

Printed in Great Britain
by Amazon